Little Tea

Claire Fullerton

FIREFLY
SOUTHERN FICTION
LIGHTHOUSE PUBLISHING OF THE CAROLINAS

LITTLE TEA BY CLAIRE FULLERTON
Firefly Southern Fiction is an imprint of LPCBooks,
a division of Iron Stream Media
100 Missionary Ridge, Birmingham, AL 35242

ISBN: 978-1-64526-259-6
Copyright © 2020 by Claire Fullerton
Cover design by Hannah Linder
Interior design by AtriTex Technologies P Ltd

Available in print from your local bookstore, online, or from the publisher at: ShopLPC.com

For more information on this book and the author visit: ClaireFullerton.com

Brought to you by the creative team at LPCBooks: Eva Marie Everson, Lucie Winborne

Library of Congress Cataloging-in-Publication Data
Fullerton, Claire.
Little Tea / Claire Fullerton 1st ed.

Library of Congress Control Number: 2020934013

Printed in the United States of America

Praise for *LITTLE TEA*

On the surface, *Little Tea* is about three forever friends, Celia, Ava, and Renny, who come together to do what they've always done best: love and support each other through the uncertainties and difficulties life brings to each of us. But in this compelling story, much more lies beneath the surface. Clare Fullerton skillfully draws us into a lost world of Southern traditions and norms where past tragedies cast long, dark shadows on present-day lives, and no one ever truly escapes.

~Cassandra King Conroy
Author of *The Same Sweet Girls*

Claire Fullerton once again delivers an emotional, lyrical tale and proves she's a writer to watch.

~Julie Cantrell
New York Times & USA TODAY
bestselling author of *Perennials*

The world of *Little Tea* comes at the reader saturated in the physical and cultural authenticity of its setting. In Claire Fullerton's trademark poetic but unflinching prose, Little Tea confronts universal questions of how we define home, and where lies the tipping point between loyalty to self vs family fealty.

~Ellen Notbohm
Author of *The River by Starlight*

Fullerton delivers another poignant work of Southern Fiction in *Little Tea*. With a well-paced narrative and sense of place, we revisit the hard truths of family and friends in the Deep South, where the past is never past.

~Johnnie Bernhard
Author of *Sisters of the Undertow*

In Little Tea, Memphis native Claire Fullerton takes us on a bumpy literary journey down to Como, Mississippi during the turbulent 1980s, where the landed gentry and their black neighbors and employees are still struggling to move forward from decades of complex racial relationships. Fullerton's prose is stunning, and her characters are vividly drawn, but it's the story that kept me turning the pages late into the night, right up to an ending I never saw coming.

~**Susan Cushman**
Author of *Friends of the Library*, and *Cherry Bomb*
editor of Southern Writers on Writing

Little Tea is a simple title that belies a story both complex and compelling. Beautifully written, the novel moves seamlessly between the 1980s Memphis and the present, as we become fascinated by the family dynamics, and events that would change the lives of those touched by them. *Little Tea* is a book you will be reluctant to put down, and with some unexpected twists to the story, it will keep you captivated to the end.

~**Sally Cronin**
Author and blogger at *Smorgasbord*

Claire Fullerton writers with such depth of character, compassion, and hope. Her latest novel, *Little Tea,* draws you into the lives of longtime friends. Even though they have gone separate ways over the years, the friendship stays like a connecting thread. This story brings them together in one place as each works through their own personal conflicts to realize the true meaning of friendship.

~**Tonni Callan**
Co-host, A Novel Bee

When you sit down for a "Little Tea" with Claire, your heart will be full of warmth and sunshine. The song of the cicadas will keep you company as you read. If Southern fiction is your sweet spot, then *Little Tea* is a bullseye and Fullerton an expert marksman.

~**Kristy Barrett**
Co-host, A Novel Bee

Praise for Claire Fullerton's *Mourning Dove*

Set against the backdrop of a complicated 1970s South – one both forward-looking and still in love with the past – and seen through the eyes of a Minnesota girl struggling to flourish in Memphis society, *Mourning Dove* is the story of two unforgettable siblings with a bond so strong even death can't break it. Claire Fullerton has given us a wise, relatable narrator in Millie. Like a trusted friend, she guides us through the confounding tale of her dazzling brother Finley, their beguiling mother Posey, and a town where shiny surfaces often belie reality. Like those surfaces, Fullerton's prose sparkles even as she leads us into dark places, posing profound questions without any easy answers.

~**Margaret Evans**
Editor, Lowcountry Weekly, Beaufort, SC
Former Editorial Assistant to Pat Conroy

Claire Fullerton knows how to get a voice going. I'm talking distinctive, authoritative, original as all get out. Narrator Millie Crossan will grab you by your hand and set you down in privileged Memphis with her family and not let you go.

~**Bren Mc Clain**
author of the award-winning novel
One Good Mama Bone

In *Mourning Dove*, Claire Fullerton deftly weaves the story of a Memphis family into a fine fabric laden with delicious intricacy and heart. A true Southern storyteller.

~**Laura Lane McNeal**
Bestselling author *Dollbaby*

Every sentence tells a complete story in and of itself. A rare accomplishment by any writer! What an excellent novel—put it on your Must Read List for 2018! Millie Crossan tells the story of her brother Finley, life in the South, and the anguish and joy of growing up in an eclectic and ever-changing household with rare poetic prose. Such a wonderful book.

~**Valerie MacEwan**
Editor
The Dead Mule School of Southern Literature

A wise and brilliantly evocative Southern tale enhanced by Claire Fullerton's inimitable wit. Indulge in this eloquent exploration of colorful and complex family dynamics.

~**Gary Fearon**
Creative Director
Southern Writers Magazine

ACKNOWLEDGMENTS

Southern gentlemen are the world's finest, and there are three who helped me give shape to this book:

Sledge Taylor, of Como, Mississippi: 5th generation farmer, artist, historian, botanist, and entomologist, who took the time to drive me around Como, Mississippi for five hours in his Ford F-150 and give me the lay of the land, in one of the more memorable days this writer will ever have.

Bobby Pidgeon, Jr. of Memphis, who told me all I wanted to know about hunting and fishing in the Deep South. My gratitude is endless.

Ted O'Brien of Memphis, my go-to guy for all things pertaining to the great outdoors.

Thank you also to:

Julie Gwinn of the Seymour Literary Agency, who goes beyond the call.

Ramona Pope Richards for her full support

And yet again, Eva Marie Everson, my champion from the very beginning and a light in my life.

No author is an island. Thank you to the wonderful readers, book bloggers, book reviewers, and book club chapters I've met along the path.

Kathy Murphy of The Pulpwood Queens. I stand in line with so many who are humbled and grateful for the book-loving culture you've created.

DEDICATION

For Kakki and Bootsa.
And for Tama and Louise.
I call your name.

Malibu, California

Five rings and Renny finally answered her cell phone. I could just picture her standing in the barn of her horse ranch in Olive Branch, Mississippi. Springing to action. Reaching into the back pocket of her jeans, expecting an emergency on the line. Renny leads her life on call. Always ready for something.

"Hey," I said. "You busy?"

"Never too busy for you," she returned. I could hear voices in the background, a gate latching, metal jangling.

"We have to talk about Ava," I said. "Can you talk now, or do you want to call me back?"

It's a two-hour time difference between California and Mississippi—just after eleven Renny's time, all but the middle of her day.

"I swear I was gonna call you," Renny said. "Hang on, let me walk outside. Luna, come," she ordered, and I knew the black-and-tan German shepherd she'd sent me pictures of stopped on a dime and circled to Renny's heels. Renny has a tone of voice that doesn't mean maybe. Her voice is authoritative, commanding, the kind that would bring anyone to heel.

"All right, go ahead," she told me.

"So, what? Now Ava wants to move back to Memphis? Should we be worried about this?"

"I tell ya, Celia," Renny began, because she talks this way now. She never used to, but the past twenty years of working with horses in Mississippi has beaten the cultured notes of the lyrical accent we were born to right out of her diction. Her speaking voice is flat and direct now, robbed of its singing gentility, clipped to a hardened edge. "I'm just gonna support her," she stated. "Ava's unhappy; she's been unhappy. She's stuck in a Podunk town out in the sticks of Columbia, and I'm telling ya, there's nothing happening. You know their claim to fame is that they're the mule capital of the world, right? Not Tennessee. I'm talkin' the whole world. I told you I was gonna drive up and see her. I was gonna stay for the weekend. But I couldn't even take that. Let's just say the biggest thing going on in town was a bake sale. It was depressing. We ended up watching a basketball game on television. You know I love Ava, but I couldn't get out of there fast enough. I made an excuse about having to get back to the barn and left the next morning. Now what's that tell ya?"

"I thought Ava's new job was going to change everything," I said when Renny took a breath. "I mean, she's running that social services clinic, right? This is what she's been hoping for."

"Yeah, but there's a bigger picture going on. I think she's ashamed to tell you everything because she's so damn confused. Celia, I know it's a long way to go and a lot to ask, but if there's any way you could come down here, I'll take some time off and the three of us can go to the lake. because, right now, that's all I can figure."

I've had more friendships than I care to list come and go over the years. People I thought would be in my life forever fell by the wayside for one reason or another, some leaving me baffled and bruised and second-guessing. But Renny Thornton and Ava Cameron have remained. The progression of years and disparate locations has not altered our bond one iota. We became friends when we were thirteen, and now that we're "a little older," each of us realizes we're in it for life. Our dogged loyalty to each other is partially based on longevity. We've invested too much time in each other to turn back now. We overlook the fact that we're as different as night and day in what our lives have become, because we began at the same starting point. Born to a certain sect of the South so staid in its ways few people ever leave.

But the truth is, I had to.

"When do you want me to come?" I asked, my mind tripping through one resistance after another: my husband; my work; the safety zone I'd cultivated so far from Memphis.

"This weekend?" Renny suggested. "I know it's short notice, but for God's sake, there's never gonna be a good time. If we don't *make* this happen, it never will."

The things that stop me in life are mostly self-created. I've never been the spontaneous sort, unless push comes to shove, which it has at a couple of junctures during my search for identity and what should be mine. But this was a rare request from Renny. She never takes time off from her veterinarian practice and is not one to delegate responsibility. She's completely cognizant of the fact that nobody on the planet is more qualified than she to take charge. I happen to agree with her. In a world where many are trying to find themselves, Renny Thornton was born to this world knowing exactly who she is.

"I'll call you back," I said by way of answer, then hung up and went in search of my husband. David—eight years my senior—is nothing at all like me, and very little of what I do surprises him. He attributes much of my actions to my Southern eccentricities—he's from Chicago, and I'm his only Southern frame of reference. I don't mind when he tells me he thinks Southerners are offbeat. Truth is, I'm proud to be a Southerner. We're a queer breed of cat, products of a social milieu that defines us as people within it but doesn't translate well anywhere else. Being Southern has everything to do with regional mentality because Southerners grow up in packs. We aid and abet each other in upholding an endemic way of living passed down in families, which is bright, well-mannered, and tacitly nonnegotiable. I can't simply say I come from Memphis inasmuch as I come from her ways and means. It's a consciousness, really. A source of identity. A way of being in the world with all its attendant explanations and apologies.

I love almost everything about my contradictory home city, which has been trying to pull herself up by her bootstraps since I was in my teens. When the outside world tried to creep into Memphis, my parents' generation fought it tooth and nail, which, for me, had far-reaching repercussions.

"I just got off the phone with Renny," I said, when I found my husband. He was out back in his recording studio, separate from our house. David's a "sound guy," which is another way of saying he's an audio engineer, working as a composer for movies and television. When he's in his studio, he's happy as a pig in mud. Sometimes I think California is wasted on David completely. He can stay in his cave of a studio all day and not even know the sun is shining or the Pacific tide is rolling in.

"Renny wants to know if I can go to the lake," I announced, as though he knew what I was talking about. As though he'd been sitting there all morning thinking about Greer's Ferry Lake in Heber Springs, Arkansas.

David turned in his swivel chair to face me.

"The lake? What lake? When?" He pushed errant graying hair from his forehead to expose gray-green eyes that had an unsettling way of looking through me instead of at me and always made me feel one tenuous step away from being called out.

"Renny has a house in Heber Springs, Arkansas," I clarified with a cursory shrug, as though what I was considering were the most reasonable idea in the world. "It's about three hours outside of Memphis. Ava's going. They want me to come down there too."

In a movement that told me I had his full attention, David reached over and pressed stop on his workstation and leaned back. "Do you think that's wise?" he asked, all cautionary business now. "I'm not suggesting you shouldn't, but seriously, after all this time—what's it been, ten years? Why now?"

"It does seem a little impulsive, but Renny can be persuasive. To tell you the truth, I'm thinking if I don't go down there this way, I'll come up with a million reasons not to. I don't like the idea of that," I said, giving him what I hoped was a confident smile. "Maybe this time I can create a good memory."

David's eyes studied my face in a lengthy pause. "That's one way of looking at it," he said. "I'm just looking out for you. You know that."

My heart warmed, and I stood straight, the picture of decisiveness. "I know, and I appreciate it," I said. "It'll be fine."

★ ★ ★

I've never entered an airport in all my life without feeling I've entered a time machine. I walk in shouldering my current caseload: hopes, fears, worries, concerns, all the things that keep me myopically focused in the bubble of my life. But somewhere around 33,000 feet up, I manage to switch the channel en route to my destination. I park the past and disembark ready for adventure.

Except when I'm going to Memphis.

There, the past comes hurtling full throttle to meet me. If it's not at the gate, it's waiting in the parking lot, smiling sardonically and holding the form-fitting coat of my childhood.

Ava waited in one of the black leather chairs at the bottom of the escalator as I descended.

"I saw your shoes coming down first and just knew the rest was you," she said, when I rushed into her arms. She wore a knee-length, cotton floral-print dress and matronly cardigan. On anyone else the ensemble would have looked frumpy, but on Ava's willowy frame it looked bohemian cool. Her wavy, red-blond hair floated just above her collarbone, held back by a tortoiseshell headband. She looked somewhat polished and put together, until I scrolled down to her flip-flops and discovered her personal flair. I hadn't seen Ava in ten years, but it sure didn't feel like it. Some people are so much a part of your day-to-day psyche that their physical absence means very little.

"Well done on the flip-flops," I said, watching her smile crease her straight, aristocratic nose. Even at our age and with not a single strand of gray in her hair, Ava impressed me the way she impresses most: fairylike, fragile, will-o-the-wisp. But I happened to be privy to her real strength. Ava glanced at her feet then back at me. "You like them? I wore them for you. Doesn't everyone wear flip-flops in California?"

"They do," I confirmed. "Where I live, they're considered fancy. People in Malibu barely get dressed."

"Really?" She sounded incredulous. "I thought you were surrounded by the fashion trendsetters."

"Well, kind of," I said. "It's just that there's a certain angle brought to the idea of surfside chic. I've seen people at the grocery store in the middle of the day wearing pajamas. Nobody thinks twice."

"Well, everyone out there is either rich or famous. You can do whatever in the Sam Hill you want, if that's the case," Ava lilted.

"True," I said, thinking of Ava's use of the words "out there." To a Southerner, any place outside of the South is "out there."

There's the South, and then there's everywhere else.

"Have you seen Renny?" I asked.

"Not yet, but I did three weeks ago, when I came home to see Mama. I drove straight from Columbia to get you. It's only about three and a half hours away. Renny said to call her when we got close to Olive Branch." Ava squeezed my hand and took a step back to assess me. "You haven't changed a bit," she enthused. "I'm so glad to see you haven't cut your hair. Here, let me get your bag."

"Thanks, but I've got it," I said, following behind as she headed for the sliding glass doors. "You haven't changed a bit, either."

"Oh, come on. I've changed a lot, and you know it," Ava laughed. "Don't you get off the plane and start lying to me. I'm surprised you haven't said I look rode hard and put up wet."

"Actually, I was going to mention you look like the hind axle of hard times," I said, and we both reeled with what I always considered our secret laughter, born of and part and parcel to the history of our friendship.

Ava and I have a surfeit of Southern expressions we've used since high school. They were funny then but funnier now that they're inside jokes. We take rapturous joy in using them. We get on a roll and try to top each other with the creative use of backwoods Southern parlance, lobbying colloquialisms at each other by getting into character and spinning them in an exaggerated accent. Many of them have a history, like the time when we were sixteen and Ava had recently acquired autonomy by driver's license.

We were lost, driving around downtown Memphis, desperately needing directions. Ava pulled into a gas station and rolled down her window. An overweight attendant wearing a "How Bout Them Vols?" baseball cap leaned in and gave directions by drawling out, "Well, yer best bet is to go up to the first red light and take yer left."

"What do we do if the light isn't red?" I'd asked as we pulled out of the filling station. We're still not over that one. Even after all these years, there are times I'll ask Ava a question, and she'll begin her answer by drawling out, "Well, yer best bet..."

I wheeled my bag to the automatic doors. When they swished apart a humid inferno slammed against me and held on all the way to the car. I lifted my hair off my neck and said, "Good God, how does anyone live here?"

"Welcome to Memphis in the summertime," Ava said.

I'll always have a homing instinct that pulls me to Central Gardens from Memphis International Airport. My heart will always leap at touchdown to a rolling, manicured lawn, where a series of magnolias shade the front of a Southern Colonial house. There, my past lies waiting: my mother in the kitchen, my brother, Hayward, in the living room playing the piano. My eldest brother, John, of course, will be nowhere around, but my father will arrive home from work any minute. In my mind, my blue-and-white uniforms from Immaculate Conception High School—white short-sleeved blouses and blue button-back vests to match the blue tartan skirts—hang in the front of my closet. Nostalgia has selective memory; it softens the heart and strips the details to leave you with what should have been instead of what was.

Ten minutes into the twenty-five it takes to drive to Olive Branch from Memphis International Airport, Ava pulled curbside. "Wait a minute. I better check my GPS. We need to get on I-78. I don't want to call Renny and tell her we're lost. We'll never hear the end of it."

I didn't bother to offer rebuttal, for the thing of it was, Ava was right.

I have a relationship with Ava that's different than the one I have with Renny. I understand them both but have always wondered if they understand each other. I'm the friend in the middle, the interpreter, the neutral ground. I can't say how this happened, other than to say Ava and Renny are at opposite ends of the personality spectrum. Ava is light and airy. She has a deep internal life she doesn't easily reveal and there's something about her that is not of this world. Renny, on the other hand, is earthy and practical, born with a take-charge ability that gets anything done. Both tell me I'm aloof and introspective but that's only because I experience the world from the outside looking in and am not given to extremes. I know now, since I'm well into my adulthood, that there's a side to the unions made in high school that has perpetual resonance, a side that remains in arrested development that will never let you forget who you essentially are.

★ ★ ★

There's a damp, verdant feel to Olive Branch, Mississippi, in the summertime. From the side of the road, everything is a chiaroscuro of overgrown, tangled green. Moss drips sultry from kudzu-covered oaks, shading twists of the road in canopies of diamond-dappled sunlight. The world there is flat, expansive, and quiet, evoking a mood both eerie and somber. One step outside Ava's car and I knew I was out of sync with the environment. I figured I'd need to slow down, ease into the heat, try it on for a spell.

Renny couldn't have known Ava and I were out in her driveway. In the summertime, people down South live in air-conditioned wind tunnels that drown out all sound. I rounded the car and walked to the side of Renny's quarter-mile driveway. With my hand on the weathered, wooden plank fence, I stood gazing around. Before me, five paddocks stretched in a blanket so green it cast a blue, shimmering edge in the menagerie of clover and lespedeza. Horses sauntered slow and lazy in the distance, dipping their heads rhythmically with each rise of their bended knee. All around, rural, earth-toned colors hung in chestnut and agate, ivory and hunter green. Through the flatwoods behind the barn, buttonbush, red buckeye, and tag alder spread beneath red and white oaks rambling down to the lake. Renny's farm was dedicated to her horse clinic, a purposeful, synergistic society in all ways that matter, a testament to harmonious efficiency, and the conglomerate of her life's work. At one time Renny had a husband, and although the marriage was over in less than three years, it graced her with a daughter, now seven years old, whom I'd never met.

"Celia, what are you doing over there, waiting on Christmas?" Ava called.

I turned and started toward the house just as Renny burst through the garage door.

"Y'all are here? I thought you were going to call first," Renny said, sounding more surprised than annoyed. She swept me into a two-step hug, the kind that dances and jumps and won't hold steady. "I'm so sorry you just missed Sammie. She'll be at her father's this weekend while we're at the lake. Y'all go on inside and put your stuff down then come back outside. I have to run out to the barn."

"Okay," I said. "Ava, let's go."

Back outside, the oppressive humidity tugged at my emotional heartstrings, reeling me back to a time when I was a part of this sultry, Spanish moss-dripping environment and knew very little outside it. Once inside the barn, Renny's German shepherd sidled up beside her as she walked to an area at the right of her office's glass door where two technicians were ministering fluid intravenously to a majestic, tethered horse. As Renny settled onto a three-legged wooden stool by the horse, I walked into the middle of the cavernous barn and looked up. The wood beams of the pitched ceiling were coal black and dense, supporting a lattice pattern roof where sunlight seeped in and bathed the twelve stalls below. The brass-hammered tack fixture nailed to the left of each stall's half-wood, half-steel bar door was draped with lead ropes and sinuous, leather bridles. Sober black eyes loomed steady and unblinking from most of the stalls. In the middle of the scattered sawdust sat a Ford FX4 the size of the great outdoors. I motioned for Ava to join me. "Have you seen this before?" I asked her. "It's the size of a football field. Who in the world would take the risk of driving this thing? It'd be like driving a mountain."

"Me," Renny fired over her shoulder. "I drive the heck out of that truck."

One look between Ava and me, and we broke out laughing, not quitting until we'd gone a few rounds mimicking that line in our best country accents. "Yes ma'am, umm-hmmm, gonna drive me the heck outta this here truck."

"Hey, that baby's got six-speed transmission and tow-haul mode," Renny said with reproach, and Ava and I couldn't help but start in again.

"Corinna Thornton, your mama didn't raise you to drive a truck with tow-haul mode," I said.

"That's it, keep laughing," Renny said. "I paid a fortune for that truck. We take it to every horse show."

Because Ava's eyes were now watering, she ran the back of her hand over one eye and said, "Celia, cut it out, I can't take it."

"Oh, I promise you, I won't be through with this one until I go home. It's the kind of thing that wouldn't be funny anywhere else, so I'll be milking it," I said.

Ava, in her endless pursuit of trying to top me, came back with the perfectly delivered, "I heard that."

Renny dusted her hands off and walked toward us. "All right, if y'all've had enough, I want to take Celia down to the lake before the sun sets."

Ava started walking to the barn's entrance, but Renny redirected her. "It's out back, Ava. We can take the Mule." The Mule was an all-terrain utility cruiser parked beneath a slated roof. Handing me a single key, Renny said, "Celia, get in and pull forward, I'm gonna open the gate."

It took three attempts for me to start the cart. It lurched and stalled until I put my foot on the brake and told Renny I was more qualified to handle the gate. "This thing's bucking," I said, "no wonder they call it a mule."

"You're doing fine," Renny said, but she came to the driver's side and took the wheel, and the three of us jostled side by side on the single seat, down to the water's edge.

"I have to tee-tee," Ava announced. "All this jumping around tickles my bladder."

"Ava, your bladder was born tickled," Renny said, which wasn't entirely inaccurate.

"I can't help it. We don't have to go back to the house. I can go in the woods," Ava offered.

"You sure? I don't mind driving you back, Ava." Renny looked over at me.

"She can tee-tee in the woods," I said. "It's not like this is anything new. We spent half our youth waiting on Ava to tee-tee."

"Go on ahead," Renny said to Ava, and Ava bounded off, fleet of foot, a woodland creature traipsing spritely into parts unseen.

Renny parked the Mule and turned to me. "She seem all right to you?"

"Yeah," I answered. "She seems fine."

"Has she said anything to you about moving to Memphis?" Renny pressed, her eyes on mine, level and steady.

"No. We didn't discuss any of that on the way here. What is it I'm waiting for her to say? I know they're exploring their options, but what's weird to me is they haven't been living in Columbia for even a year. Just seems like a lot of moving around these last few years."

"Well, the 'they' isn't necessarily part of the equation. That's what I wanted to tell you—wait, here she comes. We'll talk about this later."

Once Ava was settled in the Mule again, we rolled forward toward the dock while Renny's dog ran beside us, darting through a jungle of tall grass mixed with Bermuda and fescue, St. Augustine and zoysia, bending and rippling in a concert of beige, blending in a vista like Cream of Wheat. In the air, a vibrato of cicadas pulsed so discordantly as to be concordant, like one wall of sound that tricked the ear until I could feel its heartbeat.

All manner of movement stirred the deceptive stillness in dragonflies and mosquitos, mayflies and moths. Ankle-deep, I knew there were no-see-ums, chiggers, and anybody's guess, creeping and crawling, waiting to inflict the kind of scratching misery that keeps a person up at night.

Ava leaped out of the Mule and sprinted to the dock's edge. She stood on her toes, hands wide apart on the battered wood rail, and leaned over the placid, gray water looking for her reflection. "If I were Renny, I'd be out here all the time," she mused over the water. "It's so peaceful here, it's a wonderful place to dream."

"I'd dream if I had the time," Renny snorted. "There's always some life emergency happening around here. So I'll dream when I'm dead."

I admired Renny's purposeful life. I was two years out of college before I focused on my future. While I was floating around taking life as it came to me, Renny adhered to a paradigm gifted to her in childhood by her parents, who lived in Memphis and owned inherited land in the Delta that reached back pre-Civil War. Renny's childhood was played out on the regional horse circuit stage. It was a way of life foreign to me, but I don't recall it impinging on our friendship. But then the passage of time can blur a friendship's edges to the point where you feel its essence but forget the logistics. Twenty-two years on, and the facts don't matter to me now. It's enough for me to retain the spirit of our friendship, the anchoring way Renny and Ava were beside me in my coming of age. Combined, we were a girl complete. Separately, we were inchoate and in need of each other, like solitary pieces of a clock that were useless until assembled, but once assembled, kept perfect time.

Renny returned to the Mule ahead of us, a sense of urgency in her stride. Taking the wheel, she called out to her dog, "Luna, come. Y'all, we need to get a move on. I'm gonna take us back the short way. I've got us some pork tenderloin in the oven." At the mention of pork tenderloin, I met Ava's narrowed eyes, and although no words were necessary, she whispered, "Should I remind Renny I'm a vegetarian?"

I bumped against Ava's shoulder; a let's get going gesture. "Ava, you're not a vegetarian, and neither am I, not technically. It's just that neither of us likes meat. I'm not going to say anything to Renny. There's nothing more insufferable than a house guest who tells you what they will and will not eat. I'm going to tell Renny I can't wait until I get my hands on that tenderloin. Come on, let's go."

Ava spun into tinkling laughter as we walked up the dock.

"Gimme some of that pork butt," she said. "Remember Fred Sanford on *Sanford and Son*? Remember how he was always talking about pork butt?"

"Why are y'all laughing?" Renny asked when we got in the Mule.

"You know how to cook, and we don't," I deflected.

★ ★ ★

Nine o'clock the next morning, Renny stretched up from the driver's seat and pivoted to see behind her, guiding the white Escalade in a smooth reversed arc as we set out for Heber Springs.

"Does this baby have tow-haul mode?" I asked from the wide, leather back seat.

I could see Renny arch her eyebrows in her rearview mirror. "Gonna keep that one up forever, Celia?"

"Probably," I said, as we scratched the serpentine gravel driveway between hushed morning fields glistening in spiderweb dew.

We drove down Center Hill Road then through the outskirts of Memphis. When I heard the Escalade wheels hit the first chords of the Memphis-Arkansas Bridge, I looked up halfway over the Mississippi river to the steel-suspended sign that read *Welcome to Arkansas*. Touching down in the town of West Memphis, we veered right at the fork to Blytheville-Jonesboro, and the land flattened to soybean fields on either side of the road. Renny and Ava sang at the top of their lungs to a song on a country radio station that had something to do with buying a boat while I looked out the back-seat window, watching sodden fields click by as though someone had divided their boundaries with a straight-edge ruler. I thought about David in California and the strange alignment of dominos that unwittingly build a life and considered the difference between random chance and unescapable fate. Never was the lens more explicitly focused on my life's evolution than being back home in this telling moment. I watched Renny and Ava dance in their seats, acting out that country song with head tilts and hand gestures, using the kind of energy we had in high school when we interpreted the world through music because it spoke for us and it was enough to be together singing. I cracked the window to the right of me, shivering as the air hit my skin and couldn't discern if I shivered from the cool morning air, or if it was the kind of shiver that spontaneously rises, when you suddenly realize the life you inexplicably missed.

★ ★ ★

Renny's lake house was in an area of Heber Springs called Tannenbaum, where the waterfront houses on Greer's Ferry Lake are large, wooden, intentionally rustic, and chalet-chic. Hers was a two-story, six-bedroom house nestled in a grove of mature maples and oaks with two lake-view porches: the one on top, railed and open, the one below, brick-floored and screened. We unloaded the car in multiple trips up the wood-slat stairs to the kitchen, where a breakfast bar partitioned the kitchen from a living room so spacious you could have landed a plane in its middle. The glass wall of the pitch-ceiling living room faced the lake with an elevated, unobstructed view. Framed family photographs decorated an earth-tone, rolled-rock fireplace, and the seating area before it was classic, cabin-comfortable, sprawled in an arrangement of a four-seat couch, a low wooden coffee table, and multiple mismatched upholstered chairs. "Y'all pick a room," Renny called, marching through the kitchen. "I'm going to take the one down this hall. There are five others. One of y'all is welcome to take the suite downstairs. Doesn't matter to me. Just make yourselves comfortable." I looked at Ava, not knowing which way to move until she said, "I'll take the one downstairs." I walked down the green-carpeted hall opposite from Renny, opening one creaking wood door after another and decided on the end room facing the lake. I scrolled up the ivory Venetian blinds hoping to replace the dimness of the room with sunlight. The high afternoon beams vaulted from the upstairs deck, flooding the serene bedroom wall to wall. Renny entered carrying an oversized pillowcase, whose stuffed contents provided everything to make the queen-size bed. "This is how we do it at the lake," she said, handing me the bundle. "Here, let me show you your bathroom." She led me back down the hall, then opened an unfinished wood door and stepped onto the brown-and-white-checked tile. "Whatever you need, you'll find in here," she directed, opening the double-door closet. "Towels, washcloths, shampoo, whatever you need. Go on and change into your bathing suit. I'll set Ava up, then let's get the boat and go out on the lake."

★ ★ ★

I've never seen anyone handle anything with the facile agility and finesse with which Renny commandeered her red-and-white Cobalt 220 Bowrider. She took full charge of the sleek, white craft, painted down the center with a racy red strip. The red canvas awning rippled over two swivel chairs in front, where the two of them sat. I took the white back-seat cushion, knowing there was nothing to do but become one with the battering wind and spraying water as the boat bounced up and slammed down, ripple upon wave, from the speed Renny assumed, spinning us around Greers Ferry's three hundred and forty miles of rock-shored lake. Ava was having the time of her life, ebullient in her Docksiders, screaming, "Yay, go faster" over the whirr of the engine. We spent three hours on the rocking lake, floating on rubber rafts, bobbing on Day-Glo-orange Styrofoam noodles, holding on to waxed lines to keep from floating away from the boat. Now that the thrill of reunion and the logistics of travel were behind us, it was our first opportunity to ease into idle banter. There was nothing here but wind and heat and the glare of water. Nothing to do but slather sunblock, then lean back and float.

"All right, Ava," Renny prompted, her right hand dangling in the water as she lay stretched out on her raft. "Go on and tell Celia."

"Tell me what?" I said.

Lying on her back, Ava removed her sunglasses, pulled her straw hat low, and fixed me with her gaze. "I'm thinking about leaving Stan," she said flatly.

"You can't leave Stan," I fired automatically. "Y'all've been together since you were twenty-two."

Ava adjusted her sunglasses and pointed her nose skyward. "Celia, you don't know how it's been. I'm sick of moving all over. In twenty-three years, we've lived in five different places because of Stan. And every time we settle somewhere, he's dissatisfied. I keep quitting my job and rearranging my life to accommodate him, and this time, I don't want to do it. I told him Columbia was going to be our last move, but now I realize I can't stay there. I hate it. Stan's already looking at another job that involves traveling, which would leave me isolated in a small town with no friends. I'm just sick of this. I'm well approaching middle age—or maybe I'm already in it—and have never lived my own life. I've been living Stan's."

I rolled off my unwieldy raft and struggled to stabilize myself, my elbows on the spongy rubber as I treaded water. "Ava, that's what married people do, isn't it? There's always going to be a certain amount of compromise. If Stan's dissatisfied, can't you just ask him to get a job somewhere you want to be? If you could be anywhere, where would that be?"

Ava took her time answering with a deflating sigh. "Maybe Memphis. At least I know people, and Mama's there. I don't know. I don't know what I'm doing."

"Remember, Celia," Renny clarified. "Ava married Stan when he was a Memphis insurance man, but he upped and became a concert promoter without even telling her. It's not the lifestyle she thought she was going to live."

"I get that. But, Ava, you're in it now. I mean, come on … you're right; we're all closing in on fifty. We no longer have the bloom of our youth to recommend us. I say be satisfied with what you've got."

Renny sat up laughing. "Where do you get this stuff, Celia? You're kidding, right?"

"I'm only kind of kidding, but you get the point. Seriously, Ava, why do you want to bail now? We should be switching to glide here."

"I knew you were going to say that, Celia." Ava sprang up, her feet stroking water on either side of her raft. "You need everything to be a safe bet. But not everybody's living large in California. I'm scratching around in a one-horse town, and it's different for me. And I don't even know if I love Stan anymore. Now that Jessica's away at school, we're just stuck in a routine and don't know how to relate to each other anymore."

I paused for a moment to let the sting out of her erroneous suppositions of my lifestyle on the West Coast. I busied myself with navigating my raft while I considered what I knew about Ava and Stan. Because the thing is, when it comes to marriage, people rarely give you the gritty minutia; what you get are the highlights, the bullet points—we went, we saw, we did, whatever is worth telling, whatever creates the general impression that they, of course, have it all sussed. Rarely will anyone mention when they're off the grid of marital harmony. The intermittent bouts with doubt or second-guessing that are bound to happen when negotiating a protracted union are a big problem once you're fully entrenched. What's more, one's struggle with equilibrium is too glaring a character confession. Best not to go there, unless it's a crisis. Best not to confess unless you're willing to concede defeat.

"You did tell me y'all are trying to quit drinking," I finally said. "Once you take the alcohol out of a relationship, it takes a while to recalibrate. What's it been now, Ava, six months?"

"Yes," Ava said, then hesitated, her eyes flickering. "Well, kind of. I can't seem to stick with it. It's no fun. I want to have fun."

Now I was worried. I knew too well what could happen to a person unwilling to consider the facts, which in Ava's case were genetic. When we were fifteen, many was the Friday afternoon I'd go home from school with Ava to spend the night. Sometimes I'd spend two, and my mother would come get me on Sunday. Our youth was neat and streamlined. We spent the summer weekends in the Camerons' backyard pool and loved every minute of it. But there was a darkness to Ava's house we never talked about, and I look back now and think I know why. Tiptoeing through the Camerons' living room, where her drunken father brooded in his armchair before the TV, was familiar terrain to me; my father was also an isolationist though his dark tendencies manifested in another form. We both had a mother born and loyal to old Southern ways, which is to say the less you talked about something, the less real it became. And because our individual family dynamics remained unnamed, Ava and I didn't think to compare notes until decades later, when the strong arm of fate met the weak link of genetics, and Ava found herself holding the wrong end of the stick. I was concerned over what I knew about Ava's struggle with alcohol. I started to say something, but she rounded on me from her raft as though intuiting my thoughts. "Celia, this isn't about alcohol, I just want to live my life. I feel like I'm standing still. I look at Stan sometimes and think I'm stuck for the rest of my life. I mean, I swear, is this *it*?"

Renny reeled the wax rope to the boat toward her. "You got married so young, Ava," she said. "You basically moved out of your mother's house straight into Stan's. You only knew Mark Clayton before that."

Ava jumped in the water and started swimming toward the boat, pulling her raft behind her. Flipping the unwieldy rubber before her, she stood in the boat and said, "Do y'all mind if I don't want to talk about this anymore? I just want to sit with all this while I'm here." She looked out over the horizon. "It's getting late. Let's go back to the house. I want to take a shower." Renny shot me a wide-eyed look, paddled to the boat, and climbed in to take the wheel.

★ ★ ★

Twilight crept through the woods in varying shades of green. Here hunter, there absinthe, and before me, incandescent chartreuse haloed the tops of trees. The sun made its descent above the road where I walked, while Renny and Ava took showers. The shady road through Tannenbaum didn't have a divider and didn't need one because there were no cars to be found. It seemed I was the only one out while the first respite of breeze sliced the late afternoon humidity. I thought it unusual that none of the houses on the lake appeared occupied. For the end of July, and what should have been the height of tourist season, it could have been any off-season time of the year. But Tannenbaum is unincorporated, primarily exclusive to vacation homes, and there's no reason to be on this side of Greers Ferry Lake unless you're a homeowner. For whatever reason, we seemed to have the entire neighborhood to ourselves, and as I walked along, content in my solitude, I started thinking enough time had passed and I'd better turn back to help with dinner.

One step through the kitchen door, and it was clear I'd stepped into the middle of something.

"Ava, if you make one more crack about pork butt, I'm gonna come over there and snatch you bald-headed," Renny said, her tone not kidding. She set out placemats and cutlery on the counter between the kitchen and living room, walking back and forth arranging salt, pepper, and linen napkins while medallions of pork tenderloin warmed in the oven.

Ava focused intently on her cell phone, presumably texting. She looked up as Renny reprimanded and gave me a conspiratorial wink. For some reason, Ava seemed jumpy throughout dinner. Her eyes were focused on her cell phone, her head bobbing like a bird on a wire toward the clock, toward her phone, toward the door. After we'd cleaned up the kitchen, Ava drifted outside to the deck and lit a cigarette. Through the window, I watched tendrils of smoke reach in gray spindled fingers as though clutching the damp mellow air. In the night's liquid amplification, a cacophony of crickets, cicadas, and katydids pulsed in a code only they understood, rioting at a pitch so overwhelming I could barely think of anything else. The new moon was symbolic of this three-day reunion. Amidst a backdrop of stars, it waxed over the lake with no other pursuit beyond its reflection.

I walked out to join Ava; Renny followed. She pulled a canvas chair forward and positioned it beside two others facing the lake. Side by side, we sat with our feet on the deck rail. Stretching her arms overhead, Renny asked Ava for a cigarette. Watching Ava lean across me to hand one to Renny, I said, "If y'all are going to smoke, I might as well have one too."

Renny sat back, studying me. She lit her cigarette with a stick match then held it to the right and lit mine. "Thank God you have a vice," she said. "I was beginning to wonder."

"Yeah, well, I gave serious consideration to applying for sainthood," I said. "But I decided it wouldn't suit me."

Renny turned to Ava, who sat at my right. "Ava, let me ask you something, and you don't have to answer, if you don't want to. Are you still taking antidepressants?"

Ava settled deeply into her chair as though wanting to duck the question. "Yes. Well … no." She leaned forward to look at me. "I was, Celia, but I don't think I'm going to take them anymore. I quit taking them five days ago."

"Ava, it's okay," I said. "I didn't know. Whatever you need to do."

"It's just that life is so messy, is all," she said. "Everything's upside down."

Renny took a drag from her cigarette then turned sharply to Ava. "Ava, life is messy in spite of what we do, not *because* of what we do," she said, and just then a knock sounded on the kitchen door. I was taken aback by the accusatory tone of Renny's voice, and it occurred to me there was much more I didn't know about Ava. Renny's eyebrows raised as she cut her eyes toward the kitchen. Glaring at Ava, she said, "Oh God. Please tell me no."

"I'll get it," Ava said, rising and skipping into the living room.

Renny scratched her chair back and stood looking down at me. "Sorry, Celia, I didn't see this coming. I swear to you, I didn't know." For a minute, I had no idea to what Renny referred, but then I looked through the living room at the kitchen's open door. There under the deck's hazy spotlight, like a ghost from the past, stood Mark Clayton.

Mark stepped onto the kitchen's linoleum floor, and already I could see little had changed between him and Ava. They swayed together like reeds in a stream, tall and lithe and fluid, complementing each other in telepathic, synchronistic gestures of action and reaction, making me feel like an interloper in their private moment.

Every group of high school friends has its dynamic center. Ava and Mark Clayton were that sparkling couple that magnetized the filaments of our group by sheer force of charisma. They were breathtaking together, in their polar opposites. In high school, they coexisted so hypnotically they seemed mythological figures borne on the wings of decree. Where Ava was light bearing and compelling—a Celtic goddess crowned with a life force of red-gold hair, Mark was dark and reflective, a mysterious black-haired, blue-eyed poetic sort, who joined our group in the tenth grade after moving from Kentucky to Memphis. We were all coupled at the time, except for Ava, but it wouldn't have mattered if she were. Like can spend an eternity trying to find its likeness, then one fateful day it rises and meets its own match.

It had been ten years since I'd seen Mark Clayton, but in no way did it lessen his impact. I assessed the physical changes time had wrought against the image I'd held of him all these years and found their subtleties inconsequential. His thick hair was short and gray at his temples yet still carried the impression of cobalt darkness. The slow, dimpled smile I remembered raised the right corner of his mouth, making his sly, aw-shucks manner all the more attractive, but then much of Mark's beauty came from the complete unawareness of his appeal.

"Celia," Mark said, coming forward to hug me. Stepping back, he gave me the once-over. "California's obviously treating you well. How you doing out there?"

"Fine," I said. "It's great. I have no complaints. I see you've changed a little. I never thought I'd see the day you'd be sporting conservative hair."

Mark ran his hand through his hair as though checking to see I was right. He swept his eyes over us, and with a slight blush, shook his head and said, "I can't believe I'm standing here with the three of y'all."

"Well, you and I both," Renny intruded, but of course, that was typical of Renny, who had a knack for reaching into the potential of a moment and slamming it to solid ground. "Are all y'all staying at the lake?" she asked. "You bring your kids?"

Mark and Ava exchanged a look that told me Ava already had the facts. "No, not this time," Mark said. "They're in Memphis with their mom."

"So you're here alone?" Renny, the mistress of inquisition.

"For now," Mark said, then he glanced at me and rerouted the scene. "Tate's coming out here tomorrow."

I needed to secure my footing. The sound of Tate's name hit me in my middle, as though there'd been no forward progress, since the time I wrote his name over and over in my ninth-grade composition book, crafting it in curlicues and hearing it in a melody that tickled my stomach. I looked at Renny and saw her head tilt as though trying to get a better view. She narrowed her blue eyes during a pause so loaded all movement stopped in the room. "Celia, can you come with me?" she directed, and without thinking, I followed her down the hall to my bedroom.

"All right, I don't believe this," Renny said, closing the door behind her. "This wasn't the plan."

"You don't have to tell me," I whispered. "I didn't fly down here from California for this."

"Let me just say it: we've been ambushed. Let's leave Mark and Ava alone for now, but I swear to you, we're gonna talk about this later."

In the distance, I heard the kitchen door squeak on its spring hinges. It bounced a few times before all fell silent, save for the cicada chorus riding the wave of the night's gentle breeze. Renny and I walked back to the kitchen, looked out the window to see Mark and Ava walking away. "So this is the way it's going to be," Renny summarized, as though she were finished with the subject. She leaned down to the swivel cabinet beneath the sink then rose holding an aluminum coffee percolator. Assembling its basket and cord, she spoke in a tone that sounded distracted. "This thing may look old because it is, but it makes the best coffee you've ever had in your life. Y'all won't have to run out to the store in the morning—not that there's a store to run out to, the nearest one is thirty-three miles away."

I continued to stare out of the window. "Where do you think Mark and Ava went off to?" I couldn't help but get back on the subject.

"Away from us," Renny stated. "That's the point. They've been communicating with each other for a while, did you know that?"

"No," I said. "I've talked to Ava a lot lately. She's been revisiting her childhood, asking me what I remember. Seems to me she's in a lot of unresolved pain over her family. I know she's been seeing a therapist in Columbia. I don't know if you know this, but this is common when someone tries to quit drinking. They're all over the place. It's like they're coming out of a haze. Everything they've been anesthetizing themselves against comes home to roost, so to speak. In her case, it's her family."

"Adult children of alcoholics, I assume. Then why has she fallen into the trap herself? You'd think it'd be the opposite."

"I don't know all the facts, but I think it's a combination of genetics and what you experience in the family."

"This is the kind of thing Ava doesn't talk to me about." Renny looked at me, her eyes devising a plan. "Let's make some tea, get the smokes, and go sit in the screened porch downstairs. There are too many bugs out."

From my position on the porch's canvas couch, I watched Renny settle into a matching slider. She kicked off her shoes, reached both hands to her ash-blond hair, and twisted it into a knot. Through the screens of the three-sided porch, an outline of pin oaks sloped down to the water, and I caught flashes of silver-edged fluid obsidian in the moonlight rippling through a menagerie of trees. It was a different vantage point from the deck up top. In this porch, we were sequestered, all but water level, tucked in a cocoon of intimacy.

It had always been my policy, with either Renny or Ava, not to talk about the other in their absence. The prospect of doing so went against my values, and I always thought one minor breach of this policy would give license to a traitorous habit without end. But on this night, I would make an exception. After all, my concern for Ava was the reason I was here. Renny had such an economic, unambiguous way of examining everything, I thought if we discussed Ava's plight, we'd jointly arrive at a sensible plan.

Renny was the one to broach the subject. "Ava's really screwed up," she began. "She's half in and half out of her marriage, and it may or may not be because of Mark. I just think she got married too young. All this moving around is Stan Thiel's fault. He's always centering his life on some band. It's not the life Ava signed up for. And I don't think they have any money either." Renny paused looking for my reaction. "Ava doesn't come from what you and I do, Celia. She hasn't had an easy life."

I wanted to say neither have I, but instead I deflected. "I still say she's in an adjustment phase." I settled back, cradled the ceramic mug in my hands, and thought about how to articulate my thoughts to the analytical Renny, who had no frame of reference when it came to life's usurping tragedies. But this is precisely why I counted on her to relegate the most layered of circumstances into black or white. She had the luxury of an unemotional view. She'd never known loss or death or betrayal. She didn't know that some turns of fate are so upending they leave part of your damaged spirit walking through life on automatic pilot. And Renny didn't know what I'd been through with Ava. I'd never mentioned our series of long-distance phone calls, when Ava was drunk and despondent. Even in protracted friendships like ours, you wonder how deep you should go. We were Southerners after all, and this inculcated us with a side that was uncomfortable with too personal of a revelation. Our tendency was to keep things light and pleasant, no matter what.

"But, Celia, you're different; you're stronger than Ava," Renny said, a foregone conclusion heavy in her voice. She reached for the Marlborough pack, lit one, then waved out the match's flame.

"Stronger meaning what?" I asked. "If you mean I've been roughed up and it's a marvel I'm still walking around, then okay."

Renny scoffed. "You've always been different. Even though you appear a little shy and cautious, we both know from your history that you're resilient. It's just that Ava's always been fragile." She took a drag, then blew the smoke into a thin line. "Besides, Celia … there's a big difference between shy and fragile."

Como, Mississippi
Sometime in the 1980s

People aren't shy when they're born to this world. Shyness evolves in increments from cause and effect until it morphs into an ingrained personality trait earned the hard way. It's a cornerstone of wariness from which one engages with the world, a hesitancy toward humanity that colors self-esteem. I was ten years old the first time I was judged as aloof, but it was the combined hand of fate and a matter of geography that contributed to this assumption. Not, I believe, the actual facts.

In the summer of my tenth year, my family moved from Como, Mississippi, to Memphis, Tennessee, where my parents had grown up. Because I arrived in Memphis as an outsider, the cautious line I trod was necessarily intact. My father, John Tallinghast Wakefield, was a gentleman farmer, who decided to accept a position with the Memphis Cotton Exchange because the high interest rates of the 1980s caused land value to plummet and commodity prices were low. Both of my brothers had embraced the move; twelve-year-old Hayward was adventurous by nature, and John Jr., at sixteen, was already a social climber, who danced with delight over the chance to ride on the coattails of my parents' social connections in the big city. My reaction to the move was complete despair, for the thing about being a Southern girl is they let you run loose until the time comes to shape you.

My first decade on earth had been spent idyllically on the plantation grounds of my family's ancestral property forty-five miles south of Memphis in the hill country bordering the Delta of Mississippi's Panola County.

My father had been appointed custodian of the vast fertile acreage of the Wakefield Plantation on Old Panola Road by his parents, who moved from Como to Memphis because they were tired of fooling with the upkeep of the white, six-pillared anachronistic domicile built in 1884.

Como is an agrarian region, whose mainstay is cotton, and although the small town has little to recommend it, the land that surrounds it is a child's wooded wonderland. My best friend was called Little Tea, though her real name was Thelonia, so named for her father, Thelonious Winfrey, who took charge of my family's cotton fields and plantation grounds. Little Tea and her parents lived in a six-room cottage beyond the fields. A pond stocked with bream and bass lay halfway between her house and mine. Many were the afternoons we fished with the poles Thelonious made, each with our name carved on its flexible handle and a cork on the line. Little Tea was my age exactly, and her mother, Elvita, helped my mother run the large, Greek Revival hip-roofed house. The two women made such a synergistic show of the finer points of domestication that the spirit of any task seemed like an exercise in harmonic beautification. They made art out of everything they touched and spent endless hours in the garden out back, tending and cutting China roses and snapdragons to arrange in porcelain vases individually assigned to each of the manse's fourteen rooms. They got along so famously that many racial barriers were disregarded, although Elvita served my mother lunch on Herend china in our formal dining room then slipped back to the brick-floored kitchen to where her sweet tea was in a Mason jar and her sandwich on a paper plate.

Thelonious used the screened door to the kitchen when he came in from the grounds to join his wife for lunch. Taciturn, dignified, and deferential, he was old-school South, and rarely spoke before spoken to. If my mother appeared in the kitchen, he leaped to his feet, hat in hand. He looked at her as though awaiting instruction, his broad shoulders squared neatly on his solid, six-foot frame, his mahogany eyes dancing askance. But I knew a side of Thelonious that belonged to the woods, a side agile and hushed, sure-footed and cautious. He was the God of the Timber, the seer of the forest who knew how to keep one step ahead of danger. Thelonious never went down to the pond or into the woods without taking his twelve-gauge shotgun. Little Tea and I trailed after him through the menagerie of broom sedge and rye grass, charged with the task of spotting water moccasins camouflaged near the water's edge. We followed Thelonious through the trees to look for the opossums and raccoons who had a nightly habit of tearing up my mother's vegetable garden. We followed deer trails and studied tree trunks for evidence of clawed feet scratching, and neither of us considered the hunt for the kill as anything out of step with the rhythm of nature or suggestive of man's supremacy. We were students of Thelonious's Arcadian dominion. We delighted in these enchanted, sylvan forays, shrouded in that prolific scent specific to the woods of Mississippi—that teeming, spawning, musky scent coaxed by heavy humidity and suggestive of something carnal and beastly. We avoided the spiky balls of the sweet gum tree, and scrounged for the brown, hard-shell fruit of the deciduous buckeye to add to our growing collection. Little Tea and I kept our buckeyes like treasure, piled in a wicker basket on the verandah beside my house's eight-foot front door. On Saturday afternoons, we painted them in vibrant colors from the art supply kit my brother Hayward gave me one Christmas. Hayward liked to encourage me in the pursuit of developing myself in life, and his magnanimity extended to Little Tea.

"Hey, Little Tea," Hayward called as she and I sat crossed legged on the north side of the verandah. "I bet I can beat you to the mailbox and back." It was a Saturday afternoon in early June, and we'd spread the church section of the Como *Panolian* beneath us and positioned ourselves beneath one of the pair of box windows gracing either side of the front door. The front door was fully open, but its screen was latched to keep the bugs from funneling into the entrance hall. They'd be borne from the current of the verandah ceiling fans that stirred a humidity so pervasive and wilting, there was no escaping until the weather cooled in early November. The glass pitcher of sweet tea Elvita gave us sat opaque and sweating, reducing crescents of ice to weak bobbing smiles around a flaccid slice of lemon.

Little Tea stood to her full height at Hayward's challenge, her hand on her hip, her oval eyes narrowed. "Go on with yourself," she said to Hayward, which was Little Tea's standard way of dismissal.

"I bet I can," Hayward pressed, standing alongside Rufus, his two-year-old Redbone coonhound who shadowed him everywhere.

Little Tea took a mighty step forward. "And you best get that dog outta here 'fore he upends this here paint. Miss Shirley gone be pitching a fit you get paint on her verandah."

"Then come race me," Hayward persisted. "Rufus will follow me down the driveway. You just don't want to race because I beat you the last time."

"You beat me because you a cheat," Little Tea snapped.

"She's right, Hayward," I said. "You took off first, I saw you."

"It's not my fault she's slow on the trigger," Hayward responded. "Little Tea hesitated, I just took the advantage."

"I'll be taking advantage now," she stated, walking down the four brick steps to where Hayward and Rufus stood.

At ten years old, Little Tea was taller than me and almost as tall as Hayward. She had long, wire-thin limbs whose elegance belied their dependable strength, and a way of walking from an exaggerated lift of her knees that never disturbed her steady carriage. She was regal at every well-defined angle, with shoulders spanning twice the width of her tapered waist and a swan neck that pronounced her determined jaw.

Smiling, Hayward bounced on the balls of his feet, every inch of his lithe body coiled and ready to spring. There was no refusing Hayward's smile, and he knew it. It was a thousand-watt pirate smile whose influence could create a domino effect through a crowd. I'd seen Hayward's smile buckle the most resistant of moods; there was no turning away from its white-toothed, winsome source. When my brother smiled, he issued an invitation to the world to get the joke.

Typically, the whole world would.

"Celia, run fetch us a stick," Little Tea directed, her feet scratching on the gravel driveway as she marched to the dusty quarter-mile stretch from our house to the mailbox on Old Panola road. I sprang from the verandah to the grass on the other side of the driveway and broke a long, sturdy twig from an oak branch. "Set it right here," Little Tea pointed, and I placed it horizontally before her. But Rufus rushed upon the stick and brought it straight to Hayward, who rubbed his russet head and praised, "Good boy."

"Even that dog of yours a cheat," Little Tea said, but she, too, rubbed his head then replaced the stick on the ground. "Now come stand behind here. Celia's going to give us a fair shake. We'll run when she says run." Her hands went to her hips. "Now what you gonna give me when I win?"

"The reward of pride and satisfaction," Hayward said, and just then the screen door on the verandah flew wide and my brother John came sauntering out.

"On *go*," I called from my position on the side of the driveway, where I hawkishly monitored the stick to catch a foot creeping forward. Looking from Hayward to Little Tea to make sure I had their attention, I used a steady cadence announcing, "Ready ... set ... *go*."

Off the pair flew, dust scattering, arms flailing; off in airborne flight, side by side, until Little Tea broke loose and left Hayward paces behind. I could see their progression until the bend in the driveway obstructed my vision but had little doubt about what was happening. Little Tea was an anomaly in Como, Mississippi. She was the undisputed champion in our age group of the region's track and field competition and was considered by everyone an athlete to watch, which is why Hayward continuously challenged her to practice. Presently, I saw the two walking toward me. Hayward had his arm around Little Tea's shoulder, and I could see her head poised, listening as he chattered with vivid animation.

"You should have seen it," Hayward breathlessly said when they reached me. "She beat me easily by three seconds—I looked at my watch."

"Three seconds? That doesn't seem like much," I said.

"Listen Celia, a second is as good as a mile when you're talking time. I'm two years older and a boy, so believe me, Little Tea's already got the makings of a star athlete." He grinned. "But we already knew that."

John called from the verandah, "Celia, Mother's looking for you." I turned to see John walking to the front steps in his pressed khaki pants and leather loafers, his hand near his forehead shading his eyes.

"Where is she?" I returned.

"Inside, obviously. Last I saw her, she was in your room."

For some odd reason, whenever my brother John had anything to say to me, he said it with condescension. His was a sneering, disapproving tone for no justification I could discern, beyond our six-year age difference. He was as hard on Hayward as he was on me, but Hayward never took John's snide remarks personally, nor did he invest in what he called his holier-than-thou demeanor.

It didn't take much to figure it out. From a young age, Hayward and I both knew he and John were two different kinds of men. Hayward once said to me, "John's just a mama's boy, which is why he calls Mom 'Mother' as though we're living in Victorian England instead of Como, Mississippi. Don't let him bother you. He has his own reality, that's all."

I skipped up the verandah's steps and put my hand on the flimsy screen door.

"You should take that pitcher inside before you forget it," John dictated, "And y'all need to pick up that paint."

"I'll get it in a minute," I said, just to spite him as I stepped into the entrance hall. I couldn't help it; it was my natural reflex in our ongoing contest of wills.

The light was always dim in the entrance hall, irrespective of the time of day. The carved crown molding on its high ceiling matched the dark walnut wood of the floor and door casings, which glowed in polished rosettes above the opening to the formal dining room on the right and the ample living room on the left, with the green-tiled solarium behind it. The entrance hall had a central catacomb feel and was always the coolest area of the house. In its cavernous elegance, footsteps were amplified on the maple floors during the months of June through September, then fell to a muted padding when Mom had Thelonious haul the crimson-and-navy runner from the attic and place it beneath the foyer's round, centered table. At the end of the hall, behind the stairs, was my father's den and attendant screened porch, but rarely did I visit the interior. My father was a private man, reclusive and solitary by nature, and whether he was in the library or not, the door was always shut. I had to skirt the gladiola arrangement on the entrance hall table. The floral design reached wide with flourishing arms toward the French credenzas against both sides of the walls. My reflection flashed in the ormolu mirror as I ran toward the stairs to find my mother. My hair crowned me with the color of night's crescendo, dashing so dark it almost looked purple. I am 100 percent Wakefield in all that distinguishes the lineage, from the dark eyes and hair to the contrasting fair skin. There has never been a Wakefield to escape the familial nose; it is severe in impression, unambiguous in projection, straight as a line, and slightly flared. John and I are mirror images of each other, the yin and yang of the Wakefield, English bloodline. But Hayward was born golden, just like our mother, who comes from the Scottish Montgomerys, whose birthplace is Argyllshire. John and I possess an unfortunate atavistic Wakefield trait, though on me the black shadow is a ready silence, but on him it plays out as something sinister. John and I are individual variations of our father's dark countenance, which is to say in our own way we are loners. People slightly removed. But Hayward got lucky in possessing our mother's shining essence. I could always see an internal light in their green eyes that set off their amber-colored hair.

I put my hand on the thick banister and climbed the stairs to the first landing, where my parents' bedroom and living quarters unfurled like wings. The bay window overlooking the garden had its draperies drawn against the searing, silver sun. Walking into the sitting room at the right, I called for my mother, thinking she may be in the adjoining master bedroom. "I'm upstairs," her voice descended. "Celia, come up. I want to see you."

I mounted the stairs to the third-floor landing and found my mother perched lightly on the sofa in the alcove that served as a central area for the other four bedrooms. Behind her, sunlight filtered through the organza window treatments, highlighting the red in her hair. Her slender hands held a three-ringed binder of fabric swatches, the swatch on top a cool, blue toile. She patted the seat beside her and I settled softly. My mother was cultivated, circumspect, and radiated a porcelain femininity. Always, in my mother's presence, I gentled myself to her calm self-possession. In my heart of hearts, it was my hope that the apple didn't fall far from the proverbial tree.

"Tell me," she said, "what do you think of this fabric for your draperies? We could paint the walls a light robin's egg and put white on the molding. I think it'd be divine." She looked around the room as though seeing it for the first time. "It's time we got rid of the wallpaper in there. You're growing up." She laid her ivory hand on my cheek. "You'll want this eventually. I think now's a good time."

I knew enough of my mother's ways to know she was engaged in preamble. She was practiced at the art of delivery by discreet maneuver, and I suspected her impulse to transform my room had hidden meaning. "Why is now a good time?"

My mother looked in my eyes and spoke softly. "Celia, I'm telling you before I tell Hayward because I don't want this to come from him. Your father's going to be taking a job in Memphis, so we'll be moving."

"We're moving to Memphis?" I gasped.

"Yes, honey. You'll be starting school at Immaculate Conception in September," she answered. "You know the school; its attendant to the big cathedral on Central Avenue."

"But that's a Catholic school, Mom. I thought we were Episcopalian."

"We are, honey, but it's highly rated academically. Your father and I think being exposed to a different religion will broaden your mind and give you beautiful advantages. We can come back here any weekend we want, and you'll have a brand-new room when we do. You'll have the best of both worlds, you'll see. You'll make new friends in Memphis, and Little Tea will still be here. It won't be a drastic change at all. Try to think of it as an addition. There now, sweetie, don't make that face. It isn't the end of the world."

But it was for me; Memphis intimidated me. Memphis was the big city compared to Como, and I found it cacophonous and unpredictable in its patchwork design. There was a disjointed, disharmonious feel to the city, what with its delineated racial relations. Parts of town were autocratic in their mainstay of Caucasian imperiousness and there were dilapidated, unlucky parts of town considered dangerous, which a white person never chanced. This much I'd learned on my visits to my grandparents' house near the lake in Central Gardens. Blacks and whites never comingled in Memphis, even though they did coexist. But there was an impenetrable wall that separated the races, and I'd been raised in a footloose environment where it didn't matter so much.

I took my teary eyes and sinking stomach to my bedroom so my mother wouldn't see me cry. Through the window over the driveway, I watched as Hayward and Little Tea threw a stick for Rufus. I hadn't the heart to run tell them our lives were about to end.

Heber Springs, Arkansas

Renny and I had just reached the top of the stairs to the lake house's living room when Ava came bounding toward us from the kitchen. She was exuberant, glowing, and the first thing I thought when I saw her was that she'd been drinking.

"What?" Ava asked, coming to a stop. One look at Renny, and her smile gave way to a look of startled entrapment. "What'd I do?"

"You tell me." Renny didn't break her stride. She walked toward the kitchen carrying the ashtray and tea cups, which compelled Ava to follow at her heels like a puppy.

"Are you mad at me? Are you mad about Mark?"

Renny turned to her from the sink. "Ava, I'm not mad. It's your business. It's just that you didn't tell us he was coming, that's all."

"Y'all want to sit down in the living room?" I intercepted. "Ava, you want some tea?"

Ava laughed as though I'd said something funny. "Tea? Come on, Celia. I know you know, but I just couldn't help it. Mark brought Veuve Clicquot, and I loved every gorgeous sip. It's been *way* too long. You know, I've decided I can drink, as long as I'm not around Stan. I swear, Stan's my problem, not alcohol. I'm fine as long as I'm not around him."

"Okay," I said. "If you're convinced, maybe you're right. Who's to say?"

"Good, then let me get the bottle outside. I was afraid of what y'all'd say if I brought it in."

I looked at Renny, who shrugged then walked back to the living room. She sat in a recliner facing the lake, so I had a seat on the sofa. The kitchen door swished open then bounced shut. Ava's steps descended on the plank stairs and her voice sailed from outside. "Just a minute, y'all. I have to look in the bushes. I stashed the bottle in them somewhere."

"Not a good sign," I said to Renny. "Obviously guilt involved here."

"You think she's drunk?" Renny asked.

"I don't know. She's probably just being Ava. The line's always been a little blurred. I know one thing—she's happy. Let's just roll with it and hear what she has to say."

Ava rifled through the kitchen cabinet looking for glasses. "Now this is a new bottle, y'all. Mark brought two and left this one for us. Y'all want a glass?"

Renny sighed. "Go on and bring them."

"Good. Now let me tell y'all about Mark," Ava gushed as she arranged the bottle and glasses on the rectangular coffee table and ceremoniously twisted off the cork. "Isn't this fun?" she twittered. "You're not going to believe what I just heard from Mark."

I rose to the bait. "What?"

"He's getting a divorce. That's why he's up here by himself." Ava exhaled, all wide-eyed and flushed. "Can you believe it? They've been married since we were all twenty-four."

"Did you know this before tonight?" Renny asked.

"No," Ava said, filling each glass. "Well, I kind of knew. He hinted at it before, but it wasn't definite until now." Ava rang with sing-song excitement as though this was good news.

Renny chose a glass, her gaze marked on Ava as she took her first sip. "Might you have something to do with his divorce being definite?" she asked with measure.

"Did you tell Celia that Mark and I have been talking?"

"She told me," I said.

"Renny," Ava whined. "You said you wouldn't. Now Celia's going to think I'm stirring everything up with Stan because of Mark. She's going to get the wrong impression."

"I don't have any impression, Ava, but I'm listening if you want to talk about it," I said.

Ava lowered herself beside me on the sofa. "I already told you today at the lake. I'm miserable with everything. I'm trapped in a little world and things keep getting smaller. I've felt like this for about a year and keep thinking there's a reason. You know, Stan has been around a lot this past year and I'm only working part time, so we're around each other all the time. It's too much. I literally cannot take it. I keep thinking my unhappiness might be part of God's plan unfolding for me. I really think I'm supposed to change my life, but I'm not sure how to do it. I must be in such discomfort for a reason." Her eyes grew larger. "What do you think, Celia? Maybe I'm being led toward change. I mean, aren't we *supposed* to be happy?"

"Of course, we're supposed to be happy," Renny answered.

"Well, then what does happiness mean exactly?" Ava continued. "I'm serious, y'all. What's it supposed to look like?" She looked from Renny to me. "Celia, why aren't you saying anything?"

I tend to wrestle with words, though it's not confusion, it's more a labor of love because using the perfect word is a pursuit that matters to me. If I'm going to say something, I want it to ring with clarity and insight or I'd rather not say anything at all. I know the words are there for the taking. They're inside me, waiting to hit the sweet spot in the land of the exact. I almost told Ava that happiness is a moving target, because in those rare moments when I'd thought I'd found it, it turned out it was too elusive for me to sustain. The way I've experienced it, life happens cumulatively with each interminably slow-moving stage. I've never known where any of it was going while I was in the middle of what seemed inconsequential; it was only in hindsight that I saw the snail's-paced build. Happiness seemed to me to be little more than intermittent highlights that faded to memory like the light of a burned-out star. And what's more, in the times I thought I had happiness by the handle, I discovered that, all along, there were subterranean forces plotting to tell the rest of the story.

I hate to nurture cynicism, but even now, when I find myself happy, there's a scale-balancing voice in my head that whispers "Wait for it." But I knew Ava wanted a concise answer. I could have given her a list of platitudes, tossed out something predictable along the lines of happiness being a sense of fulfillment, purpose, and connection, but in my mind, it's all a moving target.

"Happiness is entirely individual," I eventually said. "What it means to me could be utterly meaningless to you."

"No, it's not, Celia," Renny asserted. "It's the same for everybody, you don't have to be so complex. We all know what happiness is. Ava, you should reach out and grab it. If Stan isn't making you happy, why sit around questioning it? I swear, you and Celia examine this kind of thing to the point of exhaustion. I say make a move. Any move. If you want to move from Columbia, then move and take it from there. You don't have to know what's going to make everything work. It's enough to know what isn't working."

Again, Ava looked from Renny to me then back to Renny. "I don't know … that seems risky," she said. "The thing is, I've been trying. Seriously, I've been praying. I've asked for guidance. I just can't figure it out." She took a good swig of champagne then refilled her glass until it overflowed. Licking the rim, she set her glass on the table and leaned forward. "Y'all, I'll tell you what. I just don't want to screw up my life. And I feel guilty. I know I'm supposed to be happy. I mean, I should be happy. Mama keeps telling me I'm lucky to have a home and a job and a husband who loves me. She says all my needs are met but, if that's the case, why am I bored and uninspired? I'm afraid I'm going crazy."

"Your mother has her own frame of reference, Ava. People who've been on this planet longer than us know a lot more," I said. "They've seen more. They know what is and isn't possible. Your mother just wants to see you safe and settled."

"I know, Celia, but what I'm talking about is frustration over my lack of possibilities."

"I understand," I said, "but even if we had unlimited possibilities in life, we still wouldn't walk around all the time in an ecstatic state of bliss. We're not wired that way. The idea is to aim for harmony within our life's limitations."

Ava shook her head, not buying it. "That's too Zen for me. Thing is, I thought my life was going to be magic. But I don't feel the magic anymore." She started to reach for her drink, then drew back as though she'd thought better of it. "Remember when we were young and had that fire, that enthusiasm where anything was possible? That's what I want. I don't have that anymore, and I'm depressed by it."

"All right," I said. "Give me that bottle. I'm not trying to be flippant, but two nights with you, and I'm smoking and drinking."

Ava's laughter cornered the room. "Oh great, now Celia's depressed."

Renny joined in and said, "Ava, better get those antidepressants out."

"Cut it out, y'all," I said. "Ava, I get what you're saying. Meanwhile, back at the ranch, we grew up. Adults have responsibilities. It's not supposed to be fun all the time."

"Well, I can't figure out who's in charge," Ava volleyed. "I mean, does God have a plan for me and I'm just too stupid to figure it out? Can't I affect my own fate, or is my life up to God and I have no power? And just so you know, I'm still the good Catholic girl I was in high school. I attend Mass all the time. I asked Father McArthur about this—remember him, Celia? Even he doesn't know the answer."

"You affect your own fate," Renny stated unequivocally.

"Both," I said, which sent Ava to shaking her head.

Renny stood, set her glass on the table next to Ava's. "I hate to break this up, y'all, but I'm tired. I'm going to bed." After a few paces, she turned back to us. "The lights are on out on the deck. I'll leave them alone if y'all want to go out there, but cut them off before you go to bed." She took another step, then turned again. "And don't wake me up in the morning, if you get up early. I haven't had a day off in months."

The second Renny walked down the hall to her bedroom, Ava jumped up and said, "Let's go outside and smoke. Stan hates it when I smoke. Let's do it to spite him."

"You've got a devious attitude," I said.

"Don't I? Isn't it fun? Let's turn the lights off so we can look at the stars." She pointed over my shoulder. "Bring the champagne."

★ ★ ★

Ten-thirty at night and the air retained its breezeless humidity. Pulsing darkness deepened the woods, suggesting something lurking in the shadows of the thicket's star-lit edges. Too much deadened quiet, and my memory descends to where I start to suspect things. Images arise that aren't entirely creative because I've had experience with nighttime in the Southern woods. I looked at Ava settled into her chair. She was whispering, not wanting to be overheard by Renny, whose bedroom window faced the lake. Knowing sound amplifies over water as well as I do, Ava scooted her chair flush against mine, swept her hair to the side, and leaned in close. "Renny doesn't get it."

"Doesn't get what?"

"My dilemma. She's single; how could she know?"

"Renny's been married. She knows it isn't always easy," I said.

"Yeah, but she was only married three years. She hasn't been in a relationship that's gone on forever. Things change a lot over time. People change. Everything changes," Ava said, as though trying to convince me, her voice dropping lower. "I don't know if I've changed or what, but I'm worried about my sanity."

"Seriously? Like, you're not just saying that?"

"Yes, Celia, seriously. And you know depression runs in my family. I know you know how that is."

For a second, I was taken aback, but Ava didn't mean anything by it, this much I knew. She wasn't thinking about me in that moment. She was only being intimate in an uncensored way. Yet in that same moment, I couldn't shake the knowledge that, when it came to me, Ava had most of the facts, which is the flipside, the caveat, and sometimes the price of close friendship. I shouldn't have been surprised. I'd forgotten that after you managed to outrun something, there are those in your life who can call you back at the drop of a hat.

I switched the subject. "What's the deal with taking antidepressants? Who prescribed them?"

"I have a psychiatrist. I've been on two different kinds in the last year. But it's more than depression. I think it could be grief." She shrugged. "I don't know."

"Grief over what?" I asked.

"Everything. Daddy. Mark. My youth. I'm overwhelmed, and nothing in my life is working. Can I tell you something, and please don't laugh?"

"Sure. And I promise I won't laugh."

"Sometimes I think I'm not over Mark."

"Well … y'all broke up right before your father died," I said. "Maybe it's all tied in."

"Maybe. But don't you ever think about Tate? Don't you ever wonder what would have happened if y'all had stayed together?"

I didn't want to talk about Tate. I had way too much baggage and sat, in that time warp of a moment, thinking this is exactly what my thoughts from a moment ago had been about. There are some parts of your history your friends won't let you outrun.

Memphis, Tennessee
Sometime in the 1980s

Tate Foley would tell it differently. He forgot we were ten years old the first time we laid eyes on each other. It was a Saturday morning in late August, and my family had just moved from Como to Memphis. I'd been invited by my ten-year-old neighbor's mother to go out to their friend's pool in east Memphis. It'd taken my mother hours to quell my pout—I felt uprooted and sorely missed Little Tea—and talk me into going. She kept saying I should make an effort toward making new friends before school started in early September. After resisting for hours, I begrudgingly agreed. The heat and humidity that day turned everything in its jurisdiction to a shimmering, silver mirage. The azaleas and hydrangea bordering the rectangular pool faded in listless mid-summer defeat. Every foot of the residential grounds stood well appointed. Geraniums and black-eyed Susans surrounded two birdbaths and strategically placed concrete statuary peered through trellised vines of morning glory thicker than rope. In the midst of the blazing heat, Tate Foley slipped dolphin-like in and out of the water. Pressing himself up with sinewy arms, he mounted the diving board and stood glowing under the sun like a young Apollo, all blond and tan and golden—even then Tate was built with balanced perfection and moved with animal grace.

His metallic hair hung thick and uncompromising, waving right out of the water the moment it hit the air. I'd never given a second glance at a boy until that very moment. I was so magnetized by Tate's dazzling presence that everything around him faded to insignificance. I couldn't bring myself to speak to him that day, but I remembered him clearly five years later, when we met again at a party for the inductees of a girl's club, *Chez Nous*, in the beginning of my freshman year.

The morning had started at the break of dawn, after my mother had granted permission to eighteen girls from the Memphis social club to swarm into my bedroom carrying banners and blowing on rollout paper noisemakers, in a riotous ritual that tapped me as a club member. In Memphis society these things mattered and girls born to its sect were indoctrinated early by a jury of their peers. We were Southern belles in training, born to specific expectations developed through the channels of privilege, molded and shaped to be our mothers' replicas as we spun though life collectively.

The *Chez Nous* inductee party at the 19th-Century Club's midtown manor spilled from the ballroom to the columned verandah that faced Union Avenue. On a crisp Saturday night in mid-September, boys in tuxedos and girls in full-length gowns from Memphis' private schools milled about, testing their wings in a state of becoming. We were the high-school crowd from the same walk of life who would know each other for the rest of our lives; neither time nor space would alter the denominational sense of belonging. Our escorts had been chosen for us as a formality, but Renny, Ava, and I knew we were under no obligation to stay with our dates. I stood between Ava and Renny when Tate Foley, holding a glass of Jim Beam, walked through the Victorian mansion's double doors to its spacious verandah. "I've seen that guy," I whispered to Ava as Tate approached, brimming with insouciance over the certainty of his ready reception. Though there was nothing arrogant about Tate, he was well aware that people's eyes followed him around a room. "Who wants to dance?" he asked, and although Tate Foley's words were generally delivered, his blue eyes landed on me.

My mother was thrilled the following morning when I told her I'd spent most of that night dancing with Tate Foley. Memphis society has always been a small pond, so of course she knew his family. One is either born to it or one is not.

Tate Foley was one of three sons born to a family that earned their fortune through their affiliation with what was locally known as King Cotton. The Foleys owned much of the real estate on downtown's Cotton Row, which runs parallel to the Mississippi River on Front Street. Tate's grandfather had been a significant figure with the Memphis Cotton Exchange, whose members-only trading floor took up the corner of Union and Front. This is how the Wakefields came to rub shoulders with the Foleys generations back, and theirs was not an uncommon relationship during Memphis's growth. Because the seat of my family's business was the Wakefield Plantation, Tate's family and mine depended on each other as part of the economic synergy that made the wheels of Memphis turn—the Wakefields being sellers and the Foleys buyers of a commodity with such earthly value, it might as well have been gold. Although times changed and Memphis expanded, both families retained a prominent cache, based on a time so integral to the Delta's development that the very sound of our last names recalls Memphis' history.

"Don't tell me," my mother, as giddy as I'd ever seen her, said, "Tate has blond hair and blue eyes." She had just poured herself a cup of coffee, which she almost upended when I uttered Tate's name.

"How'd you know that?" I asked, although it didn't surprise me. My mother had her finger on the pulse of most things in Memphis. By virtue of the fact that she knew Tate's family, it told me she surely approved.

"All his people do. Every last one of them. I went to school with Tate's mother, Margaret Turner, whom we all called Missy. Her family's an old one too." She took a sip of her coffee. "Is Tate going to call you for a date?"

"I don't know," I said.

"Well, did you give him our phone number?" She pulled out a chair at the kitchen table and sat across from me, looking into my eyes as though trying to divine the future.

"He didn't ask," I said, watching her brow tighten.

"He'll know how to reach you," she decided. "Men have a way of finding out what they want to know. You just sit tight. Let him do the pursuing. You know men, they want to be the one pursuing. I guarantee you Tate Foley won't be any different."

Hayward had been playing the nine-foot Steinway in the living room. He closed the wood over the keys and came into the kitchen on the heels of my mother's last line. "Yeah, you just sit tight and wait. You have no influence over this," he said, laughing. At almost seventeen, Hayward had it all figured out. He knew the game rules of courtship but still saw its humor. "And for God's sake, when he calls, don't act like you care. If it's not going to be a cat-and-mouse game, there's no point in playing."

"Well, that's right, Hayward," Mom said in all seriousness. "You know Tate, don't you? Isn't he at MUS?"

"He's Celia's age—fifteen—and a freshman. His brother Bill is in my grade. They're both really good guys." Hayward turned to me, smiling. "So you caught Tate's eye last night? Does this imply you actually spoke to him?"

I knew what he meant. "Cut it out, Hayward." I could feel my face raising scarlet.

Hayward pulled out a chair and sat at the kitchen table. "Shyness is a virtue, Celia. It adds to the allure of feminine mystique. But on a more immediate note than your romantic future, you're still coming out to the farm with me before the party tonight, right?"

"When are you leaving?" I asked.

"Soon," Hayward said. "You can call Little Tea now, so she can get ready for that game you'll never outgrow." Hayward looked at his watch. "Tell her we'll see her at the farm in a little more than an hour."

By the farm, Hayward meant the Wakefield Plantation. It being the 1980s, few people said "plantation" anymore, not even our father, though his parents still did as though doing so would stop the world from spinning beyond their reach.

And as for the game Little Tea and I would never outgrow, Hayward liked to chide us over something that was a cornerstone to the history of our friendship. Like many things in Como, Mississippi, it involved cotton.

Every September, if the weather held, Thelonious oversaw the June planting's harvest. If it was dry the first week of September, a monstrous John Deere picker mowed through the four-foot cotton like a thunderous hovercraft, crushing everything beneath its forward thrust as it combed hundreds of acres of white yield, and its twelve menacing blades slashed the fields into rows. Bolls were snatched from their stalks and spindled by conveyor system, which suctioned the cotton into accruing, five-hundred-pound bales. From the time we could walk, Little Tea and I waited for harvest season, when the man-powered colossus wrapped each bale in industrial plastic then jettisoned it to the ground. The bales would lie like crouching cyclopes before being collected onto a flatbed that roared through Como on its way to the gin. Our game began the second a wrapped bale slammed to the ground in a thud that shook the earth. We took off running as though someone had fired a shotgun, the desiccated earth fanning behind us in lingering clouds of burnt-red dust like tongues of fire kicked from our heels. We'd run as though our lives depended upon beating the other to the top of the bale only to see who could knock the other off. We wrestled and pushed like head-butting goats in our rapturous, do-or-die game without any rules. It was basically a fight, but our safety was in the certain knowledge that we trusted each other. We knew where the line was, and never went beyond it.

Little Tea was in the cotton fields, her enthusiastic wave beckoning me as we arrived at the farm that afternoon. Hayward stopped his car when he turned off Old Panola Road, knowing there was no need to carry me up the long driveway. I leaped from his Volvo and took off running, his voice calling behind me, "Y'all don't rough each other up too bad, now. We have a big night ahead, and y'all need to be ready to dance."

Lickity-split, I tore into the field, planning to best her. Part of my strategy was to jump Little Tea with the element of surprise. I scrambled to the top of the bale before she did and turned ready-steady—Nikes planted, knees bent, arms wide, palms set to thwart any unanticipated move.

Little Tea laughed as though not taking me seriously. "If you weren't so dang skinny, you could be a wrestler. But since you are, all I have to think of is catching a bird."

"Funny, Little Tea," I said, grabbing her shoulders, "I'm quicker than you. You don't have a chance against my flat-out talent."

"I'll show you talent." Little Tea spun out of my reach, and as I stepped forward, the tip of my shoe caught a crevice and I landed in a face-plant. Because I was down for the count, Little Tea bent low and rolled me off the bale. She stood on top, laughing, rubbing in her victory. "See there, Celia? I got you again. I told you, thing about you is you too skinny."

"That's not it," I protested, propping myself on my elbows. "You're just taller than me now. I used to beat you all the time, and you know it."

"Height has nothing to do with it. The person with the lower center of gravity should be the one who wins, so I ain't buying it. Come on back up here; let me show you what's what all over again."

"No way," I said, dusting myself off and looking up at Little Tea glowing in the midday sun, her flawless skin the color of amber honey. At fifteen, she had bypassed coltish awkwardness already. She was into her own now and of this I had awestruck respect. Unlike me, Little Tea never stumbled through adolescence; she simply rose one morning fully realized, and although she was laughing at me while I looked up at her, it dawned on me then that I looked up to her in more ways than one.

"You need to come down off of there anyway," I said. "We better get a move on. Elvita's going to need our help for the party."

In one fluid move, Little Tea sprang to the ground. "I'll race you to the pig pit," she shouted, her feet already in flight.

When I said Little Tea's mother needed our help, I was talking about that night's party. Every year, my parents hosted a party on the front lawn for everyone involved in the harvest. Because the farm was run as a business, the harvest party occurred on the second Saturday in September.

My parents hired a band and had a canvas marquee set over eight, six-foot banquet tables, weighted to the breaking point with plates and cutlery, beans, slaw, cakes, and cobbler—all the fixin's that went with a respectable pig roast. Fifteen, six-seated tables draped in ivory linen were scattered throughout the yard, and a handful of vertical heaters stood on standby, in case the weather turned unseasonably cool. Every year Thelonious dug a pit in the side yard and laid it three feet high with red bricks. He constructed a grill of hay wire and rebar sturdy enough to hold the pig's weight then lit the sweet-smelling hickory and coal. Elvita shredded old table linens and t-shirts to tie on a broom handle to use as a sop mop, submerged in a bucket of water, apple cider vinegar, and salt. I liked taking my turn basting the acrid mixture that kept the meat moist and the pig encased in tough brine. The slender handle Elvita used had grooves the color of buttermilk, worn by the grip of devoted hands, and there was something sacramental about placing my thumb in a particular groove to wield the flimsy implement like a giant paint brush along the pig's burnt, glistening spine, careful not to drip the eye-stinging concoction onto the Vidalia onions and Idaho potatoes below. I knew Thelonious, Elvita, and Little Tea had taken shifts basting the pig all through the night before, and I wanted my part in it.

As Little Tea and I raced toward the pit from the cotton fields, Thelonious saw us coming and held out the mop. "Here you go, Miss Celia. High time you take your turn."

★ ★ ★

In the full swing of the harvest party, I angled down the front staircase, threading my way between groups of guests who balanced paper plates on their laps, when Hayward caught my eye from the foyer.

"What are you doing up there?" Hayward called. "Y'all need to come out and dance." In saying y'all, I knew Hayward meant me and Little Tea, so I put my index fingers together on my curled tongue and whistled above the chorus of voices in the hall. Just as I'd hoped, Little Tea whistled back, and I followed her response to the kitchen.

"Fifteen, and y'all haven't outgrown that yet," Elvita said, smoothing her hands over her apron. "It's time the two of you started acting like ladies. I'm not raising this one here to whistle in public, and Celia, I know your mama isn't, either."

"I didn't know how else to find her, Elvita," I defended. "Hey, Little Tea, what are you doing back here?"

Little Tea put a spoon the size of a baseball bat in the deep double sink and turned to me. "Helping Mama," she said. "Whatchu want?"

"Hayward's looking for us. He wants us to come outside and dance."

Elvita drew her brows together. "Thelonia, now I know I taught you better than that. Ask Miss Celia again what it *is* she wants," she said sternly.

"I'm sorry, Mama. What *is* it that I can do for you, Miss Celia?" Little Tea enunciated crisply with mirth.

"You can come on now," I said, laughing. Little Tea kissed her mother's cheek, took my hand, and we fled from the kitchen, laughing. Weaving through the dining room into the entrance hall, we sailed through the door and skipped down the steps to the yard.

At first I didn't notice Tate Foley standing beneath the oak, but then that's the way Hayward planned it. He'd taken great joy in pulling one over on me because subterfuge was my brother's idea of fun. And at first I didn't know Hayward stood beside Bill Foley, though once Bill spoke, I saw the family resemblance. The brothers had the same blond hair and wide shoulders, but Bill was a sturdier version, without the streamlined beauty. Bill Foley didn't bother to introduce himself, and Hayward seemed pleased this was the case. He stood with that mischievous smile of his when Bill said, "I heard you made quite an impression on my little brother last night. So much so, he's standing right over there."

Unbeknownst to me, Hayward had called Bill and Tate and invited them to the harvest party. He'd driven me all the way out to Como, without once letting on. I glowered at Hayward, giving him my best

I'll-get-you-back glare, then looked to the left to see Tate haloed by a string of tealights that winked from the lower branches of an oak tree.

"Well go on," Hayward encouraged. "He came all the way out here to see you."

I'd never known the debilitating power of self-consciousness until that very moment; my knees turned weak and my legs got so heavy, they all but rooted my feet. I walked with the burden of a hyper sense of myself to where Tate stood smiling. Looking up at his chiseled face, my nerves overtaking me, I couldn't think of a word to say, until Little Tea came swinging into the moment and rescued me. She elbowed me in my side. "This the boy you told me about?" she prompted. "With that head of hair, it couldn't be anyone else."

Clearly, Tate seemed taken aback for a second. "She told you about me?" he asked, looking from me to Little Tea as though trying to justify our paring. "And who might you be?"

"Thelonia Winfrey." Little Tea held out her hand. "I'm Celia's best friend."

"We call her Little Tea," I clarified. "Little Tea, this is Tate Foley."

"Nice to meet you," Tate said. He swept his eyes around, then took her offered hand.

"You, too, Tate Foley," Little Tea said, scanning him tip to toe, an amused look on her face like she knew something he didn't.

"You live around here?" Tate asked, trying to place her.

"Over back yonder on the other side of the pond. Celia and I grew up on this land."

Tate nodded, comprehending. "What school do you go to out here? My football team plays North Panola High."

"That's where I attend," Little Tea answered.

"Really?" Tate looked impressed. "They're a helluva ball club."

"They've also got a good track and field program," I offered. "Little Tea's the star."

"Is that right? What's your event?"

"Relay and the one hundred," Little Tea fired back.

"They're champions of the MHSAA this year," I explained. "Little Tea's so fast, she beats Hayward every time they race."

"Cool," Tate said, the expression on his face a sure indicator that he was warming up to Little Tea. "Maybe we'll race sometime."

"Must mean you plan on hanging around," Little Tea said. "I figured." Pausing for a beat as though thinking things over, she nodded and added, "All right, y'all. I'll leave you be." Gliding away on the air of her light step, she called over her shoulder, "See you around, Tate Foley."

Watching Little Tea saunter out of range, Tate turned and asked me, "She's your best friend?"

"Umm-hmm," I said.

"But she's black," he intoned, as though he need say nothing more.

"So what?" I said because I knew where this was going.

"So, it's a little unusual," Tate stated.

"It's not unusual for me."

"All right. I'm just saying."

"Saying what, exactly?"

"I don't know anybody white who has black friends."

"Well, you do now," I said. "Little Tea's like my sister."

"I didn't mean anything by it, Celia. I'm not saying it's wrong. I'm only saying it's different, that's all."

This wasn't the first time I'd heard this reaction. Ava hadn't balked, but Renny had taken issue the first time I brought them to spend the night in Como.

"Celia, you're the weirdest person I know," Renny had said, as the three of us prepared for bed. "Your family lives in the nicest house in Central Gardens, but you like it better out here in the sticks. Y'all belong to the Memphis Country Club, your mother was queen of Cotton Carnival, but you'd rather run around out here in the woods. And you know what? Even though you get along fine with everyone at school, I know what you're thinking. You follow the beat of your own drum."

"What drum is that?" I asked her.

"You're in it but not of it, if you know what I mean," Renny said. "And beside me and Ava, you'd rather hang around with a black girl. I don't even know anyone black, besides my family's maid."

"Oh, God," Ava said, rolling her eyes. "Renny, why can't you be open-minded? This is the eighties, for heaven's sake. Ever heard of integration? Ever noticed we have two black girls in our class at school?"

Renny sounded testy. "Yeah, because for the first time in the school's history, two black girls applied. But we're not exactly friends; we don't go to each other's house to hang out." Her eyes narrowed as though they held some lifeblood secret. "They're *different* than we are, Ava."

"What do you mean different?" Ava pressed. "Frances Wilson is black, and she's the president of our class. We voted her in, remember? I know one thing, Frances will be the only one of us to get into Harvard."

"Yeah, because she's black. If nothing else, she'll be accepted by affirmative action," Renny snapped.

"Renny, Frances is the smartest one in our class," I said. "This is ridiculous."

"Let's not talk about this anymore." Renny turned her back and settled into one of the two cots my mother had placed in my room. "We see things differently, that's all. And Celia, you were basically raised in Como. It's a different mentality out here than in Memphis. It's more permissible because blacks and whites work close together. But, my point is … they don't socialize." Taking the pillow behind her, Renny brought it to her lap and fluffed it, looking at me. "And Celia, don't give me that look. When everybody around you thinks a certain way, there's no point in questioning it. It's just the way it is." Renny, having spoken her mind, pulled the covers to her shoulders, then turned her face to the wall.

As stinging as that was, oddly, Little Tea had said something similar. She'd surprised me when I'd asked if she'd liked meeting my friends.

"That blonde one was suspicious of me," she'd finally answered, after my three failed attempts to get her to comment.

"Renny?" I responded. "No, she wasn't."

"Yes, she was. She changed her speech when she talked to me. Black folks can always tell when white folks do that. It's really kind of funny, but I know they're speaking down. They think we're foreigners, or not as smart as they are, so they talk to us like we're babies, like they're bridging a gap. You don't notice these things the way I do. How could you? You're white."

I hated having both discussions. I didn't want to be part of an "us versus them" mentality. In our insular world in Como, Little Tea and I were oblivious to outside influence because we spent most of our time on the farm's vast grounds. We'd never once broached the loaded subject. And I, in my naivete, had thought it would never be an issue between us, so tied were we at the hip. Up to this point, our interests didn't concern a wider sphere. We were focused on the business of growing into women; on this we had common ground.

Tate Foley cast his eyes downward. He must have felt my glare because he glanced up sheepishly. "I hope I didn't offend you, Celia," he tested. "Seriously, I like your friend."

"It's no big deal," I said, which wasn't the truth at all. I decided to leave it alone, when he put his hand on my lower back and guided me onto the dance floor.

Because the Southern dress code doesn't tamp itself down until the last day of September, a kaleidoscope of colors swirled on the plywood. On the periphery, John stood by the stage holding an amber drink in a plastic cup, laughing loudly with two boys I didn't know. It wasn't a stretch for me to intuit that John was engaged in his favorite pastime—ridiculing some poor woman's dress. He stood crisp in the Southern standard of khaki pants and a button-down Oxford pressed within an inch of its life.

Any minute my father would make the appearance for which everyone waited. He'd stand tall and elegant on the verandah in his cream linen suit, his side-parted hair shining like the back of a wet seal. At the start of his yearly address, all voices would hush because my father's presence was such a rare occasion. People took advantage of the opportunity while the getting was good.

Hayward flashed his full-wattage smile as Tate ushered me onto the dance floor. He was dancing "The Pretzel" with Little Tea, casting her out then reeling her in with both hands. Across the way, John watched them, his lips tight, his eyes narrowed to menacing slants. From the stage, a rhythm-and-blues band played a rendition of Wilson Pickett's "Mustang Sally," and each time the singer got to the catchy refrain, Little Tea shimmied her svelte body all the way to the ground.

I spied my mother at the foot of the verandah's front stairs. Three men in bow ties vied for her attention, seemingly encouraged by it. Because my mother was so beautiful, she deflected her looks with the art of demure deferral. She was the kind of active listener that made people animated, but when the screen door opened, she excused herself and out walked my father. He shook a few hands on his way to the verandah's standing microphone. My mother, as though on cue, rustled in blue tulle straight to my father's side.

My father didn't bother testing the microphone. He ran a hand through his collar-length hair and began, "Thank y'all, each and every one of you, for coming out tonight. This party is our way of showing our sincere appreciation for all the hard work that went into this year's harvest. We had us one long, hot summer, but by the grace of God, the plantings held, and we've something to show for it. Many of y'all have been with us year after year, and all of us here at the farm are grateful for your continued loyalty. On behalf of my wife and sons and daughter, I welcome you all to our home." Pointing to Thelonious, who stood near the pit, he smiled and added, "Thelonious wore himself out putting the pig on, so with my gratitude, please fill your glasses at the bar and help yourselves to the pig."

I felt Hayward's hand on my shoulder. "Nothing superfluous. Just shows up and gets it done," he said. "Pretty good for a man who doesn't like parties, don't you think?"

"He's completely sincere," I returned. "Dad wouldn't do this every year if that wasn't the case."

He looked at me as though I should know better. "Oh, come on, you know this is basically Mom's party."

"Hayward, Mom doesn't tell Dad what to do. She just makes suggestions."

"Exactly, it's the Southern way. It's how women civilize men. They make suggestions then pretend to wait for approval. That way men think they're in charge."

Laughing because he had a point, I said, "You're twisted, Hayward."

"No, I'm not; I'm right. This is the kind of thing Mom would never admit, but I've been paying attention, and I'm telling you, it's why their marriage works."

"Your mother is gorgeous," Tate said from behind me, startling me because I hadn't realized he was listening. "You don't favor her much, Celia, do you?"

"Way to give a compliment, Tate," Hayward erupted. He laughed so hard at the faux pas, it bent him over.

I saw the color rise in Tate's face. "Oh, wait, Celia, I didn't mean it that way," he backtracked.

Little Tea leaned into the conversation and seized the moment. "No, Celia don't favor her mother, but Hayward does. Why don't you go on now and tell Hayward how pretty he is?"

"Hayward, you're a knockout," Tate said.

Hayward batted his eyes. "Well, thank you, Tate Foley. But don't let John hear you; he'd give his eyetooth to be the pretty one in this family."

"At least y'all have a sense of humor," Tate said.

"Oh, we've got that in spades," Hayward agreed.

"So what's the story with your brother, John?" Tate asked. "He's in my older brother's group, but I never see him around."

"He's in his second year at Ole Miss. He's rarely home," I told him. "He just came from Oxford for the party."

"Well if you wouldn't mind introducing me, I'd love to meet him," Tate said, as Hayward gave me an almost imperceptible frown.

Later, on the dance floor, Hayward put his hand on my arm and whispered, "Do yourself a favor. Keep Tate away from John."

It's not that I would have jumped at the chance to introduce Tate to John on the first night of what became a relationship to see me through high school. But something in Hayward's voice rang like a caveat, and for no reason beyond intuition, I heeded the call.

Heber Springs, Arkansas

Ava whispered through my cracked bedroom door, "Celia, you awake?"

"I am now," I said, rising in bed to my elbows.

"Stan just called," she said, now standing over my bed.

"What time is it?"

"Quarter to seven."

"Which translates to a quarter to five California time. Thanks, Ava. My head's not on straight. Why'd he call you so early? What'd he want?"

"I don't know. I didn't answer my phone," she said.

"So, what's the problem?" I got up, went to the window, and reeled up the blind. The morning light crept through the trees, softening the room to a deep, hazy gold.

"Do I have to call him back?" Ava looked at me in all seriousness, as though she truly didn't know.

I turned to face her. "Yes, you have to call him back. He's your husband. What are you doing here, hiding out?"

"Kind of," she said.

"Great," I exhaled. "Is Renny awake?"

"I don't know, let's go see." Ava stepped back into the hall.

"Wait a minute, Ava. Renny said not to wake her."

"We haven't been together in fifty million years, and you're going to listen to that?"

I lifted my robe from my suitcase. "Let me get the coffee going first." I tied the sash and walked out to the hall. "Have you seen the percolator? It was made in 1842. I think we're going to have to chant over it to get it to work."

Ava's silver-bell laughter trilled down the dark, narrow hallway. One step into the living room and I noticed the sun hadn't made its full way through the glass of the front room. It was morning-damp and cabin-cool in this perch overlooking the lake's wavering silence. Outside, a communion of birdsong rang in staccato rounds of call and recall.

"You start the coffee, I'll see about Renny," Ava said. She traipsed down the hall to Renny's bedroom, and I didn't hear a sound until Renny's swearing split the air. Ava rushed back to the kitchen while I spooned coffee into the aluminum basket. "Oh no," she gasped, her eyes wide, her hand covering her mouth. "I woke her up."

"I heard," I said. "Let me finish this and then let's go."

Minutes later, Ava and I jumped onto Renny's king-size bed. Renny rolled over, put a pillow over her head, and completely missed the humor. "I swear, y'all are so immature." Ava wasn't deterred. She tugged on Renny's covers, put a knee on either side of Renny and broke into song. "Wake up, wake up, the sun is up, the dew is on the buttercup."

"What ungodly hour of the morning is it?" Renny grumbled, pushing Ava off.

"It's about seven. Coffee will be ready in a minute," I answered.

"You better bring it to me because I'm not getting up," she said. "How late did y'all stay up?"

"Around midnight," I answered.

The percolator gasped in fitful, roiling phonics that pulsed down the hall as I went to the window. "It's dark as a tomb in here. Do you mind if I open the blind?"

"Give me a minute," Renny said, which caused Ava to vault to the window and yank down the cord. Renny sat up and placed her arms crosswise over her face. Drawing her knees in, she leaned against the headboard. "Ava, I don't know why I even try with you."

"Because you love me," Ava laughed, which, of course, was true. I always thought Renny had what verged on a protective, maternal devotion when it came to Ava. But then Ava elicited this in me, too, though my alignment with her was based on identification, a somewhat empathetic, commiserative response to Ava's disassociated nature. Ava and I both considered ourselves outsiders, though Ava's reasons were subtle, far less defined than mine. Beneath Ava's dreamy remoteness was a somewhat delusional belief system, and for much of her life, that belief system worked.

"Stan called me this morning," Ava said to Renny, her way of asking for Renny's opinion.

"What'd you tell him?" Renny fired. "I know you didn't tell him when you're coming back."

I looked disbelievingly at Ava. "You didn't tell Stan when you're coming back? What's he thinking you're doing here? I thought you were kidding about 'kind of hiding out.' How'd y'all leave it?"

"I don't know, Celia, open-ended, I guess. I'm on summer break at the clinic until September. I can do whatever I want."

"I get that," I said, "but does he think this is a separation?"

"No. He thinks I've just come home to see Mama. He doesn't know I'm here at the lake with y'all."

"Or that she's confused, or that she's talking to Mark, or that his marriage hangs in the balance," Renny added. The irritation in her voice seemed to drive her from the bed. She rose quickly and walked down the hall to the kitchen, and in short order, I heard a cabinet opening, a coffee mug clatter on the counter, the carafe filling it up.

"Renny's just concerned," I said to Ava.

"I know," she said, rolling off the bed.

I followed her down the hall.

In a tone that bordered on asking for approval, Ava entered the kitchen and said to Renny, "I didn't talk to Stan when he called because I wasn't ready. I'll call him after I get some coffee."

Renny took her time responding. She sipped her coffee, took a carton of milk from the refrigerator, poured a bit in her mug, and for a minute I didn't think she'd say anything. "Well, I'm not telling you what to do, but under the circumstances it's probably best that you don't get into some long, drawn-out thing," Renny finally suggested. "I wouldn't let the cat out of the bag just yet. Best not to say anything you're gonna regret. Sweet-talk him if you have to. You know how to do that, right?"

A nose-scrunched pout flashed on Ava's disbelieving face. She tilted her head and said, "Surely you know me better than that."

I stood thinking Renny should have. If she remembered anything about that night down by the river in our sophomore year, she wouldn't have asked Ava if she knew how to sweet-talk.

Memphis, Tennessee
Sometime in the 1980s

In high school, our group called it "The Bridge," even though it was one of three straddling the Mississippi River. When our group spoke of it, we didn't mean the obvious bridge—that modern, eye-catching, steel arch that takes off from the riverfront cobblestones, soars over the water in a cursive letter M, and touches down in West Memphis, Arkansas. We had no interest in its predecessor either: The Memphis-Arkansas Bridge. To us, there was only one bridge worth talking about—the cantilevered Harahan Bridge, the old train bridge with verboten cache, for all its looming black, historic elegance. In an overgrown part of the wooded bluffs, the base of the bridge was where our group convened when we sought the underbelly of our insulated lives. We were on the cusp of adulthood now that we each had a driver's license. We were at that time in our lives where we thought we were more than we were: smarter than our parents, qualified to forge beyond the shackles of their supervision, and to be in a part of Memphis there was no good reason to be gave us a sense of walking the prohibited. It's not that we tried to get away with something for its own sake. There were simply some things we thought our parents didn't know that we did. Under most circumstances, to be down by the river at night was unthinkable. In the eighties, downtown's historic Beale Street was in the process of redevelopment and had yet to grow into the full potential of the three vibrant blocks of restaurants and nightclubs it eventually became. Back then, the shady, unkempt area of the bluffs near the Harahan Bridge was left to its own dodgy devices, fair game to anyone and anything in need of the veil of night. And we thought we were untouchable, that the shimmer of our starry-eyed youth protected us by sheer force of our specialness. The truth is, we'd been treated as such all our lives. Whatever it was our parents had gone through to achieve their standing in Memphis was something we never considered. We'd arrived on the scene privileged from birth and simply took it for granted that we'd be shielded all our lives.

What I remember most about that Saturday night was the full moon. Were it not for the luminous orb suspended over the scenery, the rest of the night wouldn't have happened as it did. But there's no fighting the black art of bad timing. When pitted against youth and optimism, bad timing will win every time.

We'd gone down to the bridge that night in three cars: Tate and I, Mark and Ava, and Renny and a guy named Hunter Phillips, whom she dated every now and again. Though Tate brought a fifth of Wild Turkey, Mark had a half keg of beer in the trunk and handed out paper cups stamped with the Budweiser logo. He'd angled his '73 Ford Falcon near the southeast end of the Harahan Bridge in a patch of clover before the cracked, weathered asphalt, where shrubbery, tallgrass, and river cane bordered the incline. His car doors were open, and Al Green's honeyed and soulful voice spilled out of a cassette. I unfurled the blanket Tate kept in his flatbed and swayed to the Memphis-classic beat of *Take Me to the River*. Ava burned bright and ethereal, more so than usual on this early June night. She was in the rapturous, first flush of love with Mark Clayton, which Renny said kept her outside her better senses. But I understood the unbalancing quality of new love, how overwhelming and consuming it could be. I'd been dating Tate exclusively for well past a year and had yet to arrive at my footing.

"I know what I want to do, y'all," Ava purred. "I want to get in the water."

"Don't be insane," Tate said. "There's all kinds of crap in that muddy water, not to mention the undertow. Bulrush, snakes … you don't know what all's in there."

Ava glided to the river's edge. "I'm not going in all the way, I'm just going to put my feet in the water."

Mark sprang from the blanket. "Wait a minute, Ava, come on back here, honey. It's too dark to see what's ahead of you."

Hunter Phillips was a clean-cut guy, steady and mature beyond his youth. There was something gangly in his whippet-thin stature, nerdy in his horn-rimmed spectacles, but his face was chiseled and defined. And although he was awkward, you could tell that, in a decade or so, he'd grow into something impressive.

Hunter was a classmate of Tate and Mark's, the son of a fowl-hunting buddy of Tate's father. Hunter had his turkey call with him that night and thrilled us by pulling the little black- and-yellow diaphragm from his pocket and putting it on top of his tongue. Pushing it to the roof of his mouth, he dropped his chin and emitted notes from high to low, the perfectly pitched yelp of a hen. We all got such a kick out of the sound, that we begged him to do it repeatedly. Which is why Hunter was demonstrating the turkey call the entire time he and Renny waded through the brush and climbed up to the train tracks. They stood beneath the moon glow, looking down at Mark and Ava at the river's edge, while Tate and I stayed on the bluff. Ava had her skirt off and wriggled in her white cotton underwear. She was making toward the water when flashing red lights whirred from two police cars patrolling Riverside Drive. Within seconds, doors clapped, and two officers appeared, sweeping flashlights too quick to avoid.

"Thanks for calling the cops, Hunter," Tate shouted, and I could hear Ava's laughter bubbling ahead. Turning from the water, she slipped into her skirt, stepped into her flats, and seemed unconcerned over the flashlights lighting her every move. Sashaying forward, she patted her hair and smiled as though she'd been expecting these uniformed men. Holding up her hand, Ava said, "Now, I know what this looks like, officers. It looks like we're up to no good. But, you see, today is my sixteenth birthday. This is my fault. I insisted we all come down to the river to celebrate, so if y'all wanna get mad, get mad at me."

The officers exchanged a wary look as though they'd seen Ava's like before. One started to speak, but Ava kept going. "My uncle is a police officer in St. Louis," she chattered. "So I have the greatest respect for the law. Seriously, officers, we don't mean any harm. If you want us to leave, we'll pack up now and won't come down here again." As the officers studied Ava, we all knew we were off the hook. There'd be no checking of IDs, no calling dispatch, and no further involvement because Ava had performed the tactical maneuver of getting to them before they could get to us.

"Bad part of town, wrong time of night to be down here," one of them said, and that was the worst that came of it. It was the first time I'd heard one of Ava's bald-face lies, when she'd made mention of her fictitious uncle. But because she was adept at spinning what people wanted to hear, in Ava's mind, her lies were little and white.

I figured Ava would use one of her little white lies when she talked to Stan, or at the least, a lie by omission. She had a circuitous way of talking as it was, a desultory way of stringing together non sequiturs that I could only characterize as classically Ava, in that there was a musing quality to her way of talking, as though the rapid succession of thoughts that ricocheted inside her head bounced at such a speed, it was all she could do to grasp the half of them. There was no taking anything Ava said literally. When it came to Ava, I was in the habit of simply following her general drift.

Since Ava had gone downstairs to make her phone call, and Renny had gone off to change into her bathing suit, I took my coffee outside on the deck, where an unsettled feeling arose that might have been anxiety. I was edgy. Out of place in a region that once gave my life context. I thought about calling the touchstone of David but decided it would be better to call at the end of the day, when there'd be more to report. Looking through the timber, I felt something within me align with the environment that reminded me of my childhood in Como, Mississippi. It was hard to say if it was the feel of the South, or the feeling I had being in it, but something soft and familiar descended, a feeling that I would always be a part of the South, even though in the moment I felt unreconciled. I sat in a canvas chair, put my feet on the rail, and thought about what Little Tea had said to me the year my family moved to Memphis. She said changing your address doesn't change who you are. At the time I agreed with her. But here's what I've learned since: a change of address might not matter, but the things that happen to a person do.

Ava crept up behind me. "Stan's either busy or he's mad at me. He's not answering his phone." She flopped heavily in the chair beside me and gave a dramatic sigh. "Just as well. I don't know what I'm going to say anyway."

"Well sooner or later you're going to have to formulate a plan," I told her.

"I know that, but for now I'm fine with winging it. Where's Renny?"

"Getting ready to take us out on the lake," I said. "In a minute, I'm going to go in and put my suit on."

"I will too, but let me ask you something," Ava said as Renny appeared on the deck.

"Am I interrupting?" Renny asked.

"Oh no, I was just going to ask if y'all mind that I invited Mark. He said he'd call me this morning."

Still behind us, Renny said, "Okay, good to know." She paused, as though considering. "Tell y'all what, go on and get it together. I want to get out there early. Mark has his own boat; you can tell him where we are when he calls."

But Mark never called, and it made Ava sullen the rest of the day. It seemed now that a dark energy surrounded her. She seemed inwardly focused and distracted, in a self-created fog that colored land and sky and water. Ava's mood influenced the entire afternoon, while Renny and I tiptoed around it, exchanging knowing glances and shrugged shoulders that spoke more than words could say. At eight thirty that night, just as I was tiring of the downtrodden climate, the sound of tires scratching in the driveway brought a spring to Ava's step. She rushed to the kitchen window and caroled, "They're here."

"They?" Renny repeated.

"Yes, Tate's with Mark. And guess what, Celia. Tate's wearing blue."

★ ★ ★

My brother, John, told Tate he should always wear blue. It was the first thing he said to him, when I finally introduced them on a Saturday morning in Como. At the time, I thought it was an unusual thing for one man to say to another, but then John was inordinately fashion conscious. My father had come out of his den at the behest of my mother, who was now on familiar terms with Tate because she always answered the door whenever he came to see me in Memphis. That I had invited Tate out to Como seemed to seal the deal of our courtship in my mother's estimation. She kissed Tate on his cheek when she saw him and showered him with attention to the point where he blushed.

My family's full assembly greeted Tate in the living room, on that early spring morning. I'd asked Tate to come out for the day to see Little Tea run in a school meet. What I really wanted was for Little Tea to like Tate better than she did, though it's not that she disliked him, it was more that she nurtured skepticism. The casement windows in the solarium were open to the scent of trellised jasmine as Elvita skirted around Hayward, who played Chopin on the grand piano.

"Y'all want the front door open to get some air in here?" Elvita asked, setting a silver tray on the coffee table.

"That would be nice, Elvita, thank you," my mother said. "Tate, sit down, honey. Can I pour you a cup?"

"Thank you, Mrs. Wakefield, I'd love that," Tate said, and it was then my brother John cleared his throat.

Unable to ignore the obvious prompt, I said, "Tate, this is my brother, John."

Tate stepped to where John stood and held out his hand. "Pleasure to meet you," he said. "I believe you know my brother Lincoln."

"Yes. I can tell by looking at you that y'all are brothers. Y'all have the same show-stopping eyes. If I had them, I'd never go anywhere without wearing a shirt the exact color of blue as you've got on. It's fabulous on you, brings out the color. Where's Lincoln now? Virginia, isn't he? I've lost track of too many people since high school."

"He's in his second year at William and Mary, studying economics," Tate said, a wash of pink rising to his face.

"Does he plan on going into the family business?" John lobbied.

"Yes, that's the plan," Tate returned.

"I admire people who know their way ahead." John lowered himself to the sofa and poured a cup of coffee, barely taking his eyes off Tate as he did. My father sat legs crossed in the wingback chair, watching the exchange with black, level eyes, a focus so steady I could feel its heat.

"Hayward," John drawled, "I think we've all had enough of the piano. Why don't you detach yourself for once and join the rest of us? Do try to act civilized."

Hayward stood abruptly. "At your command, John, though I invite you to reconsider your use of language. If you want me to socialize all you have to do is ask."

"Oh, for heaven's sake you two." My mother waved her hand. "Tate, you'll have to excuse my boys."

"I have brothers myself, Mrs. Wakefield. I know how it is."

"Civilized, socialized, they're the same thing, Hayward," John sniffed.

"No, they're not. Civilized has a broader reach. Not appropriate for this occasion," Hayward said, winking at me.

"Tate, I understand y'all are going out to the school to see Little Tea race," my father said.

"Yes sir, I'm looking forward to it." Tate sat down in an upholstered chair across from my father.

"Celia's proud of her. We all are. I'd go myself, but I have work to do. You'll have to come back and tell me about it afterwards," my father said.

John fired quickly, "Dad, you know Celia will the second she comes through that door. All we ever hear from her is Little Tea this and Little Tea that. I, for one, am not interested. Who cares if that little coon can run? It's not like it'll get her anywhere."

"Hush," my mother warned. "Elvita might hear you, John. Lower your voice."

I turned my eyes to Hayward and held my breath to stop myself from saying what I knew to be true—that John was a racist and Little Tea's God-given talent would be the ticket to her future. I could tell from Hayward's narrowed eyes that he thought the same thing too. I started thinking maybe I'd explain things to Tate later, tell him John was a contrarian by nature, that he'd been at his uncharacteristic best when he'd complimented his eyes. The curiosity was that John's compliment somehow registered with Tate, and although he wasn't possessed of vanity in any overt way, from that day onward, Tate exchanged his customary white Oxford cloth shirts in favor of blue.

Now, from the kitchen window, Ava repeated, "Celia? I hope you heard me. Tate's wearing blue," she over-enunciated.

I slid my chair from the counter and walked deep into the living room as two car doors slammed, the screen door squeaked, and a hard knock came to the kitchen door in an arpeggio that brought out my fear. I would have liked to have had more preparation for this moment. Outside, the white moon warmed eerily through the prism of gray clouds drifting. I was suspended in a pregnant pause, until the moment Tate Foley stepped in the room.

In an act of corporeal betrayal that belied the present facts, I felt my blood run hot and flush my face, fanning the embers of the infernal days when Tate and I were inseparable. I assumed I was obscured in the shadows of the living room, but when he stepped through the threshold, Tate's quick eyes cut straight to me. His blond hair grayed prominently at his hairline and temples but was the kind of gray in which true blonds are gifted, the kind that blends seamlessly. He didn't look to have gained an ounce since I'd last seen him, but he moved a bit differently, more self-consciously, the kind of walk you just can't help when you know you're being watched.

"I heard you were down here," Tate said when he reached me. "I had to come out to see for myself."

"How you doing, Tate?" I rose from my chair. "Long time."

"Years. I was beginning to think you didn't like us anymore." He stepped forward and gave me an awkward hug.

"Well, you know, a lot has changed," I said, more haltingly than I intended. "There's not as much reason to come down here as there once was."

"No. I imagine there's not. I didn't get to talk to you much the last time you were down here," Tate continued. "I'm sorry about that. There was so much going on, I thought I should give you some space. You know what I mean."

"I understand," I said.

"But I'm glad I met your husband. Y'all got married right after that, didn't you?"

"A year later," I said, deciding that the best defense was simply to be conversational. "I brought David down here, so he'd know what he was getting into with me. He'd never been to the South before, so it was an eye-opening experience. I took him down to the river for Memphis in May. He's from Chicago and loves the blues, but he'd never seen where the blues actually came from."

"Yankees," Tate laughed. "Chicago blues and the Delta blues are two different animals."

"Exactly," I said, smiling. "That's just what I told him."

Mark and Ava came into the living room while Renny stood at the kitchen sink, cracking ice from aluminum trays into a bucket. Mark produced a bottle of Wild Turkey from a brown paper bag, set it on the coffee table and said, "For old times' sake," then settled on the sofa, shoulder to shoulder with Ava.

"I remember you and David down here during Memphis in May, Celia," Renny called from the kitchen. "Jimmy and I went down there with y'all to see the Bar-Kays, or whatever version of that band it was at the time, remember? That was before I figured out Jimmy was a loser. I should have never married the guy."

"You live and learn, Renny," I said.

"Ain't that the truth." She carried the ice bucket and a stack of glasses into the living room and set them on the coffee table. "Y'all help yourselves," she invited. "Remember that time in high school when we were all at that club—Birth of the Blues—and a couple of the Bar-Kays got up on stage out of nowhere? We were the only white kids in the club. We danced our butts off. Those were some good times. I tell you what, we couldn't get away with that kind of thing now, if we had to."

Mark poured the liquor into a glass and handed it to Ava. "The funny thing was we were all underage, but back then, nobody checked IDs," he said. "I remember thinking Memphis was the most backward city on the planet when I first moved from Kentucky. We could go anywhere because there was never anyone minding the store. But boy, did we see the greats: Ma Rainey, Furry Lewis, Etta James; some of the real Mississippi Delta blues artists were still alive when we were coming up." He poured a drink for himself without pause. "It staggers the mind to think we were there. I kind of took it for granted then, but I don't anymore. Now I realize how lucky we were to grow up in Memphis."

Tate poured a drink, handed it to me, poured himself one, then sat down in a recliner. "There was still such a divide between the races though. All of it implied, of course. And since we were white kids, we were deferred to wherever we went, especially downtown. Even though it was decades after integration, Memphis was slow to embrace the change."

"Memphis was slow to embrace the mind frame, that's what it was," Ava said. "Mark, will you pour me a bit more? This is less than a finger."

"Here, I got it, Mark." Tate poured the whisky in Ava's glass. "Ava, you have to consider the setup. Memphis was much smaller back then.

Since you mentioned the mind frame, let me suggest that it was just the influence of prior generations still set in their ways. Doesn't matter that they went through the civil rights era. If you think about it, the generation that thought that way raised the next generation, so some of the pre-integration fears and attitudes remained. An entire cultural way of life had to dissipate. I think our generation saw the tail end of it. There may have been integration when we were young, but in no way was it widely accepted social integration. You have to admit that."

Ava sat taller in her seat. "I wouldn't say it's much different now," she said. "Maybe a little, but not completely. The South is still behind other parts of the country as far as that goes."

Mark reached into the ice bucket, dropped another cube in his glass. "Well, part of it was because the civil rights movement got sidelined by the Vietnam War. They got a foothold, all right, but the youth that came up behind it was spearheaded by dope-smoking, acid-dropping war protestors intent on another cause. Then feminism and all that bra-burning got into the mix. I don't know, just seemed they lost their focus." He paused then added, "The civil rights movement wasn't seen through fully the way it could have been. Yes, there was integration of the races in name, but what Ava said is right, it was the mind frame." He pointed an index finger to the side of his head. "And what Tate said holds true. There still isn't complete racial integration on a widely accepted social level." Mark cast a glance at me. "Celia, I know it's different out there in California, right?"

"Most definitely," I said. "In California people are lenient to people not exactly like them. Californians embrace growth and change. Down here, we've got to get rid of the old guard before anything—or anyone—changes."

I could feel Tate's eyes burning me. I looked over to see him blushing beneath the burden of our history before he averted his eyes and turned away.

"Not necessarily," he whispered.

Como, Mississippi
Sometime in the 1980s

Hayward opened the car door. "Here Rufus, up," he encouraged, and I swear that dog was smiling. Hayward was in the habit of taking his coonhound with him everywhere. That they were so devoted to each other tugged on my heartstrings, and rarely did I see one without the other. From a scuttling tap dance on the gravel, Rufus sprang into the back seat of Hayward's cream-colored, four-door Volvo, then arranged himself facing eagerly forward, as though ready to navigate the road.

"I'll get in the back with Rufus," I said to Tate, as Hayward slid behind the wheel.

Hayward turned to look at me. "All right, we all set?" There was such fire in his eyes, such life-enhancing enthusiasm that I could feel my soul rise. Hayward had such a cloud-parting effect on me that he made our ten-minute ride to North Panola High School in Sardis seem like a trip to the beach. He turned the volume up on the radio and Bruce Springsteen's "Thunder Road" rang door-to-door. "You're going to love this, Tate, trust me," Hayward said. "Little Tea's going to show you how it's done."

Behind the small, two-module brown-and-white school, bleachers rose at the north end of the cinder track. We were the only white people in attendance, and I could tell by his rigid posture that Tate was as uncomfortable in his blue-blooded skin as he was in the humid, lack-luster environment. Tate's peripheral vision seemed to be on red alert. He swiveled around repeatedly, looking behind his back. He slid his monogrammed handkerchief from his Oxford cloth pocket, touched it to his brow, and gave me a tight smile.

"Hey, Tate, relax, man," Hayward said lightly, giving him a light punch on the shoulder. "You're flanked by two Wakefields. Celia and I've got you covered." He patted Rufus on the head. "If all else fails, Rufus will guard you. Isn't that right, good boy?"

Down below Little Tea traipsed to the starting line in her prancing, coltish stride. Light danced around her in such a way, it dazzled my riveted eyes. She had her hair braided in tight cornrows, gathered in a band on the top of her head. They flapped with their own agenda, whirring like yarn propellers with every turn of her chin. Her sharp shoulder blades protruded from her black T-back shirt, emboldened on front with NPHS in gold. In her matching jersey shorts, she bounced like an alley cat in Nikes, waiting to position her heel on the block in anticipation of the starting gun.

"Now watch her," Hayward alerted Tate, his voice soaring with pride by association. He pointed to where Little Tea was crouching, one knee hovering on the track, one foot behind the other, hips up, fingertips on the ground. "This is Little Tea's event. One hundred meters. She wins every time."

And she did. Little Tea was first to launch from the blocks; the race was over in thirteen sprinting seconds. While her competitors grimaced, Little Tea maintained a smile through the race. I looked at Hayward to see his lips curled in satisfaction. For a fleeting second, I thought I saw mist in his eyes. He stretched from his seat and said, "I told ya, didn't I? Y'all watch Rufus for a minute. Good boy, Rufus, stay." In a flash he descended the bleachers, two at a time to where Little Tea smiled behind the wire partition.

"You want to go down there?" Tate offered. "I'll watch the dog."

"No, I'll wait until later," I said. "I see her parents walking toward her, and since Hayward's her self-appointed coach, he'll want a minute to praise her." I watched Hayward leaning forward, his hands on the diamond-patterned wire fence, nose to nose with Little Tea, who reached up and set her cornrows free to cascade around her face. I sat thinking it might have been any other moment, with Hayward and Little Tea joking over one thing or another. Watching them from a distance, I felt, once again, outside of their private moment.

Hayward had waited for the inevitability of good timing because he was never one to forget a slight. Once back at the farm, he found John in the kitchen. He walked to the refrigerator as though it were his destination, but I knew Hayward rarely entered any room where John was without having a specific plan.

"Y'all are back, I see," John said as Tate and I pulled chairs from beneath the kitchen table. "It's about time y'all were. Because of that race, Elvita's been gone for the better part of the day, and I want my lunch."

"She probably didn't realize it's beneath you to fend for yourself," Hayward said. "Don't worry, Elvita's on her way back. I'm only dropping off Rufus before we go into town. Oh, and by the way, that little coon, as you called her—the one who won't get anywhere in life—had two college scouts waiting to meet her. It can be time-consuming to be in demand."

John did as he always did; he got sarcastic. "Very funny, Hayward. It's not necessary to be smug. What'd you do, save up for that one?"

"I didn't have to for long, did I? It'd be different if you ever knew what you were talking about."

"So what?" John went to the refrigerator, riled enough to make his own sandwich. "So Little Tea's being watched. What's the big deal?"

"College scholarships, of course. Something you wouldn't know about."

"You wouldn't either, Hayward. I notice no one came knocking on your door to offer you academic support. The only thing you've got going for you is your musical talent, and where's that going to get you on this farm? Anyway, who cares? Little Tea's only in tenth grade," John dismissed.

"High school goes quickly, John. She'll be applying to colleges soon. You have to look ahead with this kind of thing."

John switched the subject. "Hayward, why can't you get that dog out of the kitchen?" He never admitted it, but John knew well enough when he'd been put in his place.

"Oh, for heaven's sake, John," I said. "We live on a farm. It's not like Rufus is a feral animal." I looked at Hayward. "I'll run take him to your room. We should go. Thelonious and Little Tea are probably already at Pop's Shop."

"Where is the mayonnaise?" John emoted. "And please don't tell me y'all are breaking bread with that family. Hayward, I thought you just said Elvita's on her way back."

"She is. We're meeting Little Tea and Thelonious, and breaking bread is exactly what we'll do."

"Well, I hope you don't run into any of my friends," John said flatly. "It's one thing for Celia to be running wild around here with Little Tea and quite another to go public. And Thelonious? What's he going to be doing sitting there with y'all?"

"John," Hayward said, with great satisfaction, "I'm happy to tell you we're his guests."

★ ★ ★

Always, in the month of May, there is such greening hope in Como, Mississippi. I am always awed by the breath-catching wonder of the earth born anew. May is the time of year before the summer heat freights the air, when spring settles into her teeming promise and holds for a while in the miracle of a contract cyclically fulfilled. There's a suspension of breadth, a lightness to depth of field. Colors shine from every glowing hue of the spectrum beneath a sky so endless, I grew up unconcerned with what lies beyond the loess soil that borders the outskirts of town like an aged photograph. We eased our way beneath canopies of oak trees, sweet gum, and hickory on the way to Main Street. Virginia creeper and curly dock tangled by the side of the road and, intermittently, wide open pasture. It is a wide, flat, mood-defining area of Como. It is low to the ground and holds fast to its history, whispers its stories, and calls to the blood of my lineage in a memory that still anchors me earthbound.

We turned onto Main Street, where a grass median partitioned the street from the railroad tracks separating Highway 51 on the west side of town from I-55 on the east. On the low grass, the community storm shelter's two metal doors reclined side by side like submerged coffins with rust-corroded lids, the handrails at the right of each no bigger than a coat hanger. At the north end of Main, Holy Innocents Episcopal Church loomed one-storied and impressive, its centered cross crowning the slate, A-framed roof and pillared front porch. At the south end of Main, Como United Methodist Church reigned majestic. Between these holy houses of worship, a slash of one-storied, historically preserved one-off businesses leaned against each other shotgun style telling a collective story of hard knocks and changing times.

Tate, Hayward, and I were still buzzing from Little Tea's victory as we single-filed into Pop's Shop. A string of metal balls bounced on the glass door like errant sleigh bells, the door suctioning to a hissing close behind us. Everywhere inside, varied tones of earthen russet. The constant assault of brewing coffee tainted the one-room space from its lackluster floor to its aged brick walls. The walls were cobbled in mismatched sizes. It appeared the idea of symmetry took a back seat to the more immediate priority of getting the walls put up. The "Farmer's Almanac's Gardening by the Moon Calendar" held pride of place from a nail behind the free-standing ice cream freezer, turned to the month of May. It was a come-as-you-are atmosphere in Pop's Shop, a frayed elegance to its shopworn, open floor plan with round, Formica tables scattered harum-scarum in hues of red and redder still. We placed our order beneath the whirr of a standing aluminum fan in the back. It felt like being in somebody's kitchen—somebody easy in their skin, unconcerned with appearances with their only concern being that the whole of the place worked. The first item on the walled menu was the daily plate lunch, detailing which meat came with what three sides and plenty of gravy. My family came to Pop's

Shop so often, none of us bothered looking at the menu. We ordered fried chicken and slaw, and that was the end of that.

Thelonious got to his feet when he saw us coming. He pulled a chair out for me and took off his hat. I scooted next to Little Tea, set my purse beneath the table then leaned in to give her a hug. Tate angled himself into the chair next to me. "How does it feel to be a winner?" I said to Little Tea. "You're going to be famous one day, I can feel it. If you don't believe me, then just wait and see."

"Well you're going to be broke, you don't get that purse off the floor," Little Tea said, though she was laughing. It was her way of deflecting attention, which she typically did with humor. It was one of the many things I loved about Little Tea. She wielded her arsenal of witticisms and superstitions with such rapid, intelligent timing, it seemed she walked the live wire of conversation a step ahead of the rest of us. Reaching under the table, she placed my purse on the table demonstratively. "There," she said, her tone final. "Don't make me worry about you ending up in the poorhouse."

"You're more superstitious than my mother, which is saying a lot," I said. "Between the two of y'all, I'm afraid to go anywhere."

Little Tea lifted her haughty chin and said, "Good thing you got me to save you from yourself."

Hayward pulled out a chair whose spindly legs rubbed the floor loudly. "Hey Thelonious," he started, his words running together, "what'd you think? You saw it all, right? Have you ever? I knew she'd win, but who knew it'd be by that much?"

"I couldn't be prouder of my little girl here," Thelonious said. He rolled the cuffs of his shirtsleeves past his massive wrists and smiled broadly at his daughter.

"She's a star, all right," Hayward continued. "I know you must have seen the two scouts drooling over her after she won. One day, Little Tea's going to have to pick and choose where to go to college. Not a bad position to be in. By the way, did y'all order lunch?"

"We got it all seen to it's coming," Little Tea answered, though she seemed unable to meet Hayward's eyes.

"I only wish my father could have seen her," Hayward said. "I'm sure he will next time, but, you know, he was in his den."

"Umm-hmm," Thelonious said, "I know how that be. He's a busy man. Specially this time of year. I best be getting back there myself, coming up here."

"But it's Saturday," I said.

"Time of year," Thelonious murmured. "Been this way forever."

"Don't y'all plant cotton in July? What's going on now?" Tate queried.

"We're planting soybeans now," Thelonious said. "It's the way of the seasons."

"How long have you been working the land out there?" Tate wanted to know.

"Let me see here." Thelonious looked up, calculating. "Since we was about twelve. Must be nigh on forty years now."

"We?" Tate asked.

"Mr. J. T. and me," Thelonious answered.

"That's what everyone calls my father," I clarified. "It stands for John Tallinghast. My father's father is Big John, and since Dad has his father's same given name, people have always called him J. T."

"I knew that," Tate said. "That's how my parents know him. They tell me there's only one J. T."

"That's right," Thelonious agreed. "Need not be two when you got one such as that. He done broke the mold."

"Thelonious and Dad grew up together," Hayward said to Tate. "They both lived out at the farm."

"It was a plantation back then, or so we called it," Thelonious clarified. "Times is changed now, but it's the same thing."

"Thelonious's parents worked for my grandparents," I told Tate.

"And theirs before them," Little Tea added. "We all go way back."

"I see," Tate concluded. "Must be a generational relationship built on trust."

"And common ground too," Thelonious said.

"Thelonious all but saved my father's life last year," I blurted.

Thelonious leaned forward and said, "But, Miss Celia, we don't talk about that now." It was a cautionary tone he used, with notes of discipline, more of a statement, really, and I suddenly needed something to do with my hands. I removed the napkin from my plastic cutlery and smoothed it over and over in my lap, grateful for the moment when our waitress came around with our lunch.

I never believed my father followed his true calling in life, which is what I planned on telling Tate later, since I'd unthinkingly opened my mouth. And I think Thelonious might have thought the same, though he never came out and said it. When Thelonious stopped me from elaborating, it had nothing to do with his humility, should I have embarrassed him by going on to tell about his bravery. He was safeguarding my father's image out of loyalty, for any version of the story would have portrayed my father as something other than he was. My father was a gentle soul, artistic in temperament. He had his own version of the world, which was at variance with the world he'd been born to. To look at my father, you would have never guessed he was a businessman. Should you have encountered him on the street, a poet or painter would have first come to mind. He had the look of a spring fawn in his sable eyes. They were sensitive eyes, soulful and deep-set, graced by arcs of full crescent brows. His full mouth was wide and sensuous. He wore his dark hair Renaissance style, swept back from his forehead to fall in one flowing length. There's no other way to describe my father than to say he was a beautiful man. But what to do with a man such as he, born to a life that didn't suit him? My father should have been born a Knight of the Order; a seventeenth-century stonemason in Venice; an Irish bard to a Tudor king. Instead, he was born in 1940s Como, Mississippi, into the empire of his father, Big John.

Big John was a man used to giving orders, and even more used to people falling in line. He ran the Wakefield Plantation by instilling fear, his domineering manner uncompromising, his robust stature intimidating. Big John was the kind of man who could blow any minute. People took a servile approach to keeping his temper tamped down. That my father was Big John's only child sealed his destiny. He'd inherited a life in lieu of forging his own. The weight of his father's expectation was inexorable, and although it burdened my father with a life not of his making, I can't say he was without familial pride at being born to the Wakefield plantation. I believe there were some white-collar aspects my father embraced. Once Big John retired, that he was responsible for the livelihoods of so many locals gave his innate, solicitous altruism an outlet. Being sensitive to the needs of others, he saw his vocation as something integral to a whole. But my father looked like a painter because he was one. He spoke like a poet because he was in love with language. The built-in shelves in his library housed leather-bound volumes by Shakespeare and Rilke, Pushkin and Goethe. On the wall to the right of his desk, by the cathedral glass doors leading to his private porch, an etching of William Butler Yeats in a pair of pince-nez loomed over a Demilune table, graced on its marble top with a Victorian inkwell and pen. It was a gentleman's den, a scholar's library, and I knew my father wrote poetry at his leather-topped desk, though he rarely shared it. But I could always tell when he'd been writing. He'd come out of his library with a dazed look about him, as though his head had yet to calibrate to the world as it is. I knew better than to speak to my father, when he'd come out to the foyer after one of his transcending writing spells. He wouldn't be available for quite some time; it would take him a while to acclimate to his surroundings. Many mistook my father as being aloof, but I believe he was socially reticent in fear of being misunderstood. It's almost understandable why my father was prone to depression: he had an artistic edge he simply found hard to reconcile with his surroundings. His were abysmal, gray-clouded days typically strung together in voids my mother called low tides. Although he was harmless during these episodes, and my family never discussed them, it was during one of his dark nights of the soul that Thelonious saved his life.

There was an outbuilding near the edge of the pond that was not much more than a glorified storage shed. It housed fishing tackle and ropes, grass-cutting scythes, the odd pitchfork. In the very back was deep shelving, where my father kept turpentine, easels, and paints. He was a sporadic painter, but when one of his fits became a start, it turned into an obsession. He'd be struck with inspiration at the oddest of times, and on that particular Friday night, he'd been drinking. I wouldn't have called my father a drinking man, but when he drank, he drank the quality hard stuff with full commitment. None of us knew he'd been drinking that night. Nobody ever kept tabs on his absences. When he'd wandered out to the shed that night, we were none of us the wiser, or at least I thought this was the case, when I woke to mayhem at two o'clock in the morning. Three fire engines roared onto the property, tearing up the uneven terrain on the swath they cut to the pond. Through my north-facing window, I saw the late winter grass violently aflame and heard a series of explosions coming from the shed like staccato rounds of echoing gunfire. Terrified, I ran to the hallway, straight to Hayward's bedroom. But Hayward wasn't in his room, so next I ran to my mother. It was apparent she hadn't caught wind of it yet, for she woke with a jolt when I screamed, "Fire, and it looks like it's down at the shed!"

My mother rushed to the window to see for herself then threw a coat over her nightgown. She flew down the front stairs, then rounded back to my father's den with me at her frantic heels. Finding his door open, she let out a panicked, "Oh, God, no," as we made for the front door. It was an evil, erratic torrent when we got there, a shrieking, demonic inferno that uplit the woods. I couldn't hear what my mother was shouting over the deafening drone of fire engines. She was angling between two medics who hovered over my prone father, one strapping an oxygen mask to his face. I was wet to the bone in a matter of seconds as geysers of water surged skyward through hoses the length of a football field. There was no safe quarter in this harrowing scene and, bad as it was, it was worse to consider what it might yet become should the February wind turn against us. I looked to my left to see Thelonious, a blanket draped around him, refusing the advances of another medic. I followed his gaze to Hayward who stood by the pond's edge beside Little Tea.

They took my father to the hospital in Senatobia, where they kept him two days for observation. It wasn't until six in the morning that I got the full story, which came out haltingly from Hayward. That he'd been down at the pond in the dead of night was something my altered reasoning hadn't factored. My concern was focused on the bigger framework: how the fire had started, how my father was involved. As explained by Hayward, it sounded like a list of singular variables that would have been innocuous on their own: single malt Scotch, a blustery evening, a Cuban cigar, and no forethought of risk. Hayward heard the explosion, but Thelonious beat him to it. By the time Hayward got to the shed, Thelonious was already inside. He had my unconscious father slung over his shoulder and carried his dead weight to the grass as the shed burst into a wall of flames.

When my mother telephoned my brother John in Oxford to tell him the story, he got all holier-than-thou about my father's drinking and gave her a litany of accusatory rhetoric, saying we all needed to keep a better eye on him, that when our grandfather found out, there'd be hell to pay. It was John who questioned what Hayward had been doing out at the pond that night. When my mother came to me with John's comments, I was too annoyed with John to care.

It wasn't often that Big John made an appearance at the farm. He was in his eighties now and fully ensconced in his life in Memphis. He'd been a gentleman of leisure since his retirement, which bolstered the image he had of himself as a member of the Southern landed gentry. After relinquishing operations of the farm to my father, he'd updated his wardrobe and taken to wearing a suit and bow tie to meet his cronies for lunch in the Tap Room of the Memphis Country Club, which irritated my grandmother because women were not allowed there on weekdays. Once my family moved to Memphis, we spent most weekends in Como, where my father tended to the farm's logistics—which is what Big John was really mad about—when my mother called to report there'd been a fire and Daddy was in the hospital. In Big John's mind, there was no more egregious error than shirking responsibility, and he didn't have to be told my father had been on a bender.

Little Tea and I were at the pond later that afternoon looking over the wreckage when Big John's driver came whisking him up the gravel in his silver Bentley. "Y'all are in it now," Little Tea had said, "Praise Jesus, this ain't my concern."

By the time I made it to the house, Big John was seated in the living room across from my mother. Elvita had served him a double Dewar's straight up; it looked like burnt amber in its heavy, cut tumbler, the glow from the fireplace tossing prisms off it in the dismal February light. Big John kept his double-breasted, camel-colored coat on. He intended to inspect the grounds for himself but needed a drink to do it. My mother sat with her spine straight as though braced for admonishment. I could tell she was relieved when I entered the room. Whatever words Big John might have said in my absence were withheld in my presence, but the look on his thunderous face spoke volumes.

"Tell me again what time this was. Go on, give me the big picture here," Big John said, stretching his left arm to me, in an invitation to come sit.

"It was the early morning," my mother began, as I scooted into Big John's barrel chest on the sofa and kissed his cheek.

"No, no, Shirley, you said it was night. Early morning is one thing, but it's another to be stumbling around in the dark. Nothing good ever comes of night wandering. A man has to be of a certain mind to think it's a good idea, which is why I want to know the facts. Let me hear a little something about his fool thinking. And before you lie for him, I know he was drinking. That boy never could hold his liquor."

"I don't know, Big John," my mother started. "He didn't tell me what he was thinking. I only talked to him at the hospital and didn't think it was the time to ask. Poor thing's ashamed as it is. You can ask him yourself when we go see him later, but please, do try to be gentle."

"Gentle?" Big John boomed. "Boy all but burns down my farm, and you want me to be gentle? I don't think so. Gonna give him a good what-for, is what I'm going to do. Where's Thelonious? I can depend on him."

"I just saw Thelonious back at his house," I volunteered. "I'll run get him if you want."

"Be easier to call him, so he can meet me out there. Give me a minute to finish my drink. Go on and call up to the cabin and tell him to meet me out there in twenty."

When I called from the hall phone, Little Tea answered on the first ring. "How bad is it?" she asked, her tone more a conclusion than a question.

"Bad, with the promise of getting worse."

"Don't worry, Daddy won't tell him your father was passed out when he found him. He's got it all worked out. He'll say your father was hit on the head with something that fell, make it seem more of an accident than what it was. There's plenty of stuff in that shed could have done it."

"Yeah, well, tell Thelonious to get his story together. Big John's going to be out there in twenty."

Thelonious had played it much as Little Tea predicted. To hear him recap the events, my father's actions seemed almost reasonable. "Well, you know how it is that J. T.'s a painter," Thelonious said. "He don't like taking time away from his family, nor the work he do round here, so he likely got it in his head it's better to paint at night, when folks is asleep. And that shed hadn't been seen to in ages. Ain't no light in there neither. Must have been why he took that cigar."

"Well, for God's sake, don't tell J.T's mother that," Big John warned. "Her father died of throat cancer from smoking those things. I told her no point in coming out here today, that it was nothing more than a little brushfire, so let's keep it that way, hear?" Big John pushed his wispy white hair from his creased forehead. It was windy outside, overcast and beginning to drizzle, but the brittle winter grass still crackled beneath his heavy feet. The shed had burned to the ground, and my grandfather walked over the charred remains with an appraising eye like a detective looking over a crime scene. Presently, he put his hands in his coat pockets and turned toward the woods behind the Winfreys' cabin, his dark-eyed gaze surveying the long stretch of land. "Y'all might not have considered the real danger in all this. Had that fire spread and gone into the woods, it would have gone up like a torch. There'd have been no putting it out. Might have traveled to the side here." He pointed east. "Might have gone clear to the back of beyond, gotten the fields on the way, never mind that they're fallow. I'm not looking at what happened, I'm looking at the jeopardy he put us in."

"But it didn't happen, Granddaddy," I said, looking up at him. "What's important is that nothing terrible happened to Daddy."

"That's where you're wrong, Celia, and you need to learn something here. It's not what a man does with his full potential, it's how he handles his worst. It's just as long of a road to becoming your own best friend as it is your worst enemy. Isn't that right, Thelonious?"

"Yes sir," Thelonious responded, but I stood there thinking what else could Thelonious have done but agree? My grandfather was not the kind of man you challenged. Because Thelonious had grown up beside my father, he knew that when Big John asked, "Isn't that right," what he expected was Thelonious's automatic agreement.

"And where's your brother?" Big Daddy continued, and by this I knew he meant Hayward. "He needs to be here. I want a word with him. Forget about his other talents; he's the one who'll be stepping into all this one day. I tell you, that boy knows his responsibilities as a Wakefield. He should be here right now."

"Hayward's with Dad at the hospital," I said. "I'm sure when you go, you'll see him."

"And your brother John doesn't feel moved to come home to see about this? Doesn't surprise me," my grandfather said, turning and shaking his head. "That one won't fish. He won't hunt. The only sport he plays is tennis, unless you want to count social climbing. If he wasn't the spitting image of your father and me, I'd have to double-check he's a Wakefield."

My father came home from the hospital the next day, shamefaced and bandaged and sullen. He went straight to his den and closed the door and didn't come out for a week.

Heber Springs, Arkansas

I still wasn't acclimated to the two-hour time change between California and Arkansas. It was past midnight, and I lay in bed, hoping for sleep to quell the memories playing traitorously across my heart. I felt disloyal to David for even thinking about Tate Foley. I had no ardor for Tate now yet could vividly remember how that breathless first love blurred the line between present and past, as though something obdurate inside me hadn't grown up to look at the facts. I should have hated Tate Foley, had some semblance of pride, but my heart wouldn't open the door of that chamber where he'd taken up residency in my youth. Ceratoid tissue had formed and sealed him in forever.

There's no denying people harden and change from the fate that shapes them, but what of their basic spirit that remains essentially unchanged? When it came to Tate, it was this I'd aligned with years ago, that resonate, subterranean tributary within him that flowed to the larger body of who he centrally was. The trouble was I could still see the familiar deep waters, vivid and roiling in his blue eyes. But my friends in the room made me self-conscious. I considered actions that would appear appropriate and seemly, for everyone knew my unabridged story with Tate. And Renny—dear, reliable, loyal Renny—had her back up the whole night. She looked at me sidelong at certain intervals, as though to check if I were okay. But there was something I considered that Renny might have not. I was older now. Tate Foley had never known me as a woman; he'd only known me as a callow girl.

I turned over in bed, thinking this might be the real issue. When I thought about Tate, I associated him with whom I had been. He'd buffered me from the part of my childhood I found untenable—that displaced part that longed for Como but was always frightened of when my father's moods would descend. Because there was no predicting when my father would lapse into the miasma of his dark underworld, and when he did, the air was charged with his bleak withdrawals. My mother came from a school of thought where the less said the better. Because she never referred to my father's disengagements, I grew up thinking the behavior that pained me was normal, that it wasn't him at fault but somehow me. I'd go over to Ava's house, and the atmosphere wouldn't be much difference, but by our junior year, our group had created its own self-sufficient safety zone, an insular society with Tate Foley at its clan center, and I began to explore the world as a bourgeoning adult beside him.

I flipped over in bed again in an effort to get comfortable, thinking about Tate and his family and how they once colored my world.

★ ★ ★

Tate's family was the sporting kind. They owned land inside the Delta levee system and considered hunting and fishing a way of life. Because we always operated as a pack, Tate initiated our group into his seasonal rhythms, for even in high school he was a well-rounded outdoorsman who knew every inch of the floodway systems in Arkansas's green timber like the pathways to his beating heart. He hunted duck beneath the metal-gray skies of mid-November through the end of January, when ducks flew from up north to feed in the Arkansas timber, rice, and soybean plains. Most weekends he'd settle his Labrador in the back of his truck and head over the Memphis/Arkansas Bridge to his hunting club where he'd rise at dawn to dress in brown-and-green camouflage then crouch with hushed anticipation among the cognoscenti of outdoor sportsmen wielding duck calls and guns in damp wooded blinds. At the day's end, they'd hand over their limit to a team of cooks who knew their way around recipes from roasted to cassoulet to gumbo. They drank Glenlivet by the fire in leather wingbacks in the tapestry-floored, wood-beamed living room of their southern gentleman's club. They feasted like kings in a fraternity of what I jokingly called cold-blooded assassins. I've always been a soft-hearted lover of sentient beings and had no bones about voicing my revulsion to shooting poor, pretty mallards out of the sky. Tate never once tried to sway me otherwise, beyond saying I didn't understand that there was more to it. Hunting, to him, was a strategic art. Because I had no quarrel with fishing, Tate planned a bass-fishing trip in early April, thirty-five miles outside of Memphis at his family's house on Horseshoe Lake.

We left at ten on a Saturday morning. Renny and Ava rode with Mark, while I rode with Tate all the way out the 147 to Arkansas's Crittenden County. He brought his hand-wrapped rod—a custom-made Fenwick, his blue-eye water scouts, a handful of blue gill swim baits, and an ice chest stocked with beer.

Ava bolted from Mark's car straight to the floating dock before the Foleys' two-story house.

"Y'all come on. This is it, right?" She had her hand on the pier that housed Tate's fourteen-foot Jon boat and looked as though she were poised to jump in.

"Yes, that's it, Ava. Give me a minute to untie her," Tate called, unloading his truck. "Hey, Mark, come give me a hand over here. The wind's up. We should get out by the cypress knees. Must be fifteen- to twenty-mile-an-hour winds out there. It'll be kicking the bait fish up right where the bass spawn." Tate turned toward Ava, knotting his brow. "Ava, quit fooling around over there. Mark and I will get the boat in the water. Why don't y'all girls go on and open up the house? Here, let me throw you the keys."

Ava opened a beer while Renny and I opened the living room shutters. "Look at this place," Renny said, the noon sun flooding the hardwood floors. "Nobody puts antiques in a lake house. What does this family do in here? Everything's breakable." Stepping into the center of the room, she continued. "You can't even turn around without bumping into some priceless piece. Who has a vacation home like this?"

"I don't know, Renny," I said as I assessed the room. "They live well. What can I say? You should see their house in Memphis. It's the size of the Pink Palace."

"Well, I wouldn't want to live in a museum, even if it was in Central Gardens. Think of all that upkeep, not to mention maid service," Renny said.

Ava rifled through cabinets and drawers in the kitchen. "I love scrounging around in somebody else's kitchen," she said. "You should see this, there's nothing in here but silver and good china."

"Go on … pull it out, we'll set the table," I said. "We should get things ready ahead of time. I need to be home by eleven."

"Why are your parents so strict about your curfew?" Ava asked. "My parents don't even know when I come and go."

Renny gave me a tell-all look that suggested I drop the subject. We both knew Ava's parents were never on the case. "I have to be back by then also," Renny said. "Ava, you can spend the night with me, if you want."

"We'll see," Ava demurred, all singsong and mysterious.

Once we got to the water, Tate navigated the three-seated Jon boat through russet reeds and clustered lily pads, each beaded with water on its supple, malachite surface. Deep-rooted, gray-gnarled cypress rose eerily from the water, their ridged trunks primeval beneath swaying foliage that filtered the sunlight in striations of gold. The flat aluminum vessel had an outboard motor on back and a trolling motor on front. Tate guided it, his left arm behind him, as Mark handed us each a lightweight Tenkara rod and reel.

Ava didn't bother to feign enthusiasm. She rolled her eyes and said, "You know I don't work for my supper. I'm just going to sit here and look pretty."

"You do that, honey," Mark said. "You could help us with the lures; they're in the tackle box right by your feet."

"I can do that," Ava said, unlatching the metal box. Holding a lure up, she said, "Look at this, it's looking at me. Tate, do the fish think these are alive because they've got little eyes?"

"That, and it has multiple joints. It has great sink and swim characteristics. Moves like the real thing."

Ava set her mouth in a pout. "It's sad to think they go to take a bite and get hooked by these sharp wire things. I feel sorry for the fish."

"That's what we're doing out here, Ava," Tate said. "You want your supper or what?"

"I want another beer," she said, and walking three paces to the ice chest, she pulled out a Budweiser and popped the top. "You want one, Celia?"

"Okay, thanks." I reached out my hand. "Renny, how about you?"

"I'll take one too. Hand it over here," Renny said, standing, and just as she did, the boat rocked.

Had Ava not been drinking, she might not have stumbled, but as it was, she lost her footing and teetered at the exact moment the boat caught a ripple that sent her reeling, landing heavily on the back seat.

"Ow," she shrieked. "Something bit me." Leaping to her feet, she turned around and tugged on her dress. But the cotton fabric stuck to her backside and her desperate attempts at yanking it loose proved futile. Soon spots of blood appeared.

Tate leaned in for a closer look. "That's it, fishing trip's over. We're going to have to take Ava back and cut that baby out," he said in full-blown laughter.

"It's not funny," Ava wailed.

"Oh, yes, it is," Renny joined in. "This would only happen to you."

"Celia, try to get this out, it hurts," Ava pleaded. "I can't see what I'm doing."

I kneeled behind Ava, the boat pulsing beneath me, and took a hook between my index finger and thumb, only to discover there were three hooks embedded. Alarmed, I looked behind me at Tate, but Mark said, "You hold right where you are, mister. That's *my* girlfriend."

"Get out of the way, Mark. Let me see," Renny said, approaching Ava with her clinical eye. Because Renny's father was a surgeon, she knew her way around an emergency. "This isn't good," Renny grimaced. "Three hooks are lodged at three different angles."

"Tate," Ava whined as though it were his fault, "take me back right now. I'm not going to die out here on Horseshoe Lake."

"Ava, you're not going to die. Let me come over there; just hold steady. I know what I'm doing. Those hooks are probably in deep. Good news is they're J-hooks, not circles. It'd be a bigger mess if the hooks were jogged over. Mark, go on and cut me some fishing line. Give me two monofilaments about a foot and a half each. Celia, there's a first aid kit underneath that seat. Better get hydrogen peroxide ready. I'm going to need another pair of hands, so who's in?"

"I am," Renny said. "I'm not afraid of blood."

"Know how to tie a good larks knot?" Tate kneeled over Ava, who presented her rump in all its hooked glory as she folded over the middle seat. "Ava, you got these in good, girl."

"Where do I tie the knot?" Renny said, all business now.

"Knot the line through the eye of the hook then hold the end bent down. I'll tie the other end under the hook's bend and slowly lift up. You gotta hold it there real still while I remove it. After this, we've got us two more."

"Hurry up," Ava said. "I'm going to bleed to death."

"You have too many layers of skin on your fat behind. You won't bleed to death. This should be painless," Tate said.

"My behind is not fat," Ava said, and Tate looked up at me and winked.

Mark hovered over Tate and Renny. "Where'd you learn to do this, watching Bill Dance Outdoors?"

"Stand back, Mark. You're casting a shadow. And no, my brother taught me. Caught a hook in the palm of my hand one time right beneath my thumb. Trust me, we don't need to go to an emergency room because they'd remove it this same way. Let me get these out, and we'll head back. Ava, your big, fat behind is going to smart for a while."

"Ava, darling, looks like you ruined everyone's dinner," Mark said, trying to lighten the mood.

"Don't worry about it," Tate said. "Celia and I will go out later and catch us some fish."

★ ★ ★

On the lakefront screened porch, four metal chains secured a hunter-green upholstered bed. Ava lay turned sideways in its middle and said, "Renny, push this a little, I want to make this bed swing."

I stood over the card table where Mark and Renny were deep in a game called "Boureé." "Are y'all playing for money?"

"Heck yeah," Mark answered. "It's not as much fun with only two people but we'll make do until y'all bring us back some fish."

Tate and I left with The Marshall Tucker Band on the stereo and a fifth of Jim Beam shared between them. Out on the dock, as I stepped into the boat, my attention was drawn to the sounds of high laughter and vigorous splashing. I looked right to the neighboring pier at the same time Tate did.

I didn't make the connection immediately, for the incongruous reason that the four boys in the water were playing with joyous abandon. They appeared to be having the time of their lives, wrestling and knocking each other off the large raft bobbing between them. To see my brother John so dramatically out of context made me question what it was I was seeing. "That can't be my brother John over there. I know he's in Oxford." I shielded my eyes from the sun. "Sure looks like him, though. Whose house is that over there?"

Tate straightened and planted his feet wide. He lowered the bill of his UT Vols hat and followed my gaze. "No, can't be John with that guy," he said. "That guy's queer as a three-dollar bill."

★ ★ ★

Sitting up in bed, I turned my memories off and the lamp on. I looked at the time displayed on my cellphone and thought about calling David. I wanted to pull myself out of the past and ground myself in the reality of my current life, which hummed along without me in California, two thousand miles away. I picked up my phone from the bedside table as a knock came on the door. Ava slipped into the room and closed the door behind her.

"I knew you'd still be awake," she whispered. "I've had an epiphany." Planting herself on the end of my bed, she sat cross-legged, her cotton robe fanned beneath her, her hair a disheveled mess. "I think my problem is I can't let go of the past." She looked at me with such agony in her eyes, such swimming, inarticulate torment that I sat upright.

"All right," I said. "Let's hear it."

Ava spoke as though releasing a pent-up exhale. "When we were young, we had fun. Everything was exciting. But now I feel boxed in. I'm sick of the same routine with Stan. I'm bored. We don't do anything at night but watch TV. We're living like old people. We married so young that I never figured out who I was. I want to find out now. And I still feel the exact same about Mark as I did in high school. It hasn't changed at all. The only reason we broke up is because I was stupid."

I leaned back against the headboard. "I can't remember why y'all broke up."

"That's because Mark and I were away at college in Virginia. I cheated on him—kind of. Not really cheated, I just didn't discourage the advances of someone else. I wasn't even serious, but Mark never got over it, and that was the end of us. I screwed up. Then I met Stan."

"I don't know, Ava, you make your choices," I offered. "All that was a long time ago. We're no longer in high school when practicality had little to do with our decisions. Now, we have to be practical. It's enough to have life nailed down by its brass tacks."

"Brass tacks?" Ava repeated. "You're just talking about security."

"Well, yeah. There are many people out there without it. I mean, seriously, after a certain point, you have to ask yourself what the aim is, or at least what's possible in a relationship. If you're looking for Stan to make you happy, then it's never going to happen."

"Why not? All Stan has to do is get his act together and stop moving us around."

"But people are going to be people. Eventually, it's all a negotiation anyway. Stan's a dependable, loyal guy. He's not out there gambling or screwing around or raging in alcoholism. There are worse things. Most women want exactly what you've got: stability. All this other stuff is inside your head, so the task is to line it up in some manageable system. I don't know, Ava. I'd rather see you safe."

"Well, I don't want to be like this for the rest of my life. And now, every time I look at Stan I want to scream. He's oblivious, on top of everything else. I swear, he's happy to keep going along in the same old way. He goes through stretches when he's working, then he comes home and just hangs around underfoot, and I'm supposed to keep him happy. I feel like I'm his maid when he's home. Now that Jessica is off at college, it's just the two of us, so there are no distractions."

"Speaking of Jessica, have you thought about how leaving Stan would impact her? You think she'd be fine with her parents divorcing at this stage in the game?"

"She's in college now. She's grown up."

"Oh yeah? Does anyone ever grow up completely? Look at how you keep going over and over your childhood. You ever going to grow beyond it?"

"I can't help it," she said, and I knew what she meant, which is what scared me. As I heard myself speak, I thought I sounded jaded. I thought maybe I am, but it's been a hard race run.

"It's impossible to forget the past, Celia," Ava said.

"No, it isn't, and this is my point. Part of letting go of the past is your decision to do it. Because you keep going over the past, you can't move forward. I say you're wasting precious time. I'm all for glancing at the past. I get that. But you're staring at it. I mean, what if we get to heaven and God says, 'Here's where you went wrong: on earth, you were given the possibility of ten full experiences, but you only experienced five because you got stuck in the middle of one of them. You basically chose to live your life on a hamster wheel.'"

Ava burst out laughing and keeled over backward at the end of the bed. "Unreal, Celia. Just when I'm trying to be serious, you come out with that."

"Look, we're not going to solve this tonight," I said. "I just hate to see you jeopardize a good thing because of the nonsense in your head. If Stan finds out you've been over here playing footsie with Mark, it'll be all over."

Ava sat up and looked at me in all seriousness. "He's not going to find out because I'm never going to tell him. You have to swear to me you'll never say anything to Stan."

"Like I talk to Stan," I scoffed. "Don't be ridiculous. What do you think I'm going to do, call him?"

"Renny might," Ava clipped. "I wouldn't put it past her."

"Ava, Renny's not going to call Stan. Unless you pull some life-threatening histrionic that puts you in danger. Come on. Cut it out."

"Well, Renny already told me I'm not making any sense. Your grandmother was the one who told you when people make no sense, comes a time when you have to step in. Remember your grandmother telling you that one?"

"Yes, I remember." I glanced at the door before eyeing my cell phone. "We've covered enough for the night. Ava, go on to bed."

Later, as I drifted to sleep, the face of my grandmother came to mind. Behind her, unbidden, the faces of Hayward and Little Tea.

Como, Mississippi
Sometime in the 1980s

My grandmother Wakefield was born Cecelia Bridgewater. She, like me, was dark-haired and dark-eyed. In the photograph album of their 1910 wedding, she and Big John stand like a pair of bookends, their noses sharp as the angles of pyramids, their impenetrable eyes hawkish and steady. She came to a respectable three inches below Big John's massive shoulders and her raven, straight hair was styled to frame her porcelain face.

Despite being delicate as a sparrow and light on her feet, Cecelia Bridgewater was no shrinking violet; she'd grown up with four strapping North Carolina Bridgewater boys. She came from mountain folk and was distantly related to my grandfather's family. Hers was a take-no-prisoners way of dealing in the world. Because she'd grown up poor and fearful of deprivation, she tended to stake her claim before it was taken. This suspicious way of being in the world shaded every aspect of her dauntless character. Although she had married up and knew it, hers was no obsequious way of relating to my grandfather. She exuded an exotic, carnal resonance, gifted to her by nature and fostered in the state's ribald mountain society, where a woman knew good and well what could hook a man and, having hooked him, keep him.

My father inherited her sensuous mouth, but he lacked her powers of self-preservation and cunning, which my grandfather came to rely upon. Together, my grandparents were a pair with which to be reckoned. My grandmother was Big John's sidekick, his better half, and never were two people more in accord. They built a prosperous fiefdom of the Wakefield plantation over a forty-year residency, and it was this my father took over as their only child, though their shadows remained looming and large. As intimidating as it was to have Big John's supervisory opinion, in everyone's mind, Cecelia's tight-lipped disapproval was worse. My father feared his mother, who had few maternal instincts, and many who knew her remarked in hindsight that Cecelia Wakefield had been saving up her love all those years until I, her namesake, was born.

My grandmother was provident of me and took full credit for every dark hair on my head. She'd take me into the woods to show me the sylvan magic that sprang to life beneath her nimble feet. She was a chameleon in the tangle of verdant colors lying dappled beneath canopies of timber, the wind acting in concert to fan out her onyx hair as I trailed behind her.

I never knew her age until after she died, so to me, she was ageless. My grandmother never aged because she refused to; she kept herself youthful through sheer force of will. Walking in the forest with her was a tutorial in small details. She identified shagbark hickory and claimed it's the best for smoking meat. She said the Potomac Indians had used it to carve their hunting bows. She was an archivist of snakes and taught me the differences between the eastern diamondback, timber rattler, cottonmouth, and coral. Once, when a pygmy rattler lay across our path, she hushed me with her hand on my arm and said, "There's nothing to fear here, take two steps back and you're out of harm's way." But I was fearful and couldn't help but turn to run. "Hold on there, Celia, here's what you should know—ninety percent of snakebites come from fools trying to kill it. Hold where you are, we'll just turn quietly and go."

But there was something contradictory to my grandmother's benevolent sentiments toward all things great and small, and it was her staunch standpoint against those she called "coloreds." When in their presence, she assumed a mountaineer's air, a prideful reserve cold as an Arctic blast, and there wasn't a black person who ever came into her sphere who couldn't feel it. It was disorienting for me to feel the barometric pressure rise when Thelonious, Elvita, and Little Tea were around her. They'd each don a game-face bland as a lizard, and their demeanor changed to something sinuate and stoic. My brother John subscribed to our grandmother's cultural divide completely, but Hayward and I never had cause to confront it until the night of Little Tea's prom.

My mother loved to stand on ceremony and was good at it. For weeks she wove great enthusiasm into every waking hour before Immaculate Conception's upper-school prom. And knowing Little Tea's prom would be two weeks before mine, in early April of that year, she invited Little Tea to spend the night with us in Memphis and planned the following afternoon around shopping for our dresses. Never one to risk bad timing, she had phoned ahead to an upscale women's dress shop named Tallulah's in East Memphis. When the three of us arrived, two attendants stood waiting in stockings and heels. They were thin and streaked blond, and both wore bangle bracelets and matte lipstick that matched the color of their dress. Practiced in the art of gratuitous fawning, the attendants twittered and swayed like balls of dancing light and showered us with over-the-top attention, saying our youth was our best makeup, and oh what they wouldn't give to go back to their proms, which, of course, led to full disclosure of their high school stories. I had no way of knowing what my mother had said in her preliminary phone call, but I found it worth noting that blacks and whites didn't shop in the same dress shops in 1980's Memphis. That these two manicured women extended themselves to Little Tea in such a deferential manner didn't escape her for one minute. She pulled me into her dressing room under the pretext of zipping up the back of her full-length dress and whispered, "Sweet Jesus, will you call the dogs off? What is this, white guilt?" I laughed so hard it drew the attention of my mother, who parted the white hanging curtains and peered inside. "Y'all doing all right in here? I can hear y'all laughing. What's so funny?"

"Nothing, Mom," I said. "We're just having a good time."

It was my mother's pleasure to buy both of our dresses, for what she called a rite of passage we'd never forget. She took us to lunch at a restaurant named Ruby Tuesday's, where the wooden tables and floors were light-colored and the walls dark wood panel dripping with kitschy art, including regional license plates and a neon sign flashing Coca-Cola. Beneath piped-in, power-pop music, we talked about fashion, boys, and future plans. It was the first time I'd heard Little Tea say she planned on leaving the South after high school, that she wanted to study business in another part of the United States. She told us she thought her athletic performance in high school would be the ticket to her future. She said she was certain her record would warrant a scholarship.

Across the table, my mother freshened her lipstick. "Why, Little Tea, I think that's wonderful," she encouraged. "Of course, you should apply for scholarships. J. T. and I will help you any way we can. Senior year will be here before you girls know it. Y'all should know where you're going as soon as possible. Now then, Little Tea, tell me about this young man who'll be your date for the prom."

I cut to the chase. "He wears black-framed glasses and is sweet on Little Tea."

"Celia, you've met him?" my mother queried.

"Just once. He came to Little Tea's house in a coat and tie to bring her a book."

"That's right," Little Tea said. "His name's Wilson Atkins, and he's a junior."

"Well, are you sweet on him?" my mother asked, animated by her inclusion in the world of youth's concerns.

"I might be if I wanted a boy underfoot, but I don't," Little Tea said. "Wilson's president of our class. He's way too serious for me."

"Serious in what way?" I asked.

"I'm not saying it's a bad thing to know what you want out of life, but he's the kind that's always looking to get into the middle of a cause. Right now, he's all over civil rights. He'll be beating that drum for the rest of his life. Wilson will end up in politics one day, I'm sure. He's a good, responsible guy, but I'm not like you, Celia, all moony over a boy. I don't play that way. I've got my own plans."

My mother jumped to my defense. "I think that's sensible, Little Tea, but Celia can't seem to help herself. And it does seem Tate feels the same for her. Sometimes these things work out. J. T. and I met in high school. There was never a question of us not marrying—we knew it right off the bat. It all comes down to what you want out of life. J. T. and I both wanted the same things: marriage, a family, ties to home. I think Celia is just like I was at her age. I think she's met her match. I'd be perfectly happy to see Celia and Tate married and living near us one day."

Little Tea smiled at me. "It looks to me like that's going to happen." She reached over and pinched my cheek.

"Quit it, Little Tea," I swatted her away. "You don't know everything. I might pick up and move to California someday, who knows? And if you don't quit pinching me, I'll pull your hair."

"Go on with yourself; you know I'm not hurting you," Little Tea laughed. "Anyway," she turned back to my mother, "Celia's not going to California or anywhere else. She's made for domestication. She'll have a good life here for sure. As for me, if I'm ever going to make something of myself the way I plan to, I'll *have* to leave the South. I know times have changed for people of color, but there's a residue that'll stick around here forever. It's a small world in Mississippi. People are slow. Even my parents want to see me spread my wings."

My mother caught the eye of our waitress and pointed to her glass of iced tea with a smile that implied a refill. "I'm not going to sit here with my head in the sand and pretend you don't have a point," she said with a sigh. "When J. T. and I were growing up, it was a rough time between the races. I know y'all know the history. Girls from my background simply didn't get involved. We were sheltered from most of the turmoil and went right along with segregation, even though we were all but in the regional thick of the upheaval."

"But times are different now, Mama," I said. "This is the eighties. I hear what Little Tea is saying, but I don't think prejudice is all that bad. Certainly not what it once was."

My mother paused then shared her thoughts. "There's a residue that lingers, Celia. You know there are those in our own family who can't bring themselves to think progressively. I will say that your generation has better opportunities than mine and hopefully your children's generation will be better still." Addressing Little Tea, she added, "I think you're sensible. One must consider the attitudes of the people around them in weighing their options. Just because other people can't move forward doesn't mean you can't. So much is in our attitude, girls."

Given my mother's warm way of encouraging Little Tea to go out in the world to make something of herself, it both saddened and hurt me to see my grandmother's heavy-handed reprimand of Hayward the night we came in from the Winfreys' house, after going to see Little Tea in her prom dress. It was Hayward's first weekend home since he'd started his freshman year at the University of the South in Sewanee. I'd asked him to come with me to the Winfreys' to see Little Tea in all her glory, wearing her full-length dress. Little Tea had never been one to utilize her uncommon beauty to her advantage. Instead, she used her intelligent sense of humor and a manner so feisty most people couldn't get around them to notice anything else. She typically wore baggy shirts that hid her sculpted body and panther grace. One had to peek behind the veil, so to speak, to spy her physical perfection. But I knew it was there, and one look at Hayward's face told me he did too.

Hayward didn't often cease his running commentary on life, but you would have thought he'd taken a vow of silence when we stood in the Winfreys' living room and Little Tea appeared from down the back hall. Her dress was a seraphic antique ivory, showcasing a wingspan of ebon shoulders, diagramed to such precision they seemed drawn to architectural specification. She carried herself steadily, for any shift in her carriage would have caused the strapless, heart-shaped neckline to falter. Her swan neck had a dancer's camber. Above it, her chin was level and proud. Seeing her step into her family's living room in strappy, gold kitten heels was breathtaking. She was statuesque and regal, and it wasn't so much that she wore the dress as it was that the dress wore her.

"Mister Hayward, you can go on pick your chin up off the floor," Thelonious said, his cheeks raised, the corners of his mouth angled down in a suppressed smile.

"What are you looking at?" Little Tea dared Hayward to confess.

"What'd you do to your hair?" he asked.

"I straightened it," Little Tea said.

"It's so long," Hayward said.

"Black folk can straighten their hair. You want to make something of it or what?"

"I didn't mean anything by it. I'm just saying, is all."

"Celia, would you take your brother home? He's making me nervous. And I don't want y'all standing here when Wilson drives up. It'll look like y'all are making too much of this. It's a prom, that's all."

"You look fit for a coronation, Little Tea," I said. "Seriously, you're beautiful."

"Y'all go on and stand on either side of Thelonia. Let me get your picture," Elvita said, stepping toward the front door to frame us in a photograph I knew I'd treasure for the rest of my life. In it, Hayward and I have our arms behind Little Tea's cinched waist. She stands taller than me, an inch below Hayward in her heels, her figure balanced in an hourglass, her hands linked in front as Hayward and I shine like grinning fools in her glow.

"All right, that's enough. Y'all go on now," Little Tea said, patting Hayward and I on our backs in dismissal.

"We're going," I said. "Elvita, Hayward and I both want a copy of that picture. Don't forget."

"I'll get it to you, don't you worry," Elvita said. "I'll send it out to the Rexall and bring it on sometime when I make y'all breakfast. Thelonia, thank your friends for coming around to see you tonight. They're paying you a big compliment."

"I know it, Mama. I'm just messing with y'all," Little Tea said. Her tone softened to a note of silken sincerity, and I knew she was touched. It was then that a knock came to the wood of the screened door, and I realized that no one had heard the pad of Wilson Atkins's leather loafers up the porch steps.

Elvita opened the door. "Why, Wilson, don't you look nice? Come on in. We're taking pictures. Why don't you go stand next to Thelonia and let me snap y'all together?"

In his blue seersucker suit and striped matching bow tie, Wilson Atkins flashed an even smile with accordion white teeth. He was a good-looking boy; tall and thin and aerodynamic, his straight-edged posture militant, the color of his skin like rubbed onyx beneath black-framed glasses over the quadrants of his sharp, boxy face. "Thelonia, you're pretty as a picture. It'd be my honor to stand next to you. Hey there, Miss Celia. And who is this standing here?" Wilson extended his right hand to Hayward, man-to-man style, a plastic-boxed, pink-and-white orchid in the other.

"Hayward Wakefield, pleasure to meet you," my brother said, his smile broad and honest.

"Wakefield? You Miss Celia's brother? Y'all don't favor at all. I wouldn't have guessed it."

"Everyone says that," Hayward returned. "Makes it easy not to claim her." He winked at me.

"Wilson, you want me to pin that corsage on Thelonia's dress?" I offered.

"Oh, no, I got it," he said, and with that, Hayward and I kissed Little Tea's cheek, said our goodbyes, and then walked through the field to our house. Hayward clipped paces in front of me as though in a hurry, so it wasn't until I closed the front door in the foyer that I said, "Can you believe how beautiful she looked? We've never seen Little Tea so polished. I almost didn't recognize her, did you?"

"I've always thought that Little Tea is a star," Hayward said, as though musing aloud. "She has star quality, a presence about her not everyone has. And yes, she's definitely beautiful." Turning sharply, he met my eyes. "Is that guy her boyfriend or what?"

"No way," I deflected, "but he's a big deal at her school. You know Little Tea she gets along with everyone. It probably doesn't occur to Wilson that she's out of his league."

Hayward laughed. "What league is that, exactly?"

"Come on, you know what I mean. Little Tea's not on the same page as anyone else. She follows her own rules. She just never lets on. I was over there a few weeks ago when Wilson showed up and gave her *The Autobiography of Malcolm X* like he was handing her the Holy Grail. It was unbelievable. Little Tea took it and thanked him for thinking of her but rolled her eyes the second he drove away. She's not into all that, but Wilson doesn't know it. I told her she's encouraging him, but she doesn't care. We laughed over it forever. She told me it's not her fault she's a head-turner." I shrugged. "You know how funny she can be."

"Who's turning whose head?" my grandmother said, walking into the foyer from the living room where she and Big John had been sitting with my parents since after dinner. "Y'all went rushing off. Where'd you go?"

"Little Tea's going to her prom tonight. We went over to her house to see her in her dress. She looked stunning," I gushed.

My grandmother's eyes narrowed cobra-black and piercing. "Stunning by whose standards? Certainly not ours," she snapped. "You're not making any sense so I'm stepping in to tell you what's what. I worry about y'all being too wrapped up in that family back there; I always have. It's your mother's fault, I think. She doesn't know the line. Can't see around that big liberal heart of hers. Never could. Y'all don't know any better so I'll tell you nice and plain. We don't fraternize with the help."

"Come on, Grandmother." Hayward laughed. "Lighten up. We're talking about Little Tea."

I saw in her eyes a burning hostility. She took Hayward's full measure, lowered her voice, and growled, "Don't you tell me to lighten up, mister." Although only five-foot-five, my grandmother stood at her full height and arrested Hayward with a look that nailed his feet to the floor. "She's not like us, and don't you talk back to me. You let those hormones of yours land in the wrong place, and you're courting trouble. You cut that out right now and remember who you are, young man."

"What got into Grandmother?" I said after Hayward and I went upstairs to his room. I moved his suitcase aside and sat on his bed petting Rufus, feeling unduly rebuked, even though our grandmother had come down on Hayward, not me. "I don't know about you, but I feel like a scalded cat. You didn't do anything wrong; what's her problem?"

"Her problem is she has baggage from her childhood. She was raised that way, and you have to consider her background. Grandmother's scarred from her dirt-poor childhood. I take her with a grain of salt." Hayward seemed occupied with straightening papers on his desk, but I knew he was fidgeting.

"You'd think that'd make her compassionate," I suggested.

"You don't understand human nature, Celia," Hayward said. "People attack what they fear."

"What? She fears Little Tea? I doubt it, Hayward."

"You're missing the point. It's her own status she's guarding. It's a deep-seated inferiority complex."

"Over what?"

"It has to do with a socioeconomic hierarchy you and I will never completely understand because we weren't born into the dynamic. Grandmother comes from indigent mountain folk, you know that."

"Yeah, I know," I said, still not getting his point.

"People always have to have something to look down on. From her scratching-poor mountain view, black people are it."

My mother came up to Hayward's room after the worst of it. She sat on his bed and with a wistful shake of her head said, "I heard every word. You mustn't let it bother you. Y'all know how she is," which blanketed my grandmother's outburst in full discredit.

"I was just telling Celia not to let it bother her," Hayward said. "Grandmother comes from a region where people don't know any better."

"Of course this is what it is, and we pity her," my mother returned in a note of finality. "There's nothing sadder than a narrow mind, but she's the one who has to live with it. Doesn't make her a bad person, just a fearful one. But she has good reason. Everyone is a product of the people around them in one way or another. But y'all can form your own opinion. You don't have to agree with everyone, but you do have to have the courage of conviction. I've known your grandmother since I was sixteen. I've never let her bother me. Why should I?"

"Exactly," Hayward chimed, and I saw them exchange a look that moved mountains. Knowing them as I did, it was enough for my mother and Hayward to exchange one look and have it settle the score. Hayward was much like my mother with his talent for explaining what was really going on with people. It seemed while John and I had been genetically burdened with the Wakefield gravity, my mother had slipped her clear-sighted compassion into Hayward's DNA. He carried every one of my mother's high-minded traits. Neither saw the underbelly of life nor acknowledged the lost people in it.

The shame of it was, my grandmother had cause to elaborate on her belief that black people were not like us. First thing the next morning, I walked into the dining room to find her seated on the needlepointed Queen Anne chair at the head of the twelve-seat mahogany table. Whenever my grandparents spent the weekend in Como, my grandmother assumed her position as matron at the head of the table, my mother to her left, my father at her right. Big John loomed at the other end drinking coffee. "I don't believe it was her fault for one minute," he said, as I entered the room. "It was just a matter of being in the wrong place at the wrong time. You know the law around here; they're gunning for this kind of thing." He turned to my grandmother. "And Cecelia, you need to lower your voice. Elvita doesn't need to hear any more from us. It must have been a long night for them back there."

"Was for us too," my grandmother said hotly. "Made a big problem for all of us, as these people do. Good thing you were out here, or they'd still be locked up."

"What are y'all talking about?" I asked, pulling out a chair. Elvita appeared from the kitchen as though on cue while Hayward and Rufus clattered down the wooden stairs and landed in the foyer. When they entered the room, Hayward swept his eyes over all of us and asked, "What are y'all doing, sharing state secrets?"

Elvita set a glass of orange juice before me. "Y'all about ready for eggs and biscuits? Hayward, go on and sit, I'll be just a minute making your gravy." All of us kept silent until Elvita left the room.

"What?" Hayward fired. "What'd I miss?"

"You mean you slept through it?" My father sounded baffled. "Didn't you hear Big John leave the house at a quarter till two?"

Big John shifted his eyes to my father. "No, no, J. T., you've got that wrong. Thelonious didn't call the house until two this morning. Didn't know himself until then."

"I didn't hear the phone ring last night," I said.

"Your grandfather picked it up on the first ring," my grandmother stated, "or the father of your nigra friend back there would have gotten the whole house up."

"Well it's a damn good thing Thelonious didn't waste time going down there himself," Big John said. "Calling me was the right thing to do."

"What in the world happened?" Hayward asked.

My mother leaned forward and whispered, "Little Tea and her date were taken to jail."

Hayward didn't sit another second. He rose from the table, calling "Elvita, hold the gravy." By the time I reached the foyer, he was already through the front door with Rufus at his heels. I closed the door behind me and shouted, "Hayward, wait up."

"Grandmother was getting ready to give us chapter and verse on this one, and you know it," he said when I caught him. "Best we get over there now to hear it for whatever it was."

Little Tea sat on her front porch as though expecting us. She wore a cotton print dress, her night-before hair in a long, slender braid.

"About time y'all got here," she said as we stepped onto the porch. "What's going on over there at the house? I bet your grandmother's all over it, isn't she? She knows nothing about any of it, but wait," she held up her hand, "don't tell me. You have to expect this from people like us."

I waited for Hayward to do the talking. He was always so quick on the trigger, more so than I. I sat on the front steps and turned to the rocking chair. Little Tea rocked slowly, every muscle in her body resigned. "Celia, don't give me that hangdog look," she said. "There's not a black family in the world that hasn't had a conversation about white people like your grandmother. I know what she thinks of us. Doesn't matter the cause. Thing is, now she has something over us. And I'll tell you another thing, it won't be about just me, she'll be running down all black people."

"She won't do that, Little Tea," I defended.

Hayward sat down beside me and patted his knee to call Rufus. "Yes, she will, Celia, come on. Remember when she said—"

"She said she loves us as individuals but hates us as a group," Little Tea interrupted. "Don't bother pretending otherwise, Celia. Wilson and I make two of us, and in her book two or more black people spell trouble."

"Tell us what happened," Hayward said. "We already know it was some big misunderstanding."

"Wasn't no misunderstanding to it," Little Tea lobbied. "Two black kids out late on a dark country road, and the law understands just fine. And Wilson had him a flask. Wasn't even anything in it, it was brand new and had never been used."

"What was he doing carrying it around?" I asked.

"He wasn't carrying it around. There were two cops that searched the whole car. The flask was wrapped up in a box in the trunk. Wilson was going to give it to his father for his birthday today. It was monogrammed with initials and everything, sealed with tape, tied up with a bow. But there was also a baseball bat in the trunk. They claimed it was a weapon, so I guess they figured they'd best go on and open the box."

"What the hell?" Hayward said.

"They call it probable cause, that's what the hell. You have any idea where a cop's suspicion can take you? Straight to jail, that's where."

"So, you called your dad, and he called the house?"

"You better believe he called the house. Thank God y'alls grandfather was out here. Nobody else could have marched in and gotten us out. My father's no fool; he knows the way the game is played. We'd still be sitting there if it weren't for your grandfather."

Hayward, ever at the ready to lighten the mood, flashed his pirate smile and said, "Other than that, Mrs. Lincoln, how was the play?"

"Go on with yourself, Hayward. It wasn't funny," Little Tea chided, but she managed a smile. "I'll tell y'all right now, one day I'm going to get up out of this state, and when I do, it'll have to be a good reason that brings me back."

Heber Springs, Arkansas

I swear, this is never going to end," Renny said, walking into the kitchen at seven in the morning, barefoot in a T-shirt and shorts.

"What?" I asked.

"I just called Sammie and got in another fight with Jimmy. Of course he had to be the one to answer the phone. I'm telling you, there's a reason we divorced. We can't even say hello to each other without getting into the subject of money, and away we go." She sat at the bar, put her elbows on the counter and her head in her hands. "I'm never getting married again. By the way," she said, aiming her words at me, "speaking of married, did you call your husband?"

I stood assembling the percolator under the sunlight pouring through the unadorned window on the humid, breezeless morning. "This thing has a mind of its own, you know that, right? And yes, I called David last night after Ava went to bed."

Renny waited a few beats to comment. "I don't think Ava went to bed last night."

I turned from the window to see Renny arching her eyebrows and looking at me in a manner that asked if I caught her drift.

"Why do you say that?"

"Because Ava's not here. I think she snuck out. Gimme a cup of that when you figure it out."

"Snuck out?" I said. "What is this, high school?"

"Might as well be. She seems to be stuck in it. And you know what? I don't think she's doing anything other than looking for greener pasture. My guess is she's going to regret all this."

"Ah, I got it," I said after a final wrestle with the percolator. "In a minute, we'll have sound effects to rival an earthquake, then we'll have coffee." I removed two mugs from the cabinet and placed them by the percolator. "I'm actually kind of glad you've said this." I walked around the bar and sat next to Renny. "I wasn't going to say anything, but since you brought it up, we should probably talk about it."

"You want to discuss that she's obviously sleeping with Mark? We're talking infidelity here. It's a game changer. Let's just say Stan finds out; it'll be game over."

It sprang to mind that Ava was nervous about Renny talking to Stan. Renny knew Stan better than I did. They had an understanding between them that cast Renny in the role of confidant and translator when it came to the capricious Ava. Renny impressed everybody as the voice of reason, and although she was loyal to her girlfriends, she talked a man's game if asked.

But I wasn't going to tell Renny not to divulge to Stan because it would have sounded accusatory to suggest that she would. I've never been one to troubleshoot in the event of; I just react blindly when trouble lands in my lap. And what is there to say when a friend does something I wouldn't? After I get around the surprise of not considering the option, I think far be it from me to stand in moral judgement. Friends let friends slide and offer unconditional acceptance. They meet on the playing field of neutrality, unless they're prepared for the friendship to end. To do otherwise communicates a patent disapproval, and I've never been one to risk this. I have a history of swaying like a reed in the wind as events shape me. I never could decide if it's passivity or fear.

"I don't know, Renny. Neither of us could ever tell Ava what to do," I said.

"No, you've got that one wrong. We could tell her what to do, but only on the back end of some drama," she clarified.

"If she asked," I added.

"If she asked *you*," she continued. "Not me. With me, it's always been a whining soliloquy while she's in it, basically about missing the cause and effect connections after she set herself up. I've got half a mind to go over to Mark's cottage right now and yank her out of there. You know that's where she is, right?"

"I figured. Let me get us some coffee," I said, rising. "I'll say one thing; wherever Ava's life is going isn't up to us. She's never gotten over Mark. I think they've always been tied at the soul."

"And you've always been a hopeless romantic, Celia. I'm not faulting you for it; I'm just saying you're too understanding. Do me a favor while you're over there, will you? Pour a little milk in mine."

"Here you go," I said, setting her mug on the bar, her coffee now stirred. "You want to go sit outside?"

"Okay." Renny slid out of her chair. "But I'm going out front. I want to be sitting there on the steps when Ava comes slinking back. Girl's got the morals of an alley cat."

"An alley cat in heat," I said, and we laughed our way outside to where the sprinkler system sprayed the azaleas bordering both sides of the driveway and the jonquils surrounding the mailbox's post, which rose through monkey grass so supple and green it made me think every inch of the property had been consciously appointed. I thought the attention to detail was exemplary of Renny's neat, jigsaw puzzle life. I sat looking out toward the street thinking maybe Renny's penchant for perfect placement was the key. It would never occur to me to try and manipulate nature, yet here I sat with a bucolic view as finely wrought as a painter's palette, arranged from the hand of someone who left nothing to chance. I wondered if Renny had landscaped all this before she'd moved into the lake house or if she'd figured it all out afterward, like I'd done with most aspects of my haphazardly cobbled life.

Renny set her mug on the stairs. "I'm not going to ask you how you felt about seeing Tate. Unless, of course, you want to talk about it."

"You just asked," I said flatly.

"You know what I mean."

"Sorry, I didn't mean to be flippant. Here's what's so weird—last night, I couldn't quit thinking about all of us in high school. Remember *Chez Nous* and then that day at Horseshoe Lake when Ava sat on the lure? We operated as a unit in everything we did pretty much up until college. I don't know many people who grew up that way. I realize now how unusual it was." I took a single sip of coffee. "I've tried to give David an accurate description of how tight we all were so he can get an idea of my frame of reference, but it's almost impossible to articulate. Whenever I hear myself trying to describe those years, it sounds like a farfetched story. The further away I get from that time, the more my life seems like a story that happened to somebody else. If you want to know how I feel about Tate, all I feel is disassociated and numb."

Renny put her hand on my shoulder. She sighed audibly and said, "I understand."

We sat looking across the two-lane road to a shady, wooded knoll covered by oaks, ruddy shrubbery, and pines. The ground was dense with clover and chickweed, and every so often, shadows morphed beneath branches, buoyant with the movement of a squirrel, the landing of a bird, as my mind followed suit, drifting in free association.

"Remember how I used to be so terrified of flying?" I asked, unprompted. "I got over my fear in one fell swoop after everything happened … that night in Como. I was up in the clouds, in a fit of turbulence when it occurred to me nothing else could possibly happen to me. I mean, you can get to that point, you know?"

"Oh, I know. Knock on wood," Renny said, rapping her knuckles on the stairs.

"Yeah, really. I better do that, too."

"First love, Celia, that's what it was. It's like the deal with Mark and Ava."

"Not really," I said, "there was never the question of my going back to Tate. You know that. You were there. That one was final. But Mark and Ava could turn around and start it all up again tomorrow. They probably already have."

"Speak of the devil, and up she walks," Renny said, staring forward.

"Hey, y'all," Ava called, scratching up dust on the gravel driveway. "Y'all looking for me?"

"I'll leave this to you," I whispered.

Renny stood, shaded her eyes. "Celia wants to know where you've been. She's been worried sick and wants details," Renny called back.

Ava reached the first step of the stairs. "You were worried about me? I'm sorry, Celia. I didn't want to wake you up again. I couldn't sleep, so I walked over to Mark's." She glanced down at our mugs. "Is there any more coffee?"

"Yes," I said. "On the kitchen counter." Ava left her purse on the stairs and walked into the kitchen.

"Thanks a lot," I said to Renny.

"You like that? I thought it was funny. Let's not make a big deal out of this. Let's just hear what she has to say. This whole thing has been a moving target. After last night, maybe things have changed."

"I hope y'all aren't mad," Ava said when she reappeared. She took off her sandals, set them by the door, then sat on the stairs below us with her back against the railing so she was turned in profile, the better not to meet our eyes.

"Y'all are worse than confessing to my parents," Ava said.

"Who's asking anyone to confess?" I asked.

"I am," Renny levied. "I want to know what's going on."

"I'm just taking things step by step," Ava said. "Because I can. Y'all don't know what it's been like for me. I haven't been touched in over two years." She looked up to gauge my reaction. "Stan ignores me, and it makes me crazy. Celia, is being married like this for you?" I shrugged noncommittally. "Well Stan and I live like roommates. I feel dead inside, shut down. I don't even feel like a woman. I have no physical affection, and you know what? I looked up 'lack of affection' on the internet. There's actually a name for it called 'skin hunger.' I swear to you, if y'all don't believe me, I'll show you the piece I found on a psychology website. I saved the link."

"I ain't got no affection, and I don't care," Renny said, laughing. "It's not like I have the time. Celia? Oh, wait, Celia doesn't discuss things like this."

"Pardon me for being discreet," I said.

Ava pivoted to fully face us. "I have to talk to y'all," she said, a pleading note in her voice. "If I can't talk to y'all, then I have no one. And you know I'm not promiscuous; I never was. I've only had two boyfriends in my entire life, so keep that in mind."

"I'll tell you again, Ava, nobody's judging you here," I said. "And I hear you completely. It's just operating on the sly that'll get you in trouble. If not now, then somewhere down the line. It's not like I have any answers, but I'm hoping to help you sort it all out because I care."

"I care too," Renny said quickly. "And I do have an answer for Ava. She needs to leave Stan if it's so bad. Life's too short. Tick-tock and all that."

"But I don't want it to be my decision," Ava said. "Know what I mean?"

Renny shook her head. "Not really. You mean you don't want to be the bad guy? Somebody has to. The way I see it, you're only calling things as you see them. Stan's bound to know. Why would he be surprised? I don't get it."

But I got it immediately. Sometimes the writing is on the wall waiting for someone to point out the obvious. I've heard it said we all have our "core issues." If this is true, then I've identified mine. It's not that I can't read the writing on the wall, it's that I don't notice the wall in the first place.

"It seems to me it comes down to the question of whether you want to act, or be acted upon," I said to Ava. "You asked the other night about the meaning of happiness. I'm thinking we don't have a fighting chance without the foresight to consider cause and effect. If I would have known this earlier, I would have known the value of jumping ship *in medias res*."

Ava's face brightened. "Latin," she said. "I like it."

When Renny smiled, I could tell she found Ava's hold on the incidentals of my comment funny. "Ava, I think you're missing Celia's point. I wanted to say something too, because last night you were questioning God's plan. I get the dilemma. I say you should do the best you can do."

"You know what? I think it's all going to be okay because I know God understands." She jumped up, her countenance now changed, as though someone had waved a magic wand. Suddenly, she was Ava again—not the troubled, confused woman who'd come on this trip, but the old Ava, the one from high school. The irrepressible, effervescent girl brimming with the kind of hope and enthusiasm for life, where only her best interests could happen. Ava always said magic and spirituality were the same thing. Although she was Catholic, her version of God was half sorcerer and half watchful disciplinarian, a paternal, compassionate God who was lenient yet held her to high moral standards. Which is why I understood what she meant.

She reached for the screened kitchen door. "God wouldn't have put Mark back in my path if I wasn't supposed to be with him. I don't think He minds at all that Mark and I are together. I've decided it's part of the plan."

"Well, all right, there it is." Renny picked up her coffee mug and stood as the screened door bounced shut. "Let's review: We have alcohol, therapists, antidepressants, and now we've got God involved. You think this weekend has been helpful so far?"

I stood and faced her. "Well, yeah, Renny. I really kind of do. If nothing else it got Ava out of her box so she can take an objective look at her marriage."

"Objective look at her marriage? Mark's all she's looking at right now. You know it, and I know it. He's nothing but a distraction. All I can say is I can't tell you how glad I am I'm not married. I've fought that option tooth and nail, except for that one misstep with Jimmy. I should have had Sammie out of wedlock and been glad to be a single mother. Who wants the headache? I've never understood you and Ava. Y'all were practically planning your weddings right out of high school."

★ ★ ★

Renny was right. Kind of. The fact is, you can date a boy for so many years that he becomes part of the family. When I fell in love with Tate, I fell toward something. I think it was the lure of security. A deep part within me knew something was lacking at home, and with Tate I sensed stable ground. At a formative age, his presence in my life was like a promissory note for the future. He was such a shining, effortlessly charismatic boy that I blossomed in the warmth of his company and grew to depend on it for my well-being. That Tate Foley loved me bolstered my self-esteem. Together, we balanced each other, filled in each other's spaces. Where I was shy, he was gregarious; where I was hesitant, he jumped without looking. I never minded riding on his coattails wherever we went in public. People gravitated to Tate, and I basked in his glow. It was a foregone conclusion that Tate and I would always be together. I couldn't imagine it otherwise.

We never came out and talked about marriage, but the assumption was there, especially when Tate followed me to college, which sent my father and grandmother into the unanticipated consequences of a protest so vehement, you would have thought it was the end of the world. For once my father was in complete agreement with his mother. Which was unusual given the push and pull of their dynamic. The shame of it was that Hayward wasn't there to defend me that Sunday afternoon I announced Tate and I had both been accepted at the University of Tennessee in Knoxville. But John was there, at our grandparents' home in Central Gardens. At this point, he was back from Oxford for good and working at an upscale men's clothing store—James Davis—where Memphis's well-heeled shopped for the conservative apparel that made them all blend like threads in a fabric.

My grandmother was big on a formal display of Sunday lunch whenever all of us were in town. On this late summer day, Elvita's older sister Beneatha was in attendance. Because she didn't trust strangers, it had been my grandmother's good fortune that Beneatha was married and living in the area behind Buntyn's restaurant, on the other side of the railroad tracks down Southern Avenue. The convenience of Beneatha's geographic proximity to the residential area of Central Gardens afforded them a relationship that was all but on call. Every Monday, Wednesday, and Friday, Beneatha worked in my grandparents' three story, ivy-covered Tudor home, and although she wasn't scheduled for Sundays or holidays, I'd never been to my grandparents' house on either when Beneatha wasn't there in her white button-down uniform.

There were questions I never thought to ask about race relations when I was growing up in the eighties. But I look back now and find holes in my hindsight. People look at the past through the scrim of what's right and wrong according to now, irrespective of the general nature and context of the times as they were back then. The Memphis I knew growing up had a cushioned vantage point from inside a bubble. For me, they were soft times, gentle and synergistic, and much of its code was implied. Black women like Elvita and Beneatha were technically family maids, but they were also respected overseers, and without them my world would have lacked dimension and form. I believe the Winfreys understood this completely. Whatever it was they thought of my family, they upheld the relationship with sage solemnity. They were privy to all our flawed nuances and comported themselves with the acceptance of insiders who were in it yet detached from it. And they were multifaceted teachers. From their influence, I learned there is dignity in silence and there is wisdom in holding one's tongue. I'd keep a deep, watchful eye on Elvita whenever my father went into one of his spiraling dark spells. She'd tiptoe around the Como house and shepherd me through the foyer to the kitchen with a hand to my shoulder laid in a cautionary way I always understood. She taught me that oftentimes, nothing more's needed than a straight carriage and forward gaze. Because the ways of the South were unspoken in my youth, I learned much about civility from watching Elvita, Thelonious, and Little Tea, who collectively and stalwartly anchored my life. My family never discussed race relations within our own society. In tandem with the Winfreys, we were an ecosystem unto ourselves, each with a supporting part. But when it came to the issue of Little Tea's college education, the disparity between us hit a head in the middle of my grandparents' dining room the moment I made that grand announcement about Tate Foley and I going to the same college next year. I inadvertently let slip that Little Tea was going to a college in Boston because she wanted to get away from the South, and however it was I said it, it came out all wrong. My timing couldn't have been worse had I planned it. Beneatha was standing tableside to my right, when my grandmother registered what I'd said and blew a fuse.

"The world's gone crazy. You've all gone crazy," she emoted. "It's not enough that Little Tea is overreaching, but you, young lady, are painting yourself into a corner. I don't trust that Foley family; I never did. They're social climbers, too concerned with appearances. I know that boy's grandfather. He's a snob and thinks too much of himself. And his son, Renville Foley, Tate's daddy. He's a card-carrying prick. Mark my words," she said, shaking her finger at me, "the apple doesn't fall far from the tree. I'm surprised they think you're good enough for their boy. That family thinks they're the Kennedys. They've even got those same white teeth."

Big John threw back his head and laughed. "Settle down there, Cecelia. I play golf with Tate's grandfather. He's a gentleman through and through."

My grandmother wasn't having it. "I have a right to be riled, Big John. The Foleys are nothing but inbred blue bloods, and I don't like them. Celia, you're too young to tie yourself down. You're not even giving yourself a chance." My grandmother sputtered and fumed and picked up a saltshaker, dusting her plate with such theatrics and flair, it rattled the gold bracelets on her wrist and sent prisms flying overhead from the Austrian chandelier above the table. "I'm telling you, little missy, you've lost your fool mind," she continued. "And J. T., don't you dare defend her. And while I'm at it, I'm not in the mood to hear your bleeding heart, liberal lip about Little Tea, so spare me."

My father addressed my brother John first. "John, please don't sit there with a smirk on your face," he said with distaste. "This isn't a question of who's right or wrong, there's only the matter of opinion. And Mother, I happen to agree with you about Celia. Celia …" He turned to me. "It sounds to me like this is a statement. If you and Tate are meant to be together, you will be, but no sense in hurrying now. I'm concerned you'll miss the entire college experience if you go off to school as a couple. And Mother …" He met my grandmother's eyes. "Little Tea is going to Boston. It's done."

Grandmother fixed Beneatha with a stare. "Is that right, Beneatha?"

"Yes, ma'am," Beneatha confirmed.

"Well, you didn't mention it. I find out too much around here after everything's done. Nobody bothers to ask for my opinion anymore. Little Tea's life is up to her, but I'll tell you one thing, when she comes back here, she'll no longer fit in. They're uncultured up there, too. I've been to Boston. Everyone's Irish. Highly personable people, but they're shifty."

"Now Cecelia, you're being general. Generalizations aren't fair," my fair-minded mother put in.

"I make no apology for being general," my grandmother stated. "Where I came from, it's a saving grace. Helped me get my mind clear on what I was up against. You have to be on your toes with people. Little Tea's innocent. Child's too soft-spoken, from what I can tell. She'll never do well up there."

I sat thinking my grandmother had that all wrong. The only time Little Tea held her tongue was when she was suspicious. And of course, my grandmother gave her plenty of reason for that.

"I fully agree with Grandmother," John announced, puffed up with his own importance.

"Well, that's one of you making sense," my grandmother said. "Beneatha, I'll have more ice-coffee."

"Yes, ma'am," Beneatha said.

There was an admirable dignity to Beneatha's above-the-fray countenance. As I watched her from the corner of my eye, I thought about how good it must feel to be beyond the concern of my grandmother's supervisory opinion. Beneatha replenished the glass from a sterling silver pitcher then repaired to the kitchen, her white lace-ups rocking to the rhythm of rough, rubbing nylon as she made for the kitchen's swinging door.

"Little Tea in Boston," John flouted. "Now that's funny. She'll be a fish out of water trying to pull herself up. And you, Celia, y'all might as well go on and get married. You're not pregnant, are you? Else, what's the point?"

"Shut up, John," I said, wishing Hayward were with us. I knew if Hayward were, he'd have flattened John and had a smile on his face doing it.

Como, Mississippi
Sometime in the 1980s

Autumn is my favorite time of year in the South, for all its contemplative stillness. It's a reprieve between summer's leap and the dormant void of winter. There's something about its halting introspection compatible with my nature. I was never one to look forward; I've always been the kind to pause and reflect. Because it takes me a while to process things. I find it hard to live in the moment. I tend to register events in my own time, typically in hindsight. I was thinking about this as I walked the faded ochre field to Little Tea's house, thinking I'd better get ready. I knew she'd be moving to Boston in two weeks, so I should ponder the ramifications before they settled. What bothered me most was that there'd never been a time when it didn't seem like Little Tea was right around the corner. Even though I primarily lived in Memphis, I spent enough weekends in Como to feel secure with the knowledge that she was instantly accessible. Rather than being happy for Little Tea, all I could think of was how her absence would impact me, never mind that I'd be away at school in Knoxville. It was the idea of Little Tea no longer being a fixture at home that undid me; it left me feeling rudderless.

As I rounded the lake, Little Tea ran toward me. I wanted to stand stock-still, take hold of the moment, file it away, and get back to it when I was ready. It's not that I didn't know we'd grow up one day and forge different paths, it just hurt too much to think about being separated from my constant companion. College would change our lives forever, or so Hayward had said while the three of us walked in the woods during his last trip home. Little Tea had been lit up with the news of her acceptance to Boston University, bursting to tell Hayward what I already knew. We both thought Hayward would ride the coattails of her excitement, but he stopped in midstride, his head down heavy, his eyes fixed low, as though the wind were out of his sails. "Little Tea, why so far away?" he asked, his tone taking the news personally. "We'll never be able to see you."

Little Tea stopped walking. She put her hand on her hip in a way that told me she was put out and turned to lock eyes with Hayward. "For one thing, I was offered a woman's track scholarship from Boston University," she said. "You know I've been building my profile for years. You were the one who told me how to get recruited. I spent years connecting with coaches for a shot at this, and it happened for me. Why you so surprised? You've been telling me for as long as I can remember that running would be the ticket to the future."

"I know that, Little Tea, but folks from around here never stray so far from home. I don't see why you have to go all the way up there. You could go to Knoxville or plenty of other places. Boston isn't the only school that offered you a scholarship; you told me that a while ago. I didn't think for a minute you'd seriously consider moving so far away."

"What is this, white boy?" Little Tea said, a mocking smile on her amused face. "How can you keep her down on the farm after she's seen the world? Is that what this is?"

Hayward, like me, couldn't help but smile. It wasn't often she called either of us white, nor did we refer to her as black. If ever one of us resorted to this tactic, it was only to make fun of the region. We saw ourselves collectively as separate from the predominant regional mentality, which had made itself known in Tallulah's dress shop that time Little Tea and I shopped with my mother, and even in my own family at the hands of my grandmother and John. But the racial divide didn't touch us when we were together. Nobody knew that we were a unit. To an outsider's eye we were only representatives of the aggregate of our individual color, which was considered so disparate in manner and culture that it was an oddity to see us together, even if we were simply having lunch at Pop's Shop. We knew this and took smug pleasure in bucking the system. We had a sixth sense about furtive gazes and judgmental eyes. We were young and cavalier about what we saw as breaking the mold. And I knew Little Tea to the very depth of her bone marrow. She was so self-assured, no double take gave her pause; it only made her self-righteous. It was a joke among us, two notches to the left of our own club secret. Because we rarely discussed it among us, our bond was calcified when in the public eye. When in the face of scrutiny, I could literally feel our force field snap to a cohesive, protective circle, and within its boundary we stood up for each other and explained ourselves to no one. It was enough for us to know the line between us and them.

"Anyway, Hayward," Little Tea said, softening, "I'm going to come back." She resumed walking the path. "I mean, travel is expensive, so I won't be going back and forth like you do, but I'll be home for Christmas. There's a winter break, and you and Celia will be here, it'll be like it's always been. My parents are proud of me. It's like I've gotten up and given us all a new start."

"I understand; it's just a surprise, is all. Threw me for a minute," Hayward said, and his energy lifted to the happy-go-lucky, unstoppable boy who breezed through life on the wings of optimism.

I was thinking about Hayward's reaction when Little Tea reached me at the side of the lake. I wished I had his ability to take the facts of Little Tea's departure and smile. Little Tea looked at her watch. "I should be back by sunset, but we've got time for a good walk," she said.

Deep in the woods behind the Winfreys' house, in a clearing beneath a copse of oaks, a weathered array of patina, limestone grave markers rose at odd angles, their foundations incrementally altered from time untold of shifting soil. Though neither of us could claim relation to the bones lying beneath, Little Tea and I were in the habit of using their baleful whereabouts as a destination. It was the serpentine path to the clearing that so compelled us; it rolled unevenly beneath canopied overgrowth and ended near the mouth of a running stream. It was telling of the kind of friendship we had, those aimless walks we'd take through the woods. Neither of us was one for sitting around the house, and if the weather was fine, one of us would call the other and simply ask if she was ready to go. We'd take the narrow path from the Winfreys' back porch into the murky, halcyon woods. Even though this was our favorite place to talk, we'd enter with wordless reverence for all the endless enchantment.

Sound muffles in the woods, and there is something sacred about footfall on earth as it strikes a cadence. It has always brought an awareness of my own impermanence to be passing through something so eternal. I think this is why Little Tea and I so easily lapsed into stream of consciousness banter. There's a kind of intimacy in the seclusion of woods when two friends walk through together. I had no thought of censoring myself as we ambled along and got straight to the heart of the matter. "I don't know what I'm going to do without you this coming year," I said in all earnestness.

"Go on now, go along with yourself," Little Tea said, but her voice rang in the soft notes of someone who'd just said they understand. "You're going to have your man with you in Knoxville," she added. "You won't be missing the likes of me."

"It's not the same, and you know it," I said.

"No, not the same; but might be just as good. Why you want to court sorrow?"

"I'm not courting anything, Little Tea; it's just that Tate will never know me the way you do."

"No, I don't suspect he ever will," she said. "You're just going to have to wait and see. Fact is, Tate doesn't know you any better than you know him, but there's one surefire way to find out. Y'all just keep doing what you're doing."

"You think we're making a mistake by going to the same college?"

"Celia, I don't think so. I think y'all've already got things started."

I leaned to take a sturdy stick from the ground to use as a cane. "My father and grandmother are mad as hornets that Tate's going to Knoxville," I said.

"Your grandmother's mad as a hornet anyway. You and I both know it isn't you. But your daddy? That sweet soul could never be mad at anybody. I ain't buying he's mad at his baby girl."

"Well maybe not mad, just disappointed. He thinks I should experience more of the world."

"I don't know, Celia. I don't think that way about you. It's what I plan on doing, but I'm different than you. It's just what I tried to say to Hayward, remember?"

"Look, Little Tea, Hayward gets it. I don't know what got into him when you told him you were going to Boston, but he seemed to regroup."

"I sure hope so," Little Tea said. "Y'all are my two best friends in the world. It wouldn't do to be at odds with either of you. Here, give me that stick; what if we see us a snake?"

I handed her the stick. "That'll never happen, Little Tea," I said. "I can promise you that."

"What, seeing a snake or y'all at odds with me?" Little Tea asked.

"Oh, for heaven's sake, Little Tea. I'm talking about Hayward and me being at odds with you. Quit being funny. And snakes aren't around when the weather's this cool. My grandmother told me snakes burrow underground this time of year. They don't hibernate; they just get in the ground and slow their metabolic rate down."

"That one would know," Little Tea huffed.

Bypassing the gravestones in favor of the stream, we picked our way among haphazard rocks and boulders, the thicket on both sides of the water dark and dense as storm clouds. Sunlight eked through the treetops, forcing its way to enlightenment through a swaying, green-canvas awning. On the reed-covered banks, nothing but degradations of shadows, but on the water the descending sunshine turned the stream's ripples to a living silver sheen. Little Tea took her shoes off and stepped lightly from rock to boulder as water splashed in blue iron-gray. "Come on," she called, and I waded in behind her. We stood on a slippery rock holding on to each other, the sunlight bathing us in the day's waning heat.

"Little Tea, I hate to say it, but we should get going. If you need to be home before sunset, we better turn back."

"Okay, but you go in front of me when we pass by the gravestones," she said. "I saw the earth sinking in over one of the graves, and you know what that predicts."

"I have no idea what that predicts, Little Tea. If this is one more of your superstitions, I'm not even going to listen. Why do you always want to scare me half to death?"

"Because you need to know, that's why. I swear, Celia. you may not know it, but I've been watching your back for a long time. That earth sinking in over there is not a good sign. Never is in a graveyard. I'll be happy to tell you what it means."

"Save it, Little Tea," I said laughing.

But I should have listened. I should have stopped her right there, put my hands on her shoulders, looked her straight in the eyes, and listened.

Heber Springs, Arkansas

I was afraid it would happen. I'd been knotted up inside from the moment Tate Foley walked into Renny's Heber Springs lake house carrying our history, and all I could think at the time was *Thank God we aren't alone.* But now Tate wanted to see me by myself, which made me acutely aware that there really can come a point when there's absolutely nothing further to talk about with someone.

But what to do when the past comes back to haunt, as it typically does, sooner or later? I think what bothered me most was that I'd unwittingly gone out to meet the past halfway. The irony of my desire to help Ava turning into this reunion with Tate didn't escape me. It confirmed what I'd long suspected, that the only way to move past a hindrance in life is to face it head-on. But oh, I wasn't ready for this, and it was everything I could do not to blame Ava, until I realized she was only a convenient article used as a vehicle by fate.

"Celia, I'm sorry," Ava said with pleading measure. "I didn't think it'd be a big deal."

Renny put her cellphone in her pocket. Though she'd been talking to one of her vets at her clinic, she'd heard every word Ava said. "Celia knows that," Renny said, "but that's not the point. You should have asked her, that's all."

"Celia wasn't standing there with me when I saw Tate this morning. What was I supposed to do, say no?"

"If it'd been me, I'd have asked Tate for his number and told him I'd give it to Celia." Renny sounded exasperated. "You could have at least put the ball in her court."

"But they've been friends all their lives. It's not like they're strangers," Ava rationalized.

"Friends?" I rounded on Ava. "I believe our history argues otherwise."

"You were fine when he was here last night. I thought y'all were okay," Ava said. "He's just going to call you. What could happen?"

Renny jumped in again. "Ava, you just told us he wants to take Celia out on the lake. What this means is he wants to see her alone. It puts Celia in an awkward position. What's she going to say, 'No Tate, and here's why'?"

Thinking I should referee before it got bigger, I said, "All right. Let's drop this. I'll deal with it, if and when he calls. But we need to have some kind of understanding among us because we're winging it and failing. How about this: when it comes to Stan or Tate or Mark or anyone else, we should check with each other before we make a move. Is that fair?"

"Should go without saying," Renny said under her breath, and at that exact moment, Renny's cell phone rang. It was Stan, and Renny was uncharacteristically caught off guard. "Hello? ... Oh, hi, Stan ... No, no. I thought you were one of my vets."

I laughed so hard it doubled me over, while Ava stood looking like a deer caught in headlights.

"Perfect, it's cosmic timing," I said.

Ava waved her hand to get Renny's attention. "Don't tell him I'm here," she mouthed, but Renny held up her hand and waved her away then turned her back and walked to her bedroom, her phone to her ear, her brows knit in serious conference.

"What? We can't even *listen*?" Ava said.

"Believe me, you can trust Renny," I said. "If anyone can handle this, it's Renny."

"Why is Stan calling her?" Ava asked.

"He probably wants to know what's going on with you."

"Why doesn't he ask me?"

"I don't know, Ava. You're sneaky," I said without thinking.

"No, I'm not. How could you say that?"

"Okay, then you're a covert operator with otherworldly powers of intrigue. What do you want me to say? I don't know why anybody does anything they do. We might as well sit down and wait this one out."

In the living room, Ava and I sat across from each other like detained students waiting outside the principal's office. Ava had her head in her hands and said, "If Renny blows my cover, I'm going to be in big trouble."

Rearranging the pillows on the sofa, the truth came to me clearly. "Renny won't blow your cover. And even if she did, it's not a crime to go through a phase of questioning where your life should go next. Maybe you should just tell Stan the way it is. Maybe y'all can sort this out together. Don't you think you should address your marriage first before you look at anything else?"

"My therapist thinks I should address my drinking first. I was almost convinced, but you know what? *My therapist* showed up drunk at one of our sessions."

This almost took me over the edge, it was so funny. Ava and I were in hysterics when Renny returned to the room. "What's so funny?" she asked.

Now sidetracked from the subject of Stan, I answered, "Ava's therapist showed up drunk at one of their sessions."

Renny's low-throated laughter shook the rafters, and soon we were thoroughly overcome with the ties that bind from a shared sense of humor. Renny stood at the window, rolling the shades against the noon sun. "What do you do when something like that happens? I mean, do you fire the guy, or what?"

"You don't have to fire him, you just have to stop making appointments," I said to Ava.

"I don't know if I can do that. I mean, he knows my full story—the good, the bad, and the ugly. After all the work we've done, maybe I should just overlook it."

"Ava, you're confusing the nature of the relationship with friendship," Renny said, rounding the sofa. "You're paying him, remember? You've been going to him for his expertise."

"I know, but now he knows everything about me," she said. After a pause, she added, "I don't know how to explain it."

"I understand what you're saying," I said to Ava.

I was thinking about how seemingly unrelated scenarios can activate a similar heart chord that rings the same fear. At the bottom of Ava's feeling was the vulnerability that comes from emotionally investing in another person. It's an act of bravery built on blind trust, and nothing's more disillusioning than when it comes to a bad end. This was why I didn't want to see Tate alone, and why it was my hope he'd decide not to call after all. Sometimes something sounds like a good idea until it comes time for it. Sometimes just considering a prospect makes you realize you're better off where you are.

"What did Stan want?" Ava asked Renny.

Renny put her hand on my shoulder. "Y'all get ready for this: he wanted to know if Mark Clayton is here."

"What?" I said promptly. "What in the world makes him suspect that? Good God, what is he, psychic?"

"Stan knows Mark has a lake house here," Ava told us. "He's always been suspicious whenever I've come home to see Mama, always manages to slip something in about Mark. But I didn't tell him until yesterday that we were in Heber Springs. It's my fault, I guess. I wasn't thinking."

Renny sighed and sank deeper into the sofa. "I swear, this is like high school with y'all sneaking around with those boys. I thought for sure there'd be a time you'd outgrow it, but I was wrong. And here I am in the picture. The more things change, the more they stay the same." She shifted on the sofa to fully face me. "Celia, I'll never forget covering for you when you and Tate snuck out to Como. That was before we had cell phones, and if it hadn't been for me, it would have been game over. Your parents would have yanked you out of UT before you even got there. And I had to lie to your mother, which almost killed me. You still owe me for that one." She paused. "What were y'all, seventeen?"

★★★

I knew exactly to what Renny referred. Yes, Tate and I were both seventeen, and that was a dangerous age for us. Beneath nightfall and the shroud of love's illusion, we took a risk we shouldn't have. We thought we were immune to consequence. Fueled by alcohol and blinded with ungoverned, hormone-driven passion, we left Renny's graduation party and drove out to Como on a weekend when my family wasn't there. Renny hadn't raised an eyebrow when I told her where we were going. If she had, I might have thought twice, but as it was, her apathetic manner condoned our impromptu plan.

Tate parked his truck beneath an oak at the side of the house, and we walked with hesitant footfalls through the kitchen door. At night, without my family in residence, the house took on echoing, eerie proportions with illicit undertones. But I felt safe with Tate. His intrepid way of dealing in the world was something I servilely followed. It was his idea to spend the night at the farm and, at the time, for all the linear, sightless reasons that make a girl follow a magnetic boy such as Tate, I thought it was an innocuous idea. That if I made it back to Renny's house by sunrise, no one would be the wiser. That Tate and I were alone was a rarity. Our love had been planted and cultivated within the monitoring sequestration of our tight-knit group. Freed of all confines in the empty house in Como, nature took over, heightening all that it means to be young and on the exploratory edge of sexuality for the very first time.

These are the defining moments that bind two people for a lifetime. There is only one first. After that, there is only every other. I can recall to this day every indelible second of that night, for all its altering import—Tate Foley muscular and sinewy, foreign in every inch of his beautiful, burgeoning manhood. It was the unmasking of mysteries that brought us breathlessly into alignment, an expedition set sail from adolescence to no turning back. There, in the bed I'd slept in since childhood, the earth pivoted on its axis beneath a window propped open to a quarter moon's subtle breeze, flickering the trio of beeswax candles I'd brought upstairs from the dining room. It's the inconsequential elements that leave resounding impact. To this day, whenever I think of love, I think of candlelight soft and airborne, casting shadows on the wall beneath a dim quarter moon.

The morning's sun cornered the room in antique ivory as we woke to find Little Tea standing over the bed. "Y'all best get up and get a move on," she directed. "I know you're supposed to be anywhere else."

Tate and I tore out of Como as though the devil followed on our heels. By the time Tate dropped me off at Renny's parents' house, it was well past nine in the morning, and my mother had already called.

★ ★ ★

"I still owe you for that one?" I said to Renny. "What are you doing, keeping score?"

"As a matter of fact, I am," Renny said. "And Ava's not going to like this this one bit ... Stan said he's going to drive down here."

Ava's eyes widened, and her hand flew to her mouth. "Oh my God," she drawled out.

"You're busted," I said with a clip.

"Oh no, I'm not," she stated. "He's not coming here. I'm going to call him right now."

"Let's go outside," Renny said as Ava trudged downstairs. "You might want to bring a hat."

Side by side on the deck, we waited for Ava in the heat, our feet on the rail, our eyes scanning the lake. Renny must have felt the need to editorialize. She leaned back in her chair and began, "This is now a lover's triangle ... not to mention that it's turning into a Southern romance novel. I mean, seriously, don't you find this somewhat predictable? And I'll tell you where it's going to end. Ava's going to break Mark's heart all over again. She'll stay put with Stan, you watch. The shame is she'd like to be adventurous, but she's not. This is why she gets into one mess after another. She gets halfway into something then changes her mind and backs out."

"It's the rare person who has the courage of conviction," I said. "Most people are paralyzed at the prospect of what others are going to think."

Renny took a few moments mulling something over before she spoke. "I know you're thinking of Hayward," she said.

"Yes," I said. "How could I not?"

Memphis, Tennessee
Sometime in the 1980s

Hayward sent my whole family into a tailspin when he announced he wouldn't be working in Como the next summer, which had been his yearly habit. That He'd applied and been accepted at The Berklee College of Music's summer program in Boston without mentioning it was only part of the problem. The news of this divergent aim sent Big John into such a sputtering tizzy none of us thought he'd recover.

As it was the month of August, Hayward had issued close to a year's warning and told us that it was, after all, only a six-week program. But to Big John, it was a sweeping statement implying complete familial abdication. Big John took his time pontificating on the endless points of Hayward's insubordination as he paced to and fro, holding court like a lawyer issuing closing arguments, even though the decision had already been made. It was astounding to watch my father finally stand up to his in our Memphis living room, but then I suspected he identified with Hayward's decision and all the words he'd never said to his father in his own youth came tumbling out as though they'd been festering for decades and had finally arrived at an appropriate outlet. When the words sprang from my father, they were righteous and mighty. He spoke of passion, destiny, and heeding one's God-given call. Tall and elegant and beautiful, he stood on the jewel-toned, Oriental rug, looking every inch the dark romantic figure he was, every line from his lips singing as sacrosanct as a hymn. I found it striking to watch Big John take measure of his only son. Although I could feel his hostility bursting with the urge to attack, Big John's head was at such an angle it appeared he was at least partially willing to let my father's speech slide in, even if it were only for sport. Because you can always tell when a person isn't listening, that they're tone-deaf while mounting an attack from a recalcitrant stance.

Big John balanced his hefty weight with his hands in his suit pockets. Producing a gold watch from his vest, he glanced down as though to say he didn't have time for this nonsense. I'll give my grandfather this: he was the master of intimidating body language. Everything about him seemed designed for it. His was a stolid, lumbering bull presence that gave my father no recourse but to dance with a matador's featherweight agility. Back and forth they went in impassioned discourse, while Hayward and I exchanged dazed glances and John perched on the edge of the sofa like a cat waiting to creep low and steal the cream.

My mother knit her hands together from the edge of her upholstered chair. "J. T., I should have told you, but didn't. I encouraged Hayward to apply. Berklee's regional audition just so happened to be downtown at The Peabody. I urged him—in fact—I went with him."

"I'm glad you took the initiative," my father said in a manner that fully condoned my mother's involvement.

"Behind your back, of course," Big John flared.

My mother shifted her gaze to Big John. "If it came to anything, we wanted it to be a surprise. If nothing had, there would have been no need to mention it. Hayward and I both thought he should explore his options, but first he had to be accepted into the program."

"Yes, this is my precise point," my father said. "A man isn't thoroughly realized until he knows himself in all his compartments. It's his to choose which sides of himself to develop; nobody else should influence this. Hayward's an artist, a rare and gifted one at that. I'm proud of my son. I'm all for his exploring an artistic path. I think he's suited for it."

"While the Wakefield Plantation goes to seed," Big John boomed. "It's not as though we don't all know I've been grooming Hayward to step into your shoes when the time comes. He told me he'd be working at the farm next summer. I had plans for him. This going away to study music instead indicates a lack of commitment. John here let the world know he wasn't interested in the farm on the day he was born. Encouraging Hayward to explore other avenues discourages me. What if he decides to stay with music the rest of his life? Who will this leave to run the farm? Celia? She'll probably marry that Foley boy. Perhaps I should take a look at him." Swinging his gaze to Hayward, he continued. "Is this what this family is trying to tell me? Are we now turning over our ancestral home to outsiders? I'm telling you what, that dog don't hunt. Nobody runs with family tradition anymore; it's all I can do to keep y'all from running amuck." His head swiveled as he looked around the room. "By God, I want a drink. Somebody get me a drink."

"Celia, get your granddaddy a drink, honey," my mother directed.

I went to the silver service on the sideboard and pulled the knob from the crystal whisky decanter. Over ice, I filled a tumbler halfway and brought it to Big John. Now that I had his attention, I made what I thought was a good suggestion. "Big John, you know Hayward's an incredible musician," I said. "He's just testing the waters. Don't you think he should? Maybe Hayward can do both in life." I turned to my brother. "Couldn't you Hayward? I mean, that's not out of the question, right? Go on, tell Big John."

And yet, even as I spoke, something bothered me. What unsettled me about this living room passion play was that Hayward hadn't told *me* he'd applied to the school. And there I was jumping to his defense without understanding the whole story. Under normal conditions, Hayward would have enlisted me as an ally. We would have joined forces and stood firmly in unified defense. And even though it wasn't so much an act of betrayal as it was a lie of omission, it disarmed me in what could have been my full support. I was used to playing a bit part to Hayward's starring role out of sheer force of habit—so used to it, in fact, that at the time I didn't do what I should have done, which was not accept his decision at face value. I should have looked deeply into his motives.

"How this family produced two artists is beyond me," Big John said with deflation, though he managed to slip an accusatory look at my father. "A painter and a musician, for the love of Pete," his voice set sail to full throttle. "The Wakefields have always been people of the land. I'm telling you we scratched and clawed our way to our fortune. By God, I'm not leaving this earth until I see my investment safeguarded, which, by the way, can't be done from a piano."

Hayward spared us all, before my grandfather went any further. From the bench of the Steinway, he jumped on the tail end of Big John's monologue, with what I thought was an equitable rebuttal. "Celia's right, Granddaddy. I'm interested in both. And Dad's right too—it's about options. This is a big opportunity. I'll be able to develop what I love doing most in the world. But it doesn't mean I don't also love the farm. There's no telling what it will come to, but the idea is to be in an environment where I'm given the best chance to expand."

Rufus sidled up to Hayward at the sound of his excited voice. He nudged in between Hayward's bent knees as though awaiting instruction. "And just so you know, I want to be a composer," Hayward continued, reaching beneath the piano to pat Rufus on the head. "I don't want to be one of those guys who tours the world. A composer can be anywhere, know what I mean? I'm not saying I'm going to bail on the family business. Some of Berklee's credits will transfer to Suwannee, so I'll probably be out of college in two and a half years. I'm thinking I could build a little studio somewhere on the farm and take it from there."

But Big John wasn't having it. "Take it from there? A man has to get a concrete plan. You become in life who it is you decide to become, Hayward, and it doesn't just happen overnight. It's hard enough as it is without trying to be two things at once. Just ask your father, who all but burned down the farm with *his* idea of art. And while you're at it, you can ask your grandmother too. She's worked hard at who and what she is and was smart enough to keep a straight line about it. She's going to be sorely disappointed when she hears about this." Big John shook his head, then lowered himself into a wingback, as though resigned to sitting the rest of it out.

Hayward shot me a sheepish look, then spoke to Big John. "No, she won't. Grandmother already knows."

"I told Cecelia," my mother confessed, sitting poised while following the dynamic.

Big John reached for his drink and took a hard swallow. "She said nothing to me about it. She's probably been struck dumb and thrown up her hands with all y'all. She doesn't understand any of you anymore. It's no secret she's put out with y'all acting like Little Tea's family. Her dander's been up over that for a good while. She doesn't think any of you know about proper place."

"Here now, Daddy," my father interjected. "It sounds like you're suggesting that Mother disapproves of Shirley and me as parents. I take this rather personally. It's Mother's way to foster this antiquated divide between races, but not ours. Shirley and I will have no part in it."

"Wait a minute," John interjected with the proverbial light bulb over his head. "Speaking of Little Tea, isn't *she* also going to Boston?"

"Yes, she is, John," I answered. "So what?"

"Ah-ha!" John snorted.

"Ah-ha, what?" I challenged. I wasn't going to sit there mutely and let John make insinuations. I never liked it when he inserted himself into anything that had to do with Hayward or me, and whenever he did, I stood up for myself. He had no right, in my mind, to pass opinion, much less judgment, but in his arrogant mind, he seemed to think he did. John never once played the protective older brother to Hayward or me; he played the adversary. And whenever he held forth on the slightest of things having to do with either of us, it came to me as intrusive and affronting. I was getting ready to say something more, when Hayward beat me to the punch.

"John, I'm not going to Boston because Little Tea is going to be there. I don't need anybody to be my buddy in the big city. The Berklee College of Music is the most prestigious school I could ever hope to get into and it just *happens* to be in Boston. You can get over whatever it is you're implying."

★ ★ ★

My first year at UT Knoxville was defining. Being separated from my friends deepened the seriousness of my relationship with Tate Foley. Without Hayward, Little Tea, Renny and Ava in my daily life, I faced college hand in hand with Tate as my lifeline in that tenuous interval between adolescence and adulthood, when the self meets the self for the very first time. What I retain of that time is a sense of self-discovery. Unlike my father, I have never been prone to bouts of depression, though I have been subject to several rounds of introspection. I knew from the start of school that I wanted to study psychology.

But what kept me anchored to home was the prospect of seeing Hayward and Little Tea in Como during my winter break. I looked forward to being with them at Christmas, though the first thing I noticed when we convened was that we were each changed. College can do this to a person, it somehow refines us. I took a good look at Little Tea that December, newly returned from Boston, and felt she'd come into her own brand of feminine mystique. I kept thinking how grown up she seemed as we walked the damp, leaf-strewn path to the stream with Hayward and Rufus. Furtive looks I cast her way told me she'd gone out into the world and acquired a confidence beyond the innate propensity she'd always had for it. She held her head high and proud, which made her relaxed, rhythmic carriage all the more striking. Some people own the very air around them, grace it with their invigorating presence. Hayward and Little Tea both had this rare quality, it seemed. But whereas Hayward's countenance seemed lit by an internal flame, Little Tea's was magnetic and wholly self-contained. And it's not that I thought Little Tea had changed significantly since we'd both gone off to college, but I felt a subtle, internal distance as though something inside her had steadied, and that intuitive tether we shared felt to me slightly frayed. It had always been Little Tea and me as a team, however subtle the energy. Whenever Hayward was with us, he'd seemed attendant, but now both Hayward and I looked at Little Tea with curious eyes as she told us about the University of Boston, the friends she'd made at school, the places she'd seen in and around the historic city, and her continued progress running track. Though I tried not to be, I was envious that Hayward would soon be up there to witness Little Tea in her new environment. As we walked along, the biggest news she shared was that a major athletic shoe and apparel corporation was mounting a marketing campaign using college athletes, and she'd been selected for one of its magazine features.

"You got an endorsement deal?" Hayward exclaimed.

"Now you're a model?" I chimed.

Little Tea waved her hand, laughing. "It isn't like that. I'm just one of ten in their college campaign. They're targeting the youth of America. Quit acting like Naomi Campbell needs to get out of my way. Here's how it happened: Our assistant coach heard about it and sent in pictures of the team. It's more about Boston's athletic program than it is about me."

"How much they going to pay you?" Hayward asked.

"Enough to make it worth my while to stay up there for the shoot after school breaks for summer."

"You're going to be in magazines? That's so cool. Good for you, Little Tea," I said. "I've never known anyone famous."

A ponderous silence weighted the air as we walked along, and I knew Hayward and I were both absorbing the information. "I don't know why, Little Tea," Hayward finally said for both of us, "but I just can't picture you up there in the big city. We always had to pull teeth to get you to come up to Memphis and that's not but forty-five miles away. Now here you are up north getting in magazines, talking about entering the Boston Marathon and telling us about Boston Harbor like you've been there since the Tea Party." Hayward looked at me. "Celia, did you see this coming? Hell, Little

Tea, you've done more up there in four months than you've done at home in your lifetime. That short amount of time, and suddenly you're a city girl?"

"I know, I was thinking the same thing," I said, grateful that Hayward made a joke of it, thinking I should make light of it, too. "Sounds to me like you're covering ground. I'm glad people seem to like you. You must have forgotten to take your surly attitude and scathing sense of humor up there with you."

Little Tea threw a teasing punch to my shoulder. "Go on with yourself, Celia. You know that's not it. It's just a bigger world up there. I'd love to stay down here in this one-horse town with y'all forever, but I've got a life to live. Hayward, you'll see what I'm talking about when you're up there this summer. It's not like it is down here. There's not such a people difference, if you take my meaning."

"I get it. Not a big deal over who goes where with who and does what is what you're saying. Speaking of which, I sure would appreciate you showing me around Boston while I'm there. I'll be in an intensive, conservatory program. I don't know what the exact schedule will be, but there's bound to be some downtime," Hayward said. He looked at Little Tea sidelong. "I mean, if you think you'll have the time."

"Of course I will," Little Tea said. "I'll be there the whole time you will. Anyway, I owe you. If it weren't for y'all's family, I wouldn't have ended up there, what with you encouraging me to apply and your father's kind heart and all."

"*Our* father?" I asked. "What's he got to do with anything?"

"You didn't know?" Little Tea stopped walking. I heard her inhale as though checking herself; I thought it indicated she would have taken her words back, if only she could. To fill the dead air of Little Tea's pregnant pause, blackbirds and warblers and sparrows flit and lighted, their territorial warning notes ringing above us. In the thicket, the rustling of movement unseen, in this wintertime suspended. I looked at Hayward, who'd stopped when I stopped. Both of us fixed our eyes on Little Tea.

"What?" I prodded.

"Your father's paying the rest of my tuition beyond the scholarship. I thought y'all knew."

"We didn't know, but that's just like him," Hayward said.

"Well, it took my daddy a while to let him. He's proud, you know. Had to get it out of his head that the offer was some kind of sufferance. Your father must have put it to him like it'd be doing him a favor. You know how he spins magic with words. Y'all's daddy could talk his way out of hell and into heaven, if he had a mind to."

As though pondering aloud, Hayward said, "Yeah, he's good at doing that for other people but doesn't have a good record for doing it for himself. Lack of self-confidence, maybe. I don't know, hard to say."

"The man runs deep," Little Tea said. "Celia favors him that way. Neither likes letting on."

"Hey, Little Tea, I'm standing here," I said. "If you're going to give commentary on me, I might as well keep walking."

"Rufus, get the stick," Hayward called, lobbing a twig up ahead. "Maybe it is doing Dad a favor. Our family's lives are so intertwined, he likes to take care of all of us. These things matter to him. Seems to me in a dynamic like ours, anything's permissible. What's good for one of us is good for all, you know? Keeps things cohesive."

"You've got a good point, Hayward," I added. "All of us benefit from Dad's involvement. Just look how Little Tea being up in Boston is turning out to be great for you. Dad was behind both of y'all going up there. There's something about it so serendipitous, don't you think? I admit I'm kind of jealous. I'd love to see Boston, but this summer is probably not the right time. Y'all will be up there working."

Little Tea gave me one of her foregone conclusion scoffs. "Oh, you'll see it one day. Tate Foley's going to show you the world. He steps into his family business and y'all will be all over Europe. It'll be us riding on your coattails, for sure," she said as the graveyard came into view.

"Hayward, you better get Rufus out of that graveyard," I switched the subject. "We shouldn't go in it. It'll give Little Tea reason to go off on her superstitions, and I'm not in the mood to hear about bad luck or how I'm going to die."

"I never say *when* something will happen, just that something will," Little Tea laughed.

Four days before Christmas, and the stream ran hematite cold. Through a sky low and drifting, shooting shards of sunlight aimed for the current, refracting shades of silver, blue, and gray in a kaleidoscope of ripples. The world was in swirling movement, raising its voice in an aquatic tumbling roar from the soul of the stream. We'd been buffered from the wind under a network of limbs, but once out on the flat bank, we were suddenly and starkly exposed. When the three of us emerged from the woods, John and his companion were on the other side of the stream. It must have startled him to see us intrude upon them, at least that's what he indicated when he and his friend joined us.

John seemed uncharacteristically happy to see us. He waved from the opposite bank then picked his way over boulders at the mouth of the stream. I have to admit I liked John's friend right away. His name was Rhett Saunders, so named after Rhett Butler, and the way he told the story of his given first name had us all in stitches. "Too bad my mother didn't think to give me a name to live up to," Rhett quipped, which gave rise to the best in Hayward. That John seemed so animated lifted my heart to heights I'd never thought possible to associate with him. I'd been so long braced in his presence, it surprised me how willing I was to accept his good will.

John produced a bottle of white wine from his rucksack, passed it around like a gracious host. In that memorable pre-Christmas moment, all was harmonious in my world and I thought how time and separation can lend new perspective, that maybe there was a chance in the future to hold tight to what mattered. We were a family, no matter our differences, and maybe it was time to stop being at odds. Because I wanted this from John. I've always been hypersensitive to discord, especially when it's something unnamed. Seeing John so carefree on the banks of the stream gave me great hope for subsequent possibilities as all of us trailed after Rufus, making our way home through the woods.

In the foyer, the enveloping, anticipatory arms of Christmas reached wide and soothing, for no good reason I could fathom beyond the comforting fact I was home. Once the front door closed against the wind behind us, we peeled off our scarves and coats before the eight-foot pine tree Thelonious had brought in from the woods. It loomed with waiting potential, a blank canvas my imagination had decorated a few times since I'd returned.

It was my mother's way to make a ceremony out of decorating the tree. That night, there'd be boxes of ornaments brought down from the attic, music floating from the living room's stereo, whisky and ice on the bar, and all of us waiting for assignments. We all knew our mother was mistress of ceremony, and we counted on her direction. The downstairs reeked of pine garland. It looped from the banister with gold taffeta bows centered with holly. In the kitchen, Elvita roasted a turkey. She had her back to us and leaned low into the oven with an oversized plastic baster. After basting the turkey with pan drippings, she sprinkled the skin with salt and paprika. Turning when the five of us entered, she looked at the wall clock, whose black metal hands reached to four thirty-five. "Y'all got about an hour and a half to get ready," she said. "Your mama's been wondering where y'all been." Hayward reached for the pan of cut cornbread and lifted a slice to his mouth. He laughed in full anticipation of Elvita's reaction, before she even asked him if he'd been raised by wolves. I told Little Tea I'd see her later, then went in search of the touchstone of my mother. I didn't want anything, really; it just seemed fitting to tell her we were all home. Because there was a rhythm that went on in the Como house conducted by her delicate hand, and we all waltzed to its music. She dusted the world in iridescent beauty, and we all lived in its haloed glow.

"There you are, Celia," my mother said when I found her. She turned from the vanity table in my parents' bedroom. "Do me a favor, run tell

Elvita to set another place in the dining room. Rhett will be joining us tonight. John's asked him to spend the night."

"Okay, I'll go down in a minute." I sat on her bed. "Where'd he meet Rhett? I've never heard John mention him. And with a name like Rhett, I would have remembered."

"Rhett works with John at James Davis. I think he's the manager. Maybe he's the buyer, I'm not sure. Either way, he's an impeccable dresser and has beautiful manners. Seems a nice young man. I'm happy to have him." Rufus came trotting in the bedroom, his paws still wet from the trail's damp earth. "Hayward, honey," my mother called. "Come get Rufus before he tracks up my floor."

"Rufus, come," Hayward called from below.

I stood and made for the door. "All right, I'll go down now and ask Elvita to set another place." I followed Rufus out to the landing. As we descended the stairs, Hayward stood in the foyer, motioning me into the living room.

"What's gotten into John?" he whispered when I reached him.

"You mean why's he being so nice?"

"Yeah, you trust this?"

"Well, now that you put it that way, I don't know."

Hayward stood looking at me with the full intent of communicating something burning. "All right, listen; here's the deal: keep an eye on John. He might be saving up for something."

"Come on, Hayward. Why are you so cynical? Can't John be happy?"

"No. He can't. With him, it's never that simple. Something's up. Nobody does an about-face without something being up."

What was up was me later that night. After we'd lingered over dinner, trimmed the tree in stages of ornaments, ribbon, and tinsel then repaired to the solace of the living room, where a wood-burning fire wrapped us in aromatic ambience as we listened to Hayward on the piano dreaming up a medley of Christmas classics. Five hours in this traditional, festive assembly left me feeling live-wired well after midnight. Because the upstairs wood floors creaked, I padded across the landing on the balls of my feet, making my way lightly from one sound-muting area rug to another. Outside, the half-moon swam with gilded strokes reflected in a puddle beneath the landing's beveled window. I slipped down to the kitchen, noiselessly retrieved a glass from the overhead cabinet, and filled it with orange juice and sat in a stillness so ringing I wanted to hush my own thoughts. Eventually I made my way up the stairs past my parents' room and hesitated on the third-floor landing, noticing the guest bedroom's door was ajar. I froze for one spine-tingling moment, thinking of ghosts before I considered anything else. When I spied Rhett Saunders in his white boxers creeping across the hall to John's bedroom, it didn't surprise me.

For some deep-knowing reason, his stealthy feet didn't seem one bit out of step.

Heber Springs, Arkansas

O nce Ava gets off the phone, I say we go out on the lake," Renny said from her canvas chair. "And listen, Celia, I don't want to pry; but, you know, it's not as though you ever volunteer anything, so I'll just go on and say it: if you want to talk about your family, I'm all ears. I just don't want to push you. You've always been so private."

"I appreciate that," I said, though not a word beyond it, which was my way of saying I don't want to talk about my family. I wanted Renny to do the talking. I needed the distraction as we sat watching the quicksilver lake from the deck. As long as she got off the subject of Hayward, I'd be fine. We'd already talked about Tate Foley. I couldn't decide which was worse. I knew that what bothered me when it came to the subject of both Hayward and Tate was the sinking feeling I'd been hoodwinked by fate. At one time, I'd had a sense of my destiny. I knew exactly what my future looked like and who would stand beside me no matter what. In hindsight, I thought that's where I went wrong. I no longer said "no matter what" about anything because as soon as I did, the what of the matter manifested like a jinx. I thought this is why people say it's not wise to tempt fate. The forces that shape our lives don't take kindly to presumption. And seriously … no really … I didn't want to talk about it.

"You don't want to talk?" Renny pressed.

I shook my head.

"All right then … give me a cigarette."

"Ava has the pack," I reminded, and just as I did, Mark Clayton appeared on the deck.

"Hey, y'all. The door was wide open." He paused long enough to plant his hands on his hips. "What's going on? Where's Ava?"

"Downstairs on the phone with her husband," Renny said, emphasizing the last word.

"Ouch," Mark flinched, though he was smiling. He dropped his hands, then walked over to the seating arrangement behind us and slid a chair between us. "Okay, I get it, girls. Y'all are mad at me." Mark flopped down.

"You got a cigarette?" Renny asked.

"If I hand you one, don't bite."

Laughing, I squared my shoulders and cleared my throat demonstratively. "I'm glad you've decided to join us this morning. We'd like to push you up against the wall and ask about your intentions."

"Especially since Ava left your house less than an hour ago, and now here you are," Renny added with mock surprise. "Separation anxiety?"

"She left her wallet." Mark reached into his shirt pocket and set the wallet on the rail. "So what are y'all doing today?"

"I think we'll go out on the lake. I don't get out to Heber as often as I'd like, so I want to take advantage. We're waiting on Ava to get off the phone—"

"With her husband," all three of us said in unison.

"All right, all right." Mark leaned back then bounced forward. "Look, it's like this: I'm free and clear. I'm getting divorced. Ava told y'all that, right?"

"Darling, it's not *you* we're worried about, God love you," Renny said. "It's that Ava doesn't know what she's doing and, in my opinion, you're confusing things. Didn't occur to me y'all were going to get all hot and heavy. By the way, you're not over there serenading her with your guitar, are you?"

"Not that it's any of your business, but as a matter of fact, yes, I've played a little," Mark said. "Why do you ask?"

"Oh, dear God, she'll never leave here," Renny sighed. "Celia, Ava's never leaving."

"Mark, we're not saying it's wrong, it's just the timing," I qualified. "You know we love you."

"Oh, I know," Mark said. "But honestly, what am I going to do? Ava's here; it's happening now, know what I mean? You saying I should put the brakes on this?"

When I looked at Renny, her eyes were waiting for mine. She gave Mark a palms-up shrug with a tilt of her head and said, "I'm not telling you what to do, but it'd be easier if Ava were free and clear … as you put it."

"Well she's going to have to go home eventually. I know that," Mark said.

"Unless Stan's on his way to haul her back home," I suggested.

"He's going to do that?" Mark sounded alarmed.

"Maybe," Renny answered. "Wouldn't blame him if he did."

"Man, it's always something," Mark said.

"You sound like Ava," Renny said flatly. "Both y'all act like life just lands on your head and you've got nothing to do with instigating anything. I swear, y'all exhaust me."

I gave Mark a weak smile. "She's only saying y'all need to think this through."

Mark looked from me to Renny then leaned back in his chair, scanning the lake, where a handful of boats had appeared on this Saturday morning, sluicing through the crystalline water, a series of roiling whitecaps in their wake. "I'll tell ya what," he said momentarily. "I think I better get going. Do me a favor; don't even mention this conversation."

"Okay," I said. "We won't say anything."

"Yeah, what's the point?" Renny agreed.

Rising, Mark said, "Celia, you heard from Tate? Has he called you yet?"

"What did he do, clear the idea with you and Ava?" I asked. "Something feels kind of behind my back here."

"Celia doesn't like being discussed. You know that, Mark," Renny said. "When's Tate going to track Celia down? I think she should be prepared."

"He's not going to be here today." Mark's eyes scrutinized my face. "He'll be back tomorrow."

I nodded, wanting to drop the subject. I got up and followed Mark to the kitchen. With his hand on the screen door, he turned as though something had just occurred to him. "You happy out there with your husband?"

"Blissful," I said.

"You deserve it," he said. "He's one lucky man."

I walked back to the deck and said to Renny, "I'm going to give David a quick call before his day starts. Let me know when Ava appears." I walked down the hallway to my bedroom, thinking about Mark saying David was one lucky man. Maybe I'm cynical and overanalyze too much, but that statement seemed loaded, even though I knew Mark didn't mean it that way. Too frequently I suspect people have hidden motives, that what they say isn't half of what they've left out. There was this whole, big, dramatic history I had with Tate Foley, which Mark was thoroughly privy to. Standing there at the kitchen door, when Mark said I deserve to be blissful, I wanted to deflect by saying, "I know what you're implying, but let's forget all that." I want people to think that the tragedies of my life weren't all that bad, that I can handle them, as though what you see in my upright posture is exactly what you get. That I'm perfectly normal. And here beneath this roof was Ava, who didn't seem to fear any of this. She threw her flaws around the world for all to see and never faltered over what anyone thought. I must admit I admired this about her. She readily confessed to her adorable brand of insanity. Because she wore it so charmingly, people excused her as being ditzy; a little out there; artistically bent. "Celia," she'd once said to me, exasperated, "everybody's crazy, some people just hide it better than others. If any of us were normal, we wouldn't be here on earth. We're here trying to work all this stuff out. We graduate to heaven once we do."

And the funny thing was, at the time I understood what she was saying. It was typical of the things that would come out when I was with Ava, as though we maintained a running dialogue without an end, a deep, probing examination of life and where it was we fit in. Neither of us went anywhere near an existential subject with Renny. Ava declared the reason was because Renny wasn't lost. It occurred to me then that if I were lost, I certainly wouldn't admit it, but Ava waved her disorientation like a flag, and it suited her to an endearing degree.

I called David, and as was his way, he answered on the second ring. "I miss you," he said by way of hello.

"You always say the right thing," I said. "I miss you too. I'm glad to hear your voice. Are you in the studio?"

"Of course," he said. "I'm working on a deadline. How's it going down there? You having a good time?"

"I really am. I've been laughing with the girls since I got here. It's been interesting to say the least." I glanced out the window. "You wouldn't believe the ungodly humidity. You know I'm not a big fan of swimming, but in this weather, it's best to stay in the lake."

Ava leaned into my room just then. "Are you still using the phone?" she asked.

I met Ava's eyes and said to David, "Listen, I'm going to let you get back to work. I'll call tonight before I turn in."

"Well, I did it. I talked to Stan," Ava said, the second I got off the phone. She flicked off her flip-flops and threw herself on my bed. She hung over the edge horizontally, with her slender arms stretched overhead, trying to land in a backbend. This was not an unusual antic performed by Ava, who was always in motion. I zipped my cell phone into my purse pocket and looked at her leaning upside-down.

"What'd you say to Stan?" I asked.

"I told him I need my space, that I'm trying to find myself and need some time. He already knows I can't stand living in Columbia, but you should hear him. He's like talking to a trial lawyer. All he wants to hear are the facts." She straightened up to look at me. "You ever try talking to someone like that? It's like they only understand black and white; like they can't see shades of gray."

Laughing, I said, "You live in the gray shades; doesn't he know that?"

"Believe me, we've been fighting over this forever. I don't know if it's men and women or just me and Stan, but we speak different languages."

"It's men and women." After a pause I added, "All right, maybe it's you and Stan. Probably all your fault."

"Shut up, Celia." Ava picked up a pillow and threw it at me. "It's not funny. At least he's not coming over here. I got that part settled."

"For how long? What's your plan?"

"I said I'd come home in two weeks. I need to talk to Renny. When are we going back to Memphis, Monday morning or Monday afternoon? Let's figure this out and then I'll call Mama. She'll love having me stay with her for a while."

"Have you told your mother what's really going on?"

"Kind of, but she doesn't get it. I told you that. You were right when you said she wanted to see me safe, but in her mind, that means staying married. That's what she did with Daddy, even though he put us all through hell with his drinking. Mama had every reason to pack her bags and leave, but she never did."

"It was a different generation. Both of our mothers had their lives and identity tied up in marriage."

"Well I do too to some extent. I'm definitely a product of my mother's influence. You know what's really weird? She had concrete reasons to leave, and I don't have one. I almost wish I did."

"We're back to the subject of you not wanting to be the bad guy. I wish I had earth-shattering insight for you, Ava. I keep coming back to thinking Stan's a good guy, and I'd like to see you work this out."

"I don't think you like Mark," Ava stated, delivering her words in a way so pointed, it took me aback.

"Yes, I do, I've always liked Mark, but I never thought he was the one for you in the long run. Y'all are too much alike. It would have been like the blind leading the blind."

"What's wrong with being alike?" Now Ava sounded defensive.

"I don't know, Ava. I'm not saying it's this way for everyone, but the dumbest thing I could have done is tie up with someone just like me. I think in a marriage there needs to be some kind of balance in the partnership. I mean, this is what it comes down to eventually, after you clear the fairy dust out of your eyes and everything settles. Sooner or later you realize you're left with just another human being in a team effort, where both people are trying to support each other through life. In a best-case scenario, it's something complementary as opposed to both people having the same strengths and weaknesses. That's how I see it, anyway."

"I don't think that's entirely true. You and Tate were opposites. So much so, it may have been why y'all didn't work out."

My first reaction was to default to the line I always tread with Ava. If something she said stung, there was that split-second of surprise over the fact it had hurt me then I immediately started rationalizing and justifying how it was she'd said something that anybody else would have thought insensitive. I give my friends a pass in such straits because I shy from challenge and don't like discord. The fact that Ava had a point wasn't my concern. I just didn't want to hear it.

Renny walked into the room. "What are y'all talking about?"

"Opposites attracting," said Ava, "which I say is a myth."

Renny crossed to the tall chest of drawers by the window and pulled out the top drawer. Turning, she looked at Ava. "Y'all talking about you and Stan, or you and Mark?"

"Celia and Tate," Ava answered.

"I'm sure Celia loves talking about that, Ava. She's married to David, in case you forgot. Just because you're looking over your shoulder doesn't mean Celia's looking over hers." Suddenly Renny's voice sailed as she rummaged in the drawer. "I don't believe it. look at this, it's Bear." She turned to us, holding out a milky-gray, eyeless stuffed animal that had obviously seen better days. "My parents gave this to Sammie right after she was born. I had no idea it was in here."

"That's a bear?" I asked. "Let me see it."

Ava pitched her voice high, clearly uninterested in Sammie's bear. "Renny, why do you have to put it like that? I'm not looking over my shoulder at Mark. We're older now. It's like getting to know someone new."

"You buying that?" Renny said, handing me the bear.

"Not in the least," I answered, peering at the toy.

"Come on, why not?" Ava pressed.

Turning the bear over in my hands, I looked up at Renny. "This thing looks like it's been thrown in mud and run over by a truck."

"Seriously, Celia, you don't think getting older makes a difference?" Ava challenged, clearly convinced it did.

"Not really," I said. "I think we all reached our peak in high school. If you think about it, back then, we were all the best version of ourselves, before the world got its teeth into us. I don't think any of us is much different now. It's only that the circumstances have changed."

"I agree with Celia," Renny said, coming over and siting on the bed. She took the bear back from me and looked at Ava. "It's not as though Mark is someone new to you. I think you're wallowing in nostalgia—"

"For your misbegotten youth," I added. "Don't worry about it though, everyone does it at one point or another. What you should do is examine it, instead of rushing in."

"Even though y'all are in over your heads now," Renny said. "I'll tell you one thing, this nonsense about Mark getting divorced having nothing to do with you is something I ain't buying. There's not a man in the world who leaves a marriage without having somewhere to go. They're planners. All of them. None of them can be alone after they've been married for a while. What he's doing is switching horses. Ava, you need to keep this in mind because Mark's serious. He's betting on you. By the way, what did Stan say?"

Ava sighed. "I don't know. He's not coming here, so that's good. I just told him I need some time to figure everything out. We're going back to Memphis on Monday, right? Renny, did you say we're leaving Monday morning, or what? I need to call Mama. I'll go stay with her for a while."

"Yes, Ava. Tell your Mom you'll see her the day after tomorrow. Y'all go on and get it together now, so we can go out on the lake." Renny stood, headed for the door then turned as though remembering something. "I hope y'all don't mind, but I have to go to mass tomorrow morning. It's just down the road. Y'all don't have to come, but I told my Aunt Jean I'd see her there. She and Uncle Hank live here year-round. She's all excited over some big-deal priest who just arrived from Argentina. I told her I'd go."

Ava jumped up. "I'll go."

"Me, too" I said. "It'll bring back great memories of when I was the only outsider to Catholicism at Immaculate Conception High School."

Renny laughed at me. I knew she'd never forget that she and Ava had to direct me on what to do and when to do it during mass all through high school. "Celia, you were born an outsider, but you know that. Anyway, isn't Tate going to call you? If tomorrow's our last day, then that'll be the only time you can see him."

Ava shot Renny a wide-eyed look, as though she were surprised Renny didn't understand the real dynamic. "Renny, Celia doesn't want to see Tate; Tate wants to see her. He's the one who feels guilty. He wants to get her alone to ease his conscience."

Como, Mississippi
Sometime in the 1980s

In hindsight and moments of serenity, I no longer interpret the bond that Hayward and Little Tea formed as a delineating boundary between us. But over the following three summers, I certainly did. What bothered me was they both tried to hide it, but my radar was sharp; I'd been weeks into the summer break of my junior year, waiting for their return from Boston and was hypersensitive to what I quickly perceived as the covert language they shared. It wasn't that they intentionally excluded me. My reaction may have had something to do with the combined variables with which I impatiently waited—Tate working full time over the summer at his father's office in downtown Memphis, Renny in east Memphis, interning at a small-animal clinic, Ava and Mark remaining in Virginia, my father floating in a protracted, soul-dampening interlude, and my mother newly appointed as president of the Memphis Garden Club, which meant she was usually at a meeting or somewhere out to lunch. In the listless, sweltering days of Mississippi's crawl out of summer into autumn's faded reprieve, I wandered the humid, scratchy woods in Como most days with too much time on my hands. I'd amble to the stream by myself, thinking of this conversation I'd once had with Little Tea or that silly look Hayward had given me along this same path. I'd expected an end to my aimless afternoons once Hayward and Little Tea came back to save me. In my imagination, we'd eke out the last days of summer as we always had: a companionable threesome making the most of our time with each other until I began my last year of school.

But there's no slicing the thick air of attraction, and this is what Hayward and Little Tea had cultivated. It didn't strike me as something illicit as it did somewhat incestuous. To my bruised heart's way of thinking, a new tribal line had been drawn, and I stood sorely outside it. And it's funny what the mind does when given free rein to rankle. In my case, I constructed a list of clues I shouldn't have missed: Hayward's keen interest in Little Tea's track career, Hayward and Little Tea at the pond the night of the fire, Little Tea in a snit over Hayward's reaction to her leaving, then Hayward's enrollment in the Berklee College of Music's summer program. I look back now and know the signs were there all along, but I didn't want to see them. Intuition is a double-edged sword when it threatens to reveal what it is you don't want to admit. But John knew everything the second Hayward walked into the entrance hall on the July night he returned from his third Boston residency. John had an antenna for ferreting out things he could use should he need to and was a master at filing it away until the very moment he did.

"There you are, Hayward," my mother sang from the second-floor landing. She sailed down the front stairs in her cinched, tea-length dress. I came out of the living room to see Hayward sparring with Rufus, who zigzagged ecstatically at his every jostling touch. Hayward rose when my mother's heels tapped the cool, parquet floor and gave her a hug that took her up in the air. Setting her down and kissing her cheek, he turned to me and chided, "Miss me?" He reached into his shirt pocket just as I said yes then dangled a delicate gold chain before me.

"Bet you knew we'd bring you something back. Go on, look at it," he said, smiling. But I was too caught up with his use of the word *we* to do more than stand there gaping.

"Little Tea picked it out. What do you think?" he prompted, and I turned the charm in my hand to discover a minute grand piano. "Thank you, Hayward," I said. "That's so nice of you."

"You're welcome," he said. "Just wanted you to know we were thinking of you."

"Is Little Tea back?" I clasped the chain behind my neck.

"Yeah, she's out back with her parents. We were on the same flight, took a cab to get my car in Memphis then came out here."

"That certainly was convenient," John said, walking in from the dining room. "Elvita told me y'all were coming home together. Seems she was the only one who knew."

"Hey, John," Hayward said, holding out his hand for a quick, brotherly exchange. This was the best my two brothers could offer each other, but when John took Hayward's hand, he held it for a beat, clapped his other hand on top and said, "Keeping secrets again, Hayward?"

"Not from everybody, John, only you."

"Now boys, that's enough," my mother pretended to be firm. "John, of course I knew Hayward was coming. I bet he's hungry after the trip, aren't you, Hayward? Why don't y'all go in the kitchen?"

"Yes ma'am," Hayward said, and my mother touched her finger to her lips for a moment in a gesture begging silence then turned and walked the back hallway to my father's den.

"Dad okay?" Hayward asked, as John and I followed him into the kitchen.

"It depends on your idea of okay," John answered.

"Down again, huh?" Hayward interpreted.

"Pretty much the size of it, but he'll be all right."

"It's been six days and counting," I shared. "But who's counting?"

"Thelonious is; you know that, Celia," John said, as though it were obvious. "They've got stuff to do around here. They'll harvest in less than a month. Time for the party after that; they should be getting on it about now. Thelonious has been slinking around here all hang-faced, waiting on Dad to surface. Without you being here, Hayward, he's just been waiting. This is exactly what Big John feared. He's been out here himself recently. He never used to do that. I'm telling you, he's about ready to lock Dad up for treatment. A few more days of this, and Big John's going to lose patience."

"Mom's not going to let that happen," Hayward said. "Big John's just blowing smoke. Don't even worry about it." After pausing, he asked, "Celia, when do you go back to school?"

"Next week," I said.

"You'll be here for the harvest party, though. You're coming back, right?"

"Right," I confirmed.

"Me too. Hmm, let me think." Hayward sat down at the kitchen table. Momentarily, he looked up at me and said, "I better go see about Dad."

An hour later, the clouds lifted over our house in Como when my father came out of his den laughing beside Hayward. "I'm not kidding," Hayward was saying. "I was standing right there watching all of it. I even took pictures. I'll show you, once they're developed."

"I believe you, son," my father said, his hand on Hayward's shoulder as they came into the foyer. John and I had been standing by the stairs, waiting for the next event to happen, should my father's den door have flown open. We were prepared for any number of things yet hadn't anticipated the buoyancy in my father's step as he walked beside our animated brother.

"I'm telling you, they were wet as dogs, and it was all her doing," Hayward continued, his eyes wide and bright.

"What are y'all talking about?" I had to ask.

"Little Tea modeled for another magazine," Hayward reported. "She told you she does this occasionally, right?"

"She told me," I said.

"Not a bad way to make a bit of spare change, but anyway, I was at the shoot. Another model said something to Little Tea that got her dander up, so she hauled off and pushed her into the water quicker than the blink of an eye. I had to go referee. Thing is, Little Tea got pulled into the water too. Everyone was out on the dock, the photographer, the lighting guys, all the rest. Little Tea literally had an audience. Turned the whole production upside down. People running everywhere, the girl madder than a wet hen. It was awesome."

John followed the gist of things and said, "The obvious question concerns what the girl said to Little Tea."

"Some Southern slur, I'm not sure. Little Tea didn't elaborate," Hayward said.

"Didn't? Or wouldn't?" I asked. "That doesn't sound like her."

Hayward could barely contain himself, he thought it was so funny. "I know; usually she's all in your face, but this time she wasn't. Maybe she just didn't want to tell me. You can ask her about it, Celia. She asked me to have you call her tomorrow morning."

When I called Little Tea the following morning, she immediately asked, "Want to go for a walk? Let's get out there before the heat takes hold."

I put on my shorts and running shoes, grabbed my green canvas hat and shades. When I got to the top of the stairs, Elvita stood below holding two glass vases of light-blue, long-stemmed hydrangea packed securely with rumpled newspaper in a deep cardboard box.

"There you are, Celia. Listen, I need y'all to do me a favor. Y'all take my car and run these here out to the church. There's a christening at eleven, so these need to be there by ten. Thelonia will know where to go. I know y'all were planning on visiting, but y'all can do this for me, can't you, sweetie?"

"Of course, Elvita. We'd be happy to," I obliged, taking the box from her hands. Elvita held the front door open, and when I walked back to Little Tea's house, I called out to where she stood on the porch, "There's been a change of plans."

"God bless Mama; she keeps that church floating," Little Tea called back. When I walked onto the porch, she said, "You don't need to tell me what the plan is, I see it right there." Little Tea set her coffee cup on the porch railing, opened her arms, and said, "Come up in here and give me a hug first." And there I was, fully in Little Tea's arms, all five feet seven of her athletic body pressed against me as substantial and comforting as a puzzle piece come to find its match. There was always that flash, whenever I hugged Little Tea, where I became acutely aware of our physical differences. She surpassed me by three towering inches, was full-breasted, sharp-hipped, with a long, muscular back. Because I've always been self-conscious of my own femininity, I find it awkward and telling to hug a woman. It leaves me feeling exposed and vulnerable to be bosom to bosom, for whenever I do, I'm reminded how much I'm built like a boy. And the smell of Little Tea—her basal, earthy, deep-woodsy scent. To stretch my neck up and aim my face for her shoulder was heady and inescapable. She was like rain-dampened leaves in a night's wispy air. I almost stepped back at the surprise of it, how you can be so familiar with someone yet still caught off guard by the corporal feel of them. It made me question, in that instance, how much I really knew Little Tea. Thoroughly, I decided, but even with that, it only took me so far.

Around back of the house, blossoms from a heavy crepe myrtle covered the windshield of Little Tea's car in translucent, paper-thin purple like the detritus from a child's papier-mâché project. Little Tea switched on the windshield wipers, and they scattered like butterflies as we drove seven miles east to Tom Floyd Road.

Mt. Moriah CME Church seemed to me in the middle of nowhere. It sat low, red bricked, and A-framed down an unmarked gravel driveway, its wooden, handwritten signage forty feet away from a cemetery laid in uneven, unorganized family plots, strewn at the left beneath a copse of rustling mature elms. We took the two concrete steps through the glass double doors beneath the portico and padded the center aisle's red carpet between solid oak pews with Colonial ends. I could feel the sacred vibrancy in the dormant house of worship. On either side, the walls were unadorned, but at its raised apogee behind the pulpit, a massive wooden cross was affixed to the wall, fashioned from the same wood as the pews. I'd been to the church before, on a Sunday when Little Tea sang with the choir, Hayward and I the only white people in attendance. We'd sneaked in hesitantly to sit in the back row, not wanting to call attention to ourselves and mindful of our potential disruption, only to discover we'd misjudged the atmosphere. To watch the congregants greet us, you would have thought we were visiting dignitary long overdue. We were set upon immediately. It seemed a ripple from as far away as the front row spawned a current of well-wishers, who came sidling up smiling in fluid welcome, some holding paper stick fans decorated with images of the church. And the singing, oh the singing: it swelled to the rafters in exalted joy the likes of which breaks the heart open and coaxes the soul out to play. Hand clapping boomed percussively in time with the soloist. The choir wore floor-length, royal-blue robes with red-lined V-neck collars that matched the jacket of the conductor, who danced with abandon, his back to the congregation. It was a reverberating celebration sung in call and recall, as the chorus seconded every emphatic line of the singer, who belted out "When I Rise in the Morning." I had the impression any number of them could have taken the lead, that it just happened to be this particular woman's turn at the microphone. They were all so attuned to each other, all a part of what was, essentially, a unified display of the Lord's gift in song. Being the musician that he was, Hayward was enraptured. He kept nudging me in my side delightedly, with, "Listen to the tenor section. Can you hear the alto, over there to the right? We're coming back." I nodded, watching the congregants make interpretive gestures, their hands flailing as though coming out of the water. Just when I thought I couldn't take the joy anymore, it seemed someone flipped a switch and the entire choir fell somber as another soloist stepped forward to sing "Grace and Mercy" in a soaring lament that followed a five-minute introduction, illustrating how none of us could get up in the morning, put one foot before the other, or fix our children breakfast without Jesus. He had me so convinced, I wondered how Hayward and I had managed to find my brother's Volvo and make it to Mt. Moriah without Jesus' guidance. All throughout the rhythmic melody, I saw people place one hand over their heart and shoot the other straight up in the air as though trying to catch hold of Jesus' robe, for clearly Jesus hovered somewhere above us. I knew part of me felt that I hovered too. It was as close to an out-of-body-experience as I've ever had, and I was humbled in a way I'd never felt before, almost ashamed of myself for not being grateful enough that I'd been born to advantage. And here were these beautiful souls, born to not much in comparison, hanging onto Jesus' robe. I thought of my family's Episcopalian church and knew that it paled in light of all this.

At Holy Innocents Church, which we attended with no regularity, attendance was a mere tip of the hat to civility as opposed to this denominational sense of belonging, and I wondered what it really felt like to be so close to the Lord it made you weep shamelessly in public, like the people around me, dressed in their finery, putting their best foot forward to meet the Lord in a church down a gray gravel road in Como.

The reality was, Hayward and I never did return to Little Tea's church because we knew we could never be a part of it. We didn't want to appear like patronizing spectators of a culture to which we didn't belong. It was eye-opening to realize I'd been so used to the racial divide from the vantage point of us versus them. To be in this church, white and completely outnumbered, gave me a perspective I wished I'd had sooner. Would that I had it long before I did; it might have taken root and been there to steady me when I needed it most.

There wasn't a soul around when we entered the humble church. "Reverend Crosthwaite," Little Tea called in a voice that told me she was completely at home with her shouting. "It's Thelonia Winfrey come to bring Mama's flowers for the christening."

The reverend came bustling through the side door of the main room, all rotund and imposing in his pleated khakis and Sperry Top-Siders. I knew Reverend Crosthwaite. Everyone in Como did. He was a fixture at every local gathering and had been a guest at each of my family's harvest parties. The reverend clasped Little Tea's hand in both of his. "Thelonia, you're home. I heard you was coming. Miss Celia," he nodded at me, "nice to see you. I know you're glad to see this one here."

"I am," I returned. "It's been a long time coming. I've had no fun at all without her all summer."

"Now Boston," the Reverend addressed Little Tea, "my word, how you doing up there? I heard Mr. Hayward been up there too these past few summers."

"You hear a lot, Reverend, don't you?" Little Tea said. "I'm just glad y'all didn't forget me."

"Go on now, funning me," he said. "Your mama been counting the days until your return. How long you here for this time?"

"I'm staying for another week, then I go back for my last year. My track team has a different break than the rest of the school. We're there longer in the summer, so we start later. Good news is I'll see all y'all at the Wakefields' harvest party. I'll be home for it. You're coming, Reverend Crosthwaite, right?"

"Oh, I'm coming, God willing," the reverend said. "Can't keep me away from that pig. This here's my investment," he said, patting his thick middle and laughing in a way so infectious both Little Tea and I laughed too. "You coming to the Jacksons' christening of little Sharonda today?"

When the reverend asked this, I knew he wasn't asking me.

Little Tea shook her head. "No, I can't today. I'm just toting the flowers. But give them my love, will you?"

"I sure will, and thank your mama for me, honey. We sure do appreciate her being so generous with her garden."

In the car, Little Tea checked the clock on the dashboard. "I think it's too late to walk in the woods. With this heat and all, it'll be high heat by noon. Want to go to Pop's Shop in town?"

On the twenty-some-odd minute ride to Main Street, we settled into the business of catching up. Little Tea hit the brakes when an Eastern box turtle crept out of the woods and made its way across the road. Pivoting toward me, she said, "See there? We're in luck. Those turtles don't cross the road unless it'll rain within forty-eight hours. There's hope yet for a break in this heat."

Little Tea and I hadn't talked since Christmas. She wanted to know what I'd been doing with myself, how Tate Foley was, and what I planned on doing after I was out of school. But there was something on my mind I wanted to run by her. I wanted to talk about my brother John, for no other reason than something nagged me that I hadn't discussed with a soul. I prefaced it by recounting the night, a few winters back, in the upstairs hallway, when I'd seen Rhett Saunders steal into John's room in the dead of night.

"Rhett's around all the time now," I said. "He and John are tied at the hip."

"Shoot," Little Tea said immediately. "You just now figuring this out? I knew that boy was gay when we were five."

"Little Tea, come on, you did not," I said. "If you did, you never said anything to me."

"What was I going to say? Your brother's gay, that's what he's hiding? Listen, I'm not making a general statement—because I hate that, but if someone's going to hide who they are, it makes them guarded and mean with the secret. I know your family don't care one way or the other, but it's the secret that's in the way. He's like a cat turned over on its back with hiding it."

"Do you think Hayward knows?" I asked her.

"Now what is it makes you think Hayward would say something to me?" she said, rather quickly.

"I don't know, I was just wondering. Seems sometimes I'm the last to know things."

Little Tea didn't say anything for a minute. I assumed she was turning her thoughts over. She took her eyes off the road for a second to look at me. "That bother you?" When I didn't say anything, she continued, "Celia, I think everyone likes to protect you. You kinda fragile, you know."

"No, I'm not, Little Tea. I'm just quiet, is all. It's not the same thing."

"You quiet because you're gentle. People keep that in mind. What with you being a little bitty ol' delicate thing, I think folks want to keep you sheltered from things that might upset you. I know Tate Foley feels this way. He's the kind that likes to take care of his woman. Makes him feel like a man. Some men need that."

"Well, Hayward doesn't. He's not that kind of guy, and he never said anything about John to me."

"He probably never will, but that doesn't mean you can't talk to him. The thing is, Hayward's not going to bring it up first. He's tolerant of people in a way most folks aren't. Anyway, today's Thursday. When do you leave for school, Monday?"

"Yes." I sighed at the change of subject. "I'm glad I got to see you. I feel like you've seen more of Hayward than me this summer. By the way, Hayward told us about some girl pushing you in the water at a photo shoot up in Boston. What'd she say to you to make you do that?"

"Believe me, you don't want to know."

"Yes, I do, or I wouldn't have asked."

"It was about Hayward," she said.

"What about him? What'd she say?"

Little Tea took her time telling me. I could tell she didn't want to because I had to ask twice.

"Same old thing up there as down here," she said. "White boy hanging around a black girl, you know, that kind of thing. This woman knows we're both from Mississippi. She happens to be from South Carolina, so she knows the score. She called me a nigger, I called her a Cracker, and one thing led to another."

"So that's how y'all ended up in the water."

"Yeah, Celia, I pushed her in the water to shut her up. I'm flat tired of dealing with haters. There's no talking sense to someone like that, so I decided to wet her down. And I don't need people in my business, especially if they're out of line."

"Your business? Do you and Hayward hang out together in Boston? You must have some. By the way, I'm wearing the necklace y'all got me. Did you notice?"

"I did. I'm glad to see it on you. Hayward made a big deal out of getting it for you. You know how much he loves you."

Out the window, the dark golden woods turned to late-summer laxity, having been burned by the sun for too many months on their way to the acquittal of fall. I rolled the window down all the way and fingered the charm on my necklace. It wasn't until a few minutes later that I realized Little Tea had evaded my question about spending time with Hayward. But later that afternoon, I figured it out. As Little Tea and I made our way through the dining room on the way to find Elvita, Hayward came swinging out of the kitchen and met us halfway in the room. In a flash, I saw him reach out playfully and grab Little Tea around her waist, and although only a moment earlier he seemed to be leaving, he turned around and followed us back to the kitchen.

"Mama, we got your flowers there on time," Little Tea said. "The Reverend said to tell you he sure did appreciate them."

"Oh good, glad to hear it," Elvita said. She stood at the kitchen counter, reaching into a gray plastic bucket, retrieving handful after handful of Queen Anne's lace to dry upside down in a metal basin of Borax. "Thank y'all again for running them over. I'm going to set these to dry then want to get on with my lists for the harvest party. Hayward, you looking forward to the party? I know you are."

I saw Little Tea and Hayward look at each other as Little Tea burst out laughing. "Wild horses couldn't keep him away," she said, and Hayward said instantly, "I'm so glad you remembered."

I looked at Hayward, trying to understand the implication. I could have sworn I saw a flush of red heat on his face.

Heber Springs, Arkansas

"What in the Sam Hill is Ava doing?" Renny asked me, looking at her watch.

"She's changing her clothes. Again," I answered.

"For God's sake, we're not going to the country club; we're going to mass. Nobody cares what she's wearing."

"I'll go get her," I said. "Go on and start the car."

Descending the stairs and rounding to Ava's room, I found her tying a flower-print, wrap-around skirt on her narrow waist.

"What?" Ava asked when I entered.

"Renny says we need to get a move on. Mass starts in fifteen minutes. We're going to be late."

"She's the one who's gotten me all worked up over the new priest she keeps talking about. If we're going to meet him afterwards, I need to look good. What about my sandals, do they match?"

"Yeah. You look great, Ava," I said.

"Do I? I don't look like an old lady in this skirt?"

"Let me qualify that: you look good for your age."

"Stop it, I can't believe you said that," Ava said, laughing. "Is this where we are now? We're at the point where we look good for our age?"

"Yes, Ava. We've been there for a while now. It's over; we can no longer cash in on being young and cute."

"But I'm used to being young and cute."

"Ava, can we have this conversation later? Renny's in the car."

"Is she mad?"

"Fit to be tied," I said.

"Wound up tighter than a tick?" Ava egged on.

"Madder than a wet hen," I encouraged.

In the game now, Ava's face lit with a laughing, dancing energy that brought her latent freckles out of retirement. I could see the vestige thirteen-year-old Ava standing before me, tugging on her skirt. "I can't remember how to tie this dang skirt," she said, her eyes brimming with mischief, "but I usta could."

Matching her wit for wit in our game of Southern parlance, I looked around the room and continued, "I don't see Billy-Bob around here. Do you know where he might coulda went?"

"Well," Ava said, with her hand on her hip, "I'm not fer sure, but yer best bet to find him is—"

"To have a look-see back yonder," we howled.

"Celia, cut it out, I can't take it," Ava squealed. "Seriously, Renny's waiting in the car?"

"Yeah, let's go."

Luke Bryan boomed through the open windows of the Escalade when Ava and I got in the car. Within seconds, the three of us broke into song, riding down Tannenbaum Road. Eight forty-five on a Sunday morning, and not a creature stirred on either side of the wooded lane. Through the backseat window, dappled glimpses of Greer's Ferry Lake flashed staccato through the trees, and I knew the iridescent diamonds on the unruffled water meant this cloudless day would shape up to be a hot one.

"Y'all leave the windows rolled down," Renny said, parking beneath the flourishing limbs of a stalwart oak tree. Three claps of the car doors and we scuttled up the gravel driveway to the front of the cream-color, stucco church. I trailed behind Ava, who followed Renny through the open cathedral door and up the terra-cotta tiled aisle to the pews halfway up and at the right. We crab-walked into the pew, for the leather-padded kneeler was unfurled at full obstruction. Renny and Ava fell to their knees in hands-clasped, bowed prayer, but I did as I always do in a Catholic church, I sat hunkered and low and inconspicuous. Seconds later, the three of us were sandwiched on both sides, in this stain-glassed, incense-reeking house of symbolic holies. I fumbled through the hymnal, thinking if nothing else, at least I'd be prepared for the inevitable when the congregation broke into song. I sat wide-eyed through the rite of blessing and sprinkling of holy water and followed along through the Kyrie and Hymn of Gloria, my eyes cast forward and focused on the new priest we'd come to see. Renny had told us that the church brought this middle-aged, silver-haired man over from Argentina. She'd put a spin on the word "Argentina," wrapping it in inflections of exotic splendor. I couldn't help but wonder what the attraction of Heber Springs, Arkansas, was for him, but what did I know? I wasn't Catholic; I knew nothing of the migration of parochial priests.

He was magnificent in his ivory-and-gold-trimmed vestments. He stood regal and passive by the altar as the cantor recited the responsorial psalm. After the second reading, he stepped forward with theatrical flair, his level eyes scanning as the congregation fell to an anticipatory hush. Renny leaned forward and winked at Ava and me, as though to signal *This is it, y'all get ready*. Five sentences into his homily, and my inconvenient sense of humor kicked in and tried to fight its way out.

I've always known I'm at my funniest during the most inappropriate moments: funerals, christenings, the dentist chair. The priest's accent was so thick, I hadn't a clue what he was saying. He tripped over the words brothers and sisters by rolling the vowels with such underhanded creativity, I thought he must have stayed up all night practicing to get them wrong. This thought alone was enough for me to bite the inside of my cheeks, but I didn't flinch for what seemed an eternity, thinking if I could feign dignity in comportment it'd be the best defense in this pious moment. I wanted to give the guy the benefit of the doubt, thinking if I were patient, sooner or later it'd all even out, that I'd get the gist of his message if I put it all together in hindsight. I'd just decided to get over it when I made the mistake of looking to my right at Ava. She was convulsed with soundless laughter, and the effort to suppress it resulted in tears that were well on their way down her face. That she shook like a nervous Chihuahua and kept sweeping her hand over her eyes tickled me all over again. She must have felt me looking at her, for with a sudden gasp, she turned her face to me. Neither of us had to speak to communicate what was on our mind, and neither could we break the magnetic hold we had on each other, though I repeatedly tried. Just as I thought we were going to offend Renny if we didn't quit, Ava stood and made as though to leave the pew. Every head to my left swiveled toward us, and Ava almost mowed me over as everyone in the pew swiveled to make room for her exit. In a stroke of genius, Ava linked her fingers together at her waist, bowed her head with tears streaming, and assumed a grief-stricken stride straight up the aisle and toward the lobby with me at her fleeing heels.

Ava had her back to me and put one hand in the air to shush me then hurried down a flight of stairs descending to the basement. When we got to the bottom, a large vacant room with tables and chairs in scattered arrangements sprawled before us, and Ava turned to me and exclaimed, "Oh my God." In that moment, I had no idea if I was still laughing at the priest, or if I was laughing at Ava. Whichever it was, we were both around the bend, headed for no return.

"Renny's going to kills us," Ava managed to say, and all I could muster was, "I know." We paced the room like caged lions, aimless and antsy and laughing, with nowhere to break free. "Oh my God," Ava said again. "Could you figure out a single word?"

"No, Ava, maybe they should have screened the guy first. If they're going to keep him around for a while, somebody needs to find an interpreter."

"I literally couldn't take it," Ava continued, and just then Renny found us. She was laughing too.

"Oh my God," Renny said, which sent us all reeling again. "You know people must think Ava had to leave because somebody died or something. You're such a good liar, Ava; you scare me."

"Absolutely inspired thinking," I said.

"I know. Everyone was sitting there like it wasn't funny. You'd think Tannenbaum is a Spanish-speaking region. Maybe it's just us," Ava said.

"It's just us," I said.

"It's just y'all," Renny said. "I wasn't going to say anything until y'all started in. I had to sit there by myself after you left with everyone staring at me. You know you disrupted the whole back of the church."

"I couldn't help it," Ava said, launching into a perfect imitation of the priest's stilted speech.

"It was going pretty well until he got to brothers and sisters. That's what did it for me," I said.

"All of it was a train wreck." Renny sat in a ladder-back chair. "All right, let me think. I told Aunt Jean I'd see her after mass. We have to figure out what to do."

"Call her later and tell her you got sick," Ava suggested.

"How lame is that?" Renny said. "No. Let's get something better. How about Ava got sick, and I had to drive her home?"

"I don't want to be the one that got sick," Ava complained.

"Ava, we need a cover, what's it matter?" I said. "We can tell her I got sick if you want to. I don't care. Let's just get a graceful exit out of here. No way am I going back in the church."

"Oh, we're not going back," Renny stated. "I'll never be able to show my face around here again, thanks to y'all. Y'all go on and wait in the car. I'll go see if I can find Aunt Jean."

Aunt Jean, it turned out, was the solicitous sort. She came scurrying across the parking lot in her sensible rubber-soled shoes beside Renny and opened the door to where I sat on the back seat. "Celia, honey? I'm Renny's aunt Jean." She leaned her tawny-haired head into the car. "Renny tells me you're not feeling well." She placed her slender hand on my forehead and looked into my eyes with such sincerity, I almost felt guilty.

Ava turned around in the front passenger seat. "Celia felt faint. Maybe she's pregnant," she lilted with false concern.

Glaring at Ava, I said, "No, that's not it. I'm just not used to the time change between here and California. I'm a little whacked out, that's all. I'm okay, really."

Ava continued, "Maybe we should take Celia to a doctor."

"That's not necessary, Ava. I'm fine."

But Ava couldn't stop herself from trilling along. "She was just so excited over the priest, I bet that was it. Celia's not Catholic. She was the only one in our school who wasn't, you know. Celia's Episcopalian. They don't have regal Catholic priests in her church. Compared to Catholic priests, she's used to priests who don't even dress up."

"Too much information, Ava," I said, looking at Renny as though inviting her to jump in any time.

"We've been running for three days, Aunt Jean," Renny explained. "Celia's come a long way, and we've been going nonstop. Celia, you think we should just go back to the house and take it easy?"

I was about to say yes, when Aunt Jean interrupted in a singsong voice that covered three octaves. "Well girls, why don't y'all come over to my house? I'll fix y'all lunch, and you can relax down by the lake. I'd love to have you."

Once behind the wheel, Renny said, "Sorry, y'all," as we followed behind her aunt to the north side of Greer's Ferry Lake. "We don't have to stay long, but it's actually a great spot. There's a covered dock. Since our suits are in the car, we might as well hang out there. Do y'all mind? Tell me now, but I think it'd be rude not to."

"Yeah, Celia, especially since you're so sick," Ava chirped. "We have to let her take care of you. I hope she has some Pepto-Bismol. Or maybe she'll have ginger ale and soda crackers, I hear they're good for pregnant women."

"You enjoying this, Ava?" I glared at the back of her neck.

"Well, yes, I am, thank you."

"Good, because that's all that matters," I said. "Our last day here, and I have to play sick to save face in front of Aunt Jean."

Ava turned to look at me in mock reprimand. "That's what you get for being a heathen. Laughing at that poor priest. Shame on you, Celia."

"Ava, you liar, you best keep your head down low, so you don't get struck by lightning," Renny said, turning off the main road.

"Come on, Renny, if God was going to strike me dead for lying, I would have been dead long ago."

"You got that right," Renny said. "You would have been like that golfer on the green of the Memphis Country Club who got struck by lightning for the third time."

"What?" I said. "When was this?"

"Celia, you miss everything being out there in California. This was last summer. The first time was in the man's front yard, when he went out to his mailbox. Second time was in a boat out on the river. Then last August, I think it was, the man was playing golf and bam, he got struck again. Most people would have seen the sign the first time and righted their ways, but not this guy. As a matter of fact, he's a friend of Tate's father."

"It figures," I let slip.

"Why?" Ava asked.

"Guys like that run in packs. Misery loves company and all that. I remember my grandmother telling me Tate's dad is a prick," I said, laughing.

"Now that's funny," Ava said. "Your grandmother actually used that word?"

"Yeah, she really did," I confirmed. "With a name like Renville, how could it be any different? Who'd name a kid Renville without knowing he'd turn out to be a prick?"

"You're so right," Ava said, "but I think Tate's grandfather was worse, from what I've heard. Celia, I never wanted to mention it to you when y'all were dating. Speaking of Tate, I wonder when he's going to call you. You've got your cell phone, right?"

"Yes, Ava, and Tate's got my number, no thanks to you."

Renny stopped the car. "Y'all, we've been through this already. Let's just have a good time."

"We're just giving each other love pats, isn't that right, Celia?"

"That's right, Ava," I said.

"I get it, but try to keep it to a dull roar in front of my aunt. She's a Bible-thumper. She takes things literally. And Uncle Hank is the nicest guy you'll ever meet in your life, but he's real country. He may or may not get your humor." She paused. "Don't forget to grab your stuff."

I got out of the car and closed the door, wondering what it was one had to be around here to be called *country*.

"Does this mean I can't drink in front of them?" Ava asked. She and Renny closed their door at the same time, and Ava produced a metal flask from her purse and took a swig.

"It's ten o'clock in the morning, Ava," Renny said with alarm as she threw her bag over her shoulder.

"I know, I'm just taking one nip. I can wait until noon. How long are we going to stay?"

"At this rate, until the next catastrophe happens," Renny said. "Y'all please don't get me run outta this house." She paused, her eyes fixed on a lone figure. "There's Uncle Hank coming through the door now. Y'all be nice."

"I'm always nice," Ava said, a hint of defensiveness to her voice.

"I heard that," I inflected. There are two ways I could have spun that line: the first affirmatively, the second dripping with doubt. I chose to spin it with doubt.

"Celia, quit it," Ava said. "Renny, she's trying to wind me up. Tell her to quit."

Renny waved us away for being the pests she probably found us but in the blink of an eye, her demeanor changed. With a smile plastered on her face, she started speed-walking toward her uncle, though she managed a final jab over her shoulder. "Celia's not the one I'm worried about. Ava, put that flask away."

Renny's Uncle Hank was robust and red-faced, his paunch folding over Levi's secured by stretchy red suspenders. Renny pressed in tight over his obtrusive middle, giving him a cheek-to-cheek hug, while his voice rang out, "Now there's my girl," patting her back repeatedly with his liver-spotted hands. In a flash, his eyes found mine. "Now hold on here, don't tell me, this one's a Wakefield." He released Renny, and I stepped around her and offered my hand.

"Yes, sir, I'm Celia Wakefield. It's so nice to meet you."

"You're the spit of your daddy. Your grandmother too. I declare I 'bout thought I'd seen a ghost through the kitchen window. Y'all Wakefields with that dark hair and all. Now tell me, aren't you the one living out there in California? Married a Yankee, didn't you? I know I heard something about you back when."

"Yes, sir. My husband is from Chicago. We live in Southern California. I'm home for the weekend to see the girls," I said, but all I could do was stand there and wonder how much he knew.

"I'm Ava Theil, Mr. McCann. I used to be Ava Cameron, but I'm not as tacky as Celia. I did the right thing and took my husband's last name."

"Why, Ava, I know you're making fun. My, aren't you a pretty thing," he stated. "Nice to see y'all out here in Heber. Welcome to our home. I'll tell ya, y'all young folk do it different now, though I can't say turning loose of the name Wakefield would be easy, except it probably don't mean much out in California like it does in these parts." He smiled at me. "I grew up with your daddy. J. T. and I went way back. Fine fellow, your daddy. I grew up down the road from the plantation. I went to a few of y'all's harvest parties back when your granddaddy ran things. Now there was a man. We children were all afraid of him, but he could be kind. Taught me how to fish, in fact. You girls like fishing? I can set y'all up down there on the dock if you do."

Renny darted a split-second wink at Ava. "We'd love that, Uncle Hank. Ava's a great fisher. I hope you have those swimming lures with the three little hooks. They're Ava's favorite."

"I'm sure I can rustle something like that up. Y'all come on in the house," he said with such cheer, it made me ashamed we'd balked at coming over. "Y'all got your suits?"

"Yes, sir," we said in unison, and we followed Uncle Hank along a series of square steppingstones to the two-level wooden, waterfront house where Aunt Jean waved through the kitchen window.

With Uncle Hank a few steps ahead, Renny spoke, her voice low and wicked. "Ava, how's that old scar you got on your fat behind? I've been meaning to ask you."

"Come on into the living room, and I'll show you. Why don't I moon all y'all? Won't your aunt and uncle love that?" Ava shot back. "And my behind isn't fat."

"I swear, it's like we're in a time warp here. Just because Tate said your butt was fat a million years ago, you're still defending the size of it. And by the way, Renny, don't give Ava any ideas," I warned. "You know it won't take much for her to drop trou in front of God and everybody. She'd do it for sport."

"You're right, I wouldn't put it past her, but that's why we love her," Renny said.

"Yes, that's why y'all love me." Ava skipped around us and caught up with Uncle Hank.

"Renny wants me to show you the scar I've got from sitting on a lure," we heard her say.

"I can't believe her," Renny exhaled then rushed forward. "Uncle Hank, don't listen to her. I didn't say that. She's just pulling your leg."

"This one's a live wire, I can tell already," Uncle Hank said. "I'll tell you one thing right now, if you sat on a lure, I'm surprised it's not still in there. It takes a real sportsman to get a hook out. They're nasty little buggers. Most doctors don't know what they're doing."

"Tate Foley took it out. It was a long time ago, but he knew how," Renny said. "Uncle Hank, you know the Foleys, don't you?"

"Yes, I do. I knew Renville Foley growing up. And speaking of Tate, he ought to be back here later on. Y'all just missed him. Came by right after Jean went to mass. I loaned him my boat for a bit. I reckon they got rid of the one they kept out here." Uncle Hank tugged on his suspenders, scratched his forehead in a pause as though considering something. "You know, I don't see any of them Foleys around here these days. Guess that Tate's been keeping a low profile since he got married recently. Can't say as I blame him, things being what they are and all. Times is changed, but you know, people are still people." He opened the kitchen door, and we all went in the house. "Y'all go on and change into your suits," Hank said. "Jean and I will bring lunch down to the dock in a bit."

"Let's go this way," Renny said, leading us down a hallway to the guest bedroom so we could change into our suits.

"Tate got married?" I asked. "When? And why didn't y'all tell me?"

"I didn't know," Ava said, looking at Renny.

"All right, well, I knew it," Renny said. "I wasn't going to bring it up. Who cares? Celia, you're done with Tate. I don't think we should devote one more minute to discussing him. I'm not discussing who or where or when he married." She busied herself with pulling her suit from her bag. "Y'all don't even ask me."

Como, Mississippi
Sometime in the 1980s

Because my mother was a first-generation American, there was a side of her shining in the ancestral, red-tartan tones of her parents' native Scotland. It was more than the fresh-faced, ruddy-gold look of her, it was her way of relating to the world from a premise of earth and sky. When I think of my mother, I think of autumn, light breeze, and woodsmoke. At the memory of her face, a feeling arises to stir my soul's embers, pointing me homeward to the place I'll always belong. Though I can summon the feeling at will, it hurts too much to linger; there's too much inside of me now that can't accept she's gone.

What happens when a mother dies is that she takes back that part of herself she should have left to save you. More times than I care to admit, I've searched for that refuge, only to feel betrayed and lost. It's disillusionment, really, over life's inevitabilities. There's no reconciling any of it; it burns too close to the skin. But memory can be a sustaining thing, and when I think of my mother, I think of movement ... the way she walked across a room, the way she channeled the light when she smiled.

A list of idiosyncrasies made my mother unique to me; most prominent were the Scottish superstitions she clung to with such devotion. I could fill a notebook with the listing of these, beginning with a bonfire on Guy Fawkes Day and ending with the way she handled household scissors, the blades pointed toward her lest they sever a close, personal tie. Most of her superstitions were acquired from her Scottish mother, Aileen Montgomery, a widow by the time I was born, who died when I was eight. My vague recollection of Aileen elicits lavender dusting powder, frail arms around me, hair the color of November wheat twisted in a spiraling braid. The impression my mother's mother made on me is a lasting one, so much so that to this day I can't bring myself to cut my long hair. Gran, as we called her, was so enchanting she managed to bring out the best in Cecelia Wakefield, who gave her a pass, I suspect, because Aileen was also a mountain girl. That Gran was a Highlander abated the suspicions of my father's mother, who was Scots-Irish by heritage, and mistrusted anyone otherwise. Aileen's North Argyllshire burr touched something atavistic in Cecelia Wakefield because it marched in the same cadence and sang in the same notes as her clan's linguistic tendencies in rural North Carolina. My mother always said the two women understood each other in some intrinsic way. There was something pagan about both; they had an impulse toward navigating life's roadmap via talismans and signs. But whereas Grandmother Wakefield's understanding came from a premise both armored and fear-based, Aileen's was of the mystical variety, more awe-inspired and God-struck than anything else. In the air above my grandmothers, no bird's flight went beyond scrutiny. No phase of the moon nor owl's hoot went without specific interpretation. Under the influence of female divination, I grew up thinking coincidence and strange convergence was the language of women. And so it was when Little Tea called me in Knoxville, it took very little of her inference to set me on edge.

"Celia, listen to me," Little Tea said when I picked up the phone. "I wasn't going to say anything about the date change of the harvest party, but I just saw your mama, and she's wearing that gold charm of hers, the one with the little eye in the middle. You know the one I'm talking about?"

"Yes, it was her mother's. The eye in the middle is for protection."

"Your mama don't play when she has that around her neck," Little Tea said. "It's about the date change, isn't it?"

"Dates," I said, knowing full well of Little Tea's apprehension. "All I recall about dates is that my mother thinks they're uncanny. She's a calendar watcher, that's for sure. Let me think a minute. Sometimes she adheres to dates, and other times she avoids them. I can't tell you why she gets nervous."

"I think it's about the date change. My mother thinks the same way. The party's been on the second Saturday of September forever, but now it's been moved to the middle of October. The pattern's been broken. Your mama must be thinking something's off."

"Mom had to move the party at short notice. She didn't have a choice, and I did tell you all about it. It just couldn't be helped. But we can't think something bad is going to happen because of it. You're taking an inconvenience and making it worse with conjecture," I said.

"No, I'm not. From where I'm standing, it's tempting fate."

I tried to quell Little Tea's fear as well as my own because Little Tea's superstitions always made me nervous. "What do you think, the gods will be angry? Come on, Little Tea. Give me a break. Maybe it'll set a better standard from now on. Who's to say? You know my mother had to change the date. I told you about it. It was unavoidable."

Had it not been for another of my father's digressions, the party would have been on the same weekend as every other year, but as it was, an episode Dad had in Memphis upset the natural order of things and, in the end, it was my mother's decision to change the date. I'd seen my father at his most confessional during this usurping episode. At the end of July, the week after Hayward and I returned to school, we each got a call from John asking us, rather cryptically, to come home to see Dad. Before we rushed in urgency to Memphis, Hayward called our mother who told him our father had been found drunk, wandering the streets of midtown Memphis before a squad car picked him up and took him to jail. When Mom retrieved Dad and brought him home, she knew there would be a predictable fallout. The effects of excessive alcohol on my father's delicate psyche were such that, after each binge, he suffered a red-heated depression. When Big John heard from Thelonious that my father hadn't been out at the farm for weeks prior, he barreled to my parents' house in Memphis and arrived at the exact moment my father came home from jail. My mother told Hayward that

Big John made such a ruckus, he threatened to take action on involuntary commitment. My father, weighing the lesser of evils, checked himself into a behavioral and mental health facility for "evaluation" the very same day. The reason John called Hayward and me to come home was because there was a problem. Once my father checked into the facility, he changed his mind and wanted to check out.

★ ★ ★

I couldn't pinpoint what odor was being masked, but as I walked down the corridor of Lake View Behavioral Health System beside Hayward, a mixture of Lysol and Mr. Clean overwhelmed me. Because Hayward had brought Rufus when he sped home from Sewanee, the dog trotted obediently between us, tethered on a leash. "Once we get to the desk, they're not going to let you bring in Rufus," I said as we pushed through the glass door to the reception area, where the air conditioning hit me like a subzero storm.

"Yes, they will. Watch me," Hayward said, and I knew then he had a plan.

Behind a low counter, a heavyset woman in her forties wheeled forward in a swivel chair when she saw us coming. Though her phone rang, she rose in her navy, boucle cardigan glaring at Hayward. "Son, we don't allow dogs in here."

Hayward rested his elbows on the counter, turned quickly, and commanded, "Rufus, sit," then beamed his green eyes straight through the receptionist's soul, which, unsurprisingly, made her blush. "I'm Hayward Wakefield, come to see my father, John Wakefield. This is Rufus. He's a therapy dog. He's my dog, but he's been with our family forever. Rufus is therapy for my father. That's why I brought him."

"You got papers on that dog? I don't see it wearing a vest."

"Well, ma'am, you see, that's just the thing," Hayward said. "I didn't realize until I was halfway here—I drove all the way from Sewanee, that I left his papers at home. Can you check in my father's records? I'm sure

Rufus is mentioned. If not, I have a number you can call, but it'll be an automated response. If you've got the time, I mean. I'll just sign in here." Hayward put pen to paper on a clipboard. Setting the pen down, he turned from the desk and walked to a seating arrangement in clear view of the lounge. "My sister and I are not in a rush. We can wait while you check it out. Don't visiting hours last until four on Saturday?"

The glass door swished open, and a woman with three children walked into the reception area, diverting the receptionist's attention. "We're in luck," Hayward whispered. "A group is behind us. This is just what I was counting on. There are many more people in the parking lot. Believe me, this will be such a hassle, she'll just go on and let Rufus in."

We spotted our mother in the visitor's lounge the same moment she spotted us. Her wave compelled me to stand and wave back, and when I did, I saw the receptionist register the exchange. Hayward drew Rufus close to his side and stood, and the receptionist nodded her permission, but when I started to the lounge, Hayward put his hand on my arm and held me back. "Wait a minute," he said. "We have to be on the same page. I know that Mom has already talked to Dad about staying, but it didn't work. It'll be up to us to say something that'll make him stay."

"I'll try," I said, "but it's going to be awkward. I've never had a conversation with Dad about any of this. I've been downplaying his moods my whole life because Mom seems to like it that way."

"This isn't about moods, Celia. It's about alcoholism. The two are bound to be tied together. I don't think there's a prayer of addressing *his moods* as you put it, until he dries out. It's time we all quit tiptoeing around this. He was taken to jail this time, for God's sake. There's an opportunity here to make a little headway."

"I'm not going to assume a parental role with Dad, Hayward. I'd feel too weird telling him what to do."

"I'm not saying you should. But we need to tell him we want him to get better, and if that means he stays for thirty days, then it's a good start. We need to be encouraging. My guess is Big John took the hardline, and John probably wasn't much better."

"Yeah, John has all the sensitivity of a boa constrictor," I said, which made Hayward laugh. "Anyway, Mom's waiting for us."

"Wait, here's how I suggest we play this," Hayward said quickly. "We encourage him with the lure of something to look forward to. You know, it'll be incentive along the lines of positive reinforcement. Let's tell him we'll get everything together for the harvest party. That can be the goal. He'll get all fixed up, and by the time the party rolls around, he'll be good and ready."

"But thirty days, Hayward. That's a long time," I said.

"That's probably what Dad is thinking. Look, Celia, we have to get serious here. This has been an endless vortex with nothing changing. You know what the definition of insanity is? Repeating the same behavior and expecting different results. You have to work with me. We have to do this together."

I walked to the lounge with a sense of duty, thinking Hayward was right in how to play it. I hugged my mother and sat down on the beige, slipcovered sofa, trying not to think of what was beneath the worn, wrinkled cotton. "I don't mean to sound accusatory, Mom, but why is Dad in *this* place? Couldn't we have done better?"

"It's a state-run facility, honey. It was your father's choice. I was just so grateful he'd go anywhere, I didn't want to say anything."

"How's he doing?" Hayward asked. "John said that Dad wants to leave now."

"He does," our mother said, "but I think he's been a bit disoriented since he checked in. Things happened rather quickly once Big John got involved. I think your father was running scared, frankly. He checked himself in the afternoon he was released from jail. My feeling is he was still drunk. I was with him at patient intake, and they sensed it too. Your father was willing to go for psychological assessment, but when the conversation turned to addiction treatment, he changed his mind. This was all yesterday. I don't think he's had time to properly process his options."

"What do you want him to do?" I asked.

"Stay, as long as he's here. But I can't tell him what to do."

"Do you want Hayward and me to say something? Hayward thinks we should."

"That's why I wanted y'all here, and I'm so grateful you came. I hate that y'all had to leave school, but I think this is an emergency. I'd like your help. Your father's in his room and will be out in a minute. I'm going to leave y'all with him for a bit then I'll join you. See what y'all can do to get him to stay."

I couldn't get a handle on why I felt such stress, except to say that it took a lot of energy to act as though the parent-child role reversal didn't plague me. I've heard it said that one can expect this when their parents age, but this wasn't the case; there was no pretending my father hadn't sunk to the depths of despair of his own volition. It had nothing to do with age. It was his mind, or perhaps a crisis of the spirit, but whatever it was, it had to be addressed. I wanted answers yet couldn't bring myself to ask questions, so I decided to stay in my internal turmoil and let Hayward do the talking.

Dad walked into the visitor's lounge from down a long hallway. Hayward stood when he saw him. "Dad, Celia and I have come to see you," he began as Dad took a seat. Hayward lowered himself, positioned Rufus between his knees, and I pulled an armchair before them, in an attempt at forming a tight-knit circle, not wanting to be overheard by others in the dismal, windowless lounge.

"Y'all were just here, and now you've had to come back from school. I'm so sorry. Your mother must have told you what happened."

Hayward nodded. "Yes, she did."

My father cast his eyes to the floor and steadied them. "Never been to jail," he said. "It was demoralizing."

"I can imagine," Hayward said softly. "What happened, Dad? Can you tell us?"

"Can't seem to set myself right. Can't seem to get off the wheel. Demons, I imagine. I have plenty of them."

Hayward looked at me, but I had nothing to add. "Maybe you can sort it out here," Hayward said, "though Mom told us you want to leave."

"I do want to leave. Shouldn't have checked myself in here to begin with. I'm not interested in looking at my drinking. I'll be frank with you. I'm drinking as a symptom of something else. It's the something else I can't seem to address."

"What else is it, Dad?" I heard myself ask. "Can you tell us? We want to help." I looked at my father, struck as I always was by his courtly beauty. Even disheveled, there was something refined about him. His long slender fingers raked furrows in his coal hair, his white oxford was rolled at his forearms.

"Celia, let me say first it has nothing to do with any of y'all. I need to make that clear. You and your brothers are my life's blessing. And your mother, as you know … well, I'd be lost without her. It's something else. Something deep and insidious. Something not easily defined."

"Can you try, Dad?" I asked.

"Just a general dissatisfaction. An unnamed misalignment. Not anyone's fault, but it is why I drink."

Hayward's laser eyes focused on my father with gripping concentration. I could almost hear the wheels of his mind whirr as though piecing something together. "Misaligned? You mean in your life, or what?"

"It's more of a disharmony, I think," my father answered. "I just don't have everything in sync—thought, word, action, these kinds of things. It's why I was so adamant about you going to music school. It's important we follow what has heart and resonance in life. Life is hard enough as it is. We need to be fearless, follow the beat of our own drum. I haven't done that. I've been a coward in certain aspects. Lacked the courage of my own conviction." He put his hand on Hayward's shoulder and cast a quick, inclusive glance at me. "I want you both to promise me one thing: whatever it is you want out of life, you have to go out and get it. Hayward, you especially."

Hayward's eyebrows raised in that way that happens when one is taken by surprise. "Me?" he intoned. "I'm not afraid of anything, Dad."

"You know what I'm talking about, son. I'm your father." He set his eyes on Hayward for a few flaming beats, and I felt the heat that colored Hayward's face. "No sense in pretending you don't know what I mean."

I started to ask Hayward to let me in on the mystery, but he derailed further discussion by turning talk back to Dad. "It's not too late, Dad. You're talking as though your life is over. It's not, of course."

"Well, I might as well lie down if I'm not going to fix it," he said. "And I will. I see now I'll need to change some things. Take a harder stand. Do some work. If it's important to y'all for me to stay, and I know this is what you're doing here, then I will."

"Good, so you'll stay? That's what I wanted to hear," I said.

"Yeah, Dad," Hayward said. "Seriously, if you think your drinking isn't the problem, then I believe you. But as long as you're here, you might as well dry out, pause and reflect, and get a handle on things. At the very least, it'll get Big John off your back."

"For now," my father said with a wink.

"Yeah, for now," I agreed.

"Until the next time somebody does something he doesn't like," Hayward laughed. "Don't worry, Dad. We're on your side."

My father stayed at the behavioral facility and continued with therapy after he left. Although it was a tenuous beginning, his first step at rehabilitation proved fruitful. The good news was, now that his depression was no longer a taboo subject, it brought my family closer together. Because the harvest party was pushed forward a month, I made the four-hundred-mile drive from Knoxville to Como in mid-October. Six hours out the I-40 through Crossville, Cookeville, Nashville, Jackson, and Memphis until I dropped down the I-69 to Como, my nerves fluttering with anticipation. For the first time in years, my best friends would be at the annual party. Tate would drive up the next morning, Mark and Ava were in town because Ava's father was scheduled for a pacemaker operation at Baptist East, and Renny was nearby in vet school. I left a day early because I wanted to see more of Little Tea and Hayward. When I pulled in the driveway at six thirty, they were in the side yard, cloaked in tendrils of the roasting pig's sweet hickory smoke.

"You just missed Tate," Little Tea called out, gliding to my car, her arms reaching wide. I gave her a hug and said, "Tate was here? That's odd; he told me just yesterday he'd see me tomorrow night. Are you sure?"

Little Tea gave me her best you-silly-fool face. "Yes, I'm sure. Why would I make it up? He was in with your daddy all afternoon."

"I must have misunderstood," I said as Hayward sidled up.

"You finally made it," he said. "You just missed Tate."

"I heard. What was he doing here?"

The way Hayward glanced at Little Tea told me he questioned if he should share what they'd obviously already discussed. "I don't know for sure, but I could take a guess."

I was partway to asking Hayward to share his guess when the Reverend Crosthwaite walked through the front door and down the brick steps. He carried a gallon jug of vinegar, which he set beside Thelonious. "Your mama got the reverend here," Little Tea whispered. "He offered to bring his blended spices, so she asked him to bless the pig, long as he's here."

"Bless the pig? When?" I asked. This was a new one to me.

"Now," Little Tea said, as my mother walked out to the verandah.

"Celia, there you are, you're just in time," my mother trilled. "Come here, darling, give me a hug. You just missed Tate."

"What was Tate doing here?" I asked when she reached me.

"I haven't heard yet, he was in with Daddy. Wait just a minute, let me go back and get your father. Thelonious, y'all about ready?"

"We're ready," Thelonious said. "Now that Miss Celia's here, someone needs to run fetch John."

"I'll get him," Hayward said, and walking up the steps behind my mother, he turned and said, "This ought to be good. John thinks Mom's lost her mind."

We held hands around the spitted pig in an oval, my mother and father, John, Hayward, Little Tea, her parents, and me. The Reverend

Crosthwaite removed his hat for the occasion. He raised his solemn face skyward, the better to find the good Lord in the clouds. Presently, he closed his eyes and bowed his head in deference, as though waiting to make sure the Lord was ready. I felt a current run through the palms of my hands; my mother clasped one, Little Tea held the other. The linked oval dipped with the gravity of the moment as Reverend Crosthwaite assured the Lord that we came to Him in praise. "Heavenly Father, we give thanks and ask to be worthy in your eyes. Tomorrow we share the bounty you gave us with our friends and neighbors. We ask that you be with us as we celebrate the harvest of your fertile land. Bless this pig to your use and us to your holy service, in the name of your son, Jesus Christ, who taught us to pray, Our Father, who art in heaven, hallowed be thy name," and we all joined in for the recitation. "Our hearts runneth over with your many blessings, dear Lord. For thine is the kingdom and the power, and the glory, forever and ever, Amen." The Reverend Crosthwaite turned his eyes to my mother. He had a look on his face as though coming up for air as he replaced his hat. "That about do it, Mrs. Wakefield?"

"Oh, yes, thank you, Reverend Crosthwaite. Now come on, y'all. let's get out of this smoke and go in and have something to drink."

The wall phone was ringing when I walked into the kitchen. "Hey, Celia, it's me," Tate said when I picked it up.

"You were out here earlier?" I asked. "Why didn't you tell me? You said you were coming tomorrow."

"I said that?" Tate said, with an oh-silly-me laugh.

"Yes, you did. You said you'd see me at the party."

"Sorry, Celia. I must have misspoken. Anyway, I was wondering if I could see you before the party. It starts at two, right?"

"Yeah," I said.

"Why don't I come out around noon. We can go for a walk or something."

"For what?" I asked.

"I just want to run something by you, that's all. You'll see."

"You're being awfully mysterious, but okay, I'll be here."

The next day, I'd barely opened the front door of the house before Tate grabbed my hand and pulled me out to the verandah. I wore shorts and tennis shoes for our walk in the woods, knowing there'd be plenty of time to change into a dress later, as any Southern party that starts in the afternoon implies it's fine to arrive when it suits you. I didn't anticipate having to be front and center with a smile on my face until three o'clock or so, and by then I'd know what to wear. Mid-October in Como can take its pick of the weather. Its canter into Indian summer rides in blazing but typically turns on a dime. The rhododendron bordering the left side of the yard had long since lost its bloom, but the red woodbine on the verandah's trellis spread twelve feet high and dangling. Tate broke a sprig and put it behind my ear, saying now I wouldn't have to wear perfume. I touched the fragile honeysuckle with the tip of my finger, smiled at Tate, and waited. I was curious to learn what was so pressing that he had to come early, but Tate didn't say anything, only moved his head in a come on, let's go gesture.

Rounding back through the brittle rye grass, we skirted the pond and took the trail behind the Winfreys' house into the woods. Overhead, a cardinal called from somewhere unseen, a woodpecker drummed in encore after encore, yet there were few other sounds to be heard, save for our rustling feet upon the rich collateral of pine needles and twigs. Sixty yards along the uneven path, and I started to get antsy. Because Tate still hadn't said anything, I finally stopped, touched him on his shoulder, and said, "All right, what?"

"Something's burning a hole in my pocket," he said, reaching his right hand into his jeans. He dropped to one knee and said, "Celia Wakefield, I love you from the bottom of my heart and know I will forever. I want to spend the rest of my life with you. I'm asking you to be my wife." A shine that shattered the universe screeched into the daylight from the flip of a little red box. One look at the ring, and I knew it was nothing modern. Its three diamonds were set horizontally in white-gold filigree, all the same shape and size. If I knew anything about Tate, he'd been planning this moment forever, until we were both set to turn twenty-one. I imagined he'd declared his intentions to his parents, who'd been thrilled and gone to their vault at First Tennessee Bank to collect the ring. I had no way of knowing to whom the ring originally belonged, but I knew it was one grandmother of Tate's or the other. Boys that grew up in Tate's circle didn't go out and buy anything new; an engagement ring always came from family lines.

I'd had no doubt this moment would come one day. One rarely doubts what it is they're sure of receiving. And though the timing took me by complete surprise, I was prepared to say yes.

"Your daddy will announce our engagement tonight," Tate said putting the ring on my finger.

"So that's it," I concluded, under the light of understanding. "Y'all knew you'd have a stage and audience tonight. Now I get it."

"That's what I thought. Your father saw the wisdom also. Now that all of our friends are in town, we're going to have the night of our lives."

Hayward stood on the verandah with Rufus when Tate and I walked hand in hand toward the house. "Okay, confess," he called. "I saw y'all walking toward the woods. My guess is you went in one way and came out another. My little sister is betrothed; go on and tell me."

"Can't pull anything over on you, can I, Hayward?" Tate said, all beaming and smiling, springing up the steps. The two clapped each other on the back then Hayward reached for my left hand. "Woo-doggie," Hayward said, "now we're talking. I've got to hand it to you, brother-in-law, when you do something, you do it right."

"Mighty kind of you to notice. It's only the best for Celia. She's made me the happiest man on earth."

"Y'all come on in the house," Hayward said. "Mom's waiting. I couldn't stop myself from tipping her off."

"Surely Dad told her already," I said.

"Believe me, he didn't. He knows how to keep the cat in the bag when he needs to. He wanted the surprise to come from y'all."

Through the screen door, I walked into the foyer, Hayward and Tate at my heels. My mother stood by the stairs in a pose that told me she'd been expecting us. She had both hands to her face then waved one of them and said, "Wait, let me get ready."

"Guess what, Mom." I held out my left hand.

"Oh, I'm so happy for y'all," she exclaimed, rushing forward to hug me. "I've hoped for this day for a very long time. Hayward, go on run to the den and get your father. Ask him to bring his camera. And Hayward, if you could find John, I'd appreciate it. He should be in on this too."

"I'll go get John," I said, "I'll be right back." Ascending the stairs, I called John's name from the third-floor landing. His bedroom door was closed, so I rapped on it four insistent times. When the door swung wide, John stood dressed in a blue-and-white-striped Oxford, a monogrammed handkerchief folded in three points in his pocket. Looking at his watch, he seemed perplexed. "It's not time to go down, is it?"

"No, not yet. We've got about an hour. I've come to deliver good news." I walked into his room and sat on the twin bed beneath the curio cabinet that housed John's collection of hand-painted, metal toy soldiers. I never understood his attraction to them, though I liked their fifty-strong display in two colorful rows. John received additions to his collection each Christmas from Big John, who never tired of presenting his grandson with what he must have thought were emblems of masculinity. John sat on the other twin bed and lifted a glass of iced tea from the bedside table. "Good news?" he asked. "What is it?"

"Tate asked me to marry him," I spilled as a smile lit my brother's face.

"Oh, Celia, this is good news," John said, and I thought I saw tears spring to his eyes. I thought John may have had mercurial, Machiavellian tendencies, but his emotions were readily available. There were few I knew who didn't filter their inner life, lest they risk judgement. If nothing else, John's initial response was always reliable, and to me, it made his reaction credible. John knew how he felt about everything, whether others liked it or not.

"I won't mention that y'all are both so young," he said, "but what with you going into your last year of school, and seeing as how y'all have always been together, I'm thinking, why wait? I'm all for it."

Little Tea's voice called from somewhere beyond John's bedroom door, "Celia, where are you?" I accepted the hug John gave me and skipped lightly into the hall.

"Come here." I took her by the hand, leading her into my room. "Tate just asked me to marry him."

"I figured your fate was sealed." She pulled me into a hug then lifted my left hand. "Congratulations—no wait, you're not supposed to congratulate the bride. It's Tate to be congratulated. Best wishes, Celia," she said, smiling.

"Thank you for standing on ceremony. How did you know?"

"For starters, my mother overheard your father on the phone yesterday ordering champagne by the case. When Hayward just called me at home and said you had a surprise, I just knew. Come on, everyone's waiting for you downstairs. Get John, and y'all come on. Your father's standing down there with his camera."

"Now J. T., just a splash for everyone," my mother said as we descended the front stairs. "We really mustn't start in this early. We've got a long night ahead, so just a little bit for the pictures." Elvita held a cluster of crystal stems on a silver tray, and my father untwisted the wire over the cork of a bottle of Piper-Heidsieck then presented it by sweeping the bottle through the air, its contents cascading over his hand.

"Of course. Just a bit now, Shirley. We'll hide the tubs in the kitchen until after the announcement. Elvita, be sure to keep an eye on the ice. We'll need all the bottles chilled and brought out around nine."

I've heard it said you don't recognize the best times of your life unless you see them in hindsight, but I beg to differ. I knew every moment of this day for exactly what it was, and each crystalline variable seemed to me a highlight: the selection of the low heels and white sleeveless dress I wore, the arrival of Renny and Mark and Ava, the secret flutter of my heart every time I met eyes with Tate. My grandmother Wakefield's shrewd eyes noticed my engagement ring immediately. Because the sun had set by the time she arrived, I knew she intuited its presence more than anything else.

"I assume your young man had the decency to ask your father for your hand," she said. "It's just like J. T. to withhold information; but never mind all that, let me get a good look at that ring."

Tate's parents came to the party for the first time in its history, which could have been construed as a sign by anyone considering their attendance. The Foleys weren't the type to drive out to the country for what was essentially a glorified barbeque; they were not ones to blend where all stratums of social spectrum mixed. One look at Mrs. Foley's dainty, kitten-heel sandals spiked into the grass, and I knew she was out of her element. She clung to the arm of her husband's gold-button sport coat to leverage herself from sinking. My grandmother rolled her eyes, looking at the pair across the way, but then she never suffered people she thought were fools. I knew without question that what bothered my grandmother more than anything else was what she thought the Foleys thought of themselves, and my mother was aware of it too. It was typical of my mother to troubleshoot ahead of time, should my grandmother get too near to the Foleys. As I stood beside Renny and Ava, I saw her approach Tate's parents and shepherd them to the bottom of the house's front stairs, before she turned and signaled to me.

"Go get Tate and y'all come here," my mother said when I reached her. I spied Tate in the crowd of a hundred and fifty, laughing with his brother, who stood with a hand on Hayward's shoulder. "Here comes my sister-in-law now," Bill Foley said as I drew near. "All right, little brother, the time is nigh. Looks like you're wanted onstage. This is it. There's no turning back."

Tate held my hand beneath the starlit September night, the cool air quivering with rustling anticipation along the hem of my knee-length dress. I gathered my coral pashmina around my shoulders and held it tightly as we wove our way to my mother. It was then I noticed Little Tea standing beside a young man who seemed familiar, yet I couldn't place the dark planes of his long, chiseled face. I assumed he was one of the locals who came to the party year after year; this was probably why he seemed familiar. Seconds later, my memory asserted itself. When I zeroed in on his black-framed glasses, the name Wilson Atkins came to mind. I wondered what in the world the boy who'd escorted Little Tea to her tenth-grade prom was doing standing beside her, and Little Tea met my eyes and shrugged her shoulders, in answer to my furrowed brow. She waved her left hand, suggesting she'd talk to me later, flashed a half smile with a shake of her head, and in my imagination, I heard her say, "Go on with yourself."

"Come on up to the verandah," my mother said, placing a hand to the small of my back. Tate fell in step just as the front door opened, and a light applause lifted from those who saw my father step outside. A ripple went through the party, all eyes settled on the verandah. The band in the side yard set their instruments down, and the bass player skipped up the front stairs to assist my father, who'd been unaware the microphone was off when he started to speak.

"There we are now," my father said. "Good thing the right people are here to assist in this moment. Believe me, friends, it's a big moment. I want to thank all of you for coming to our harvest party. Many of you have had a hand in this year's crop, and our gratitude is unending. Tonight's going to be a little different because this year, I've got an announcement— we've all got an announcement," he said, turning to smile inclusively at my mother. "We're honored you're all here to share in our good news. Celia, Tate, y'all come in here close," he said. Tate and I stepped in to flank my father. He took our hands and joined them. "It pleases Shirley and me to announce that Celia and Tate plan to marry." I heard the cacophony of sharp breath intakes, hands clapping, and voices trilling in a hum that soared to the clouds. The vibrato seemed to me a laughing thing, it swelled in octaves, rode in layered harmony over my family, over the house, through the trees, and up to the moon. Prior to the moment, the thought of my marriage was an ephemeral, pending dream, but on the lips of my father's sanction, it was vibrant and fully manifest. I stood beside Tate, a part of him now, thinking it takes a host of witnesses to make anything real. Below me, Ava stood on tiptoes, lifting her bright smile toward me. Mark gave a two thumbs-up sign, while Renny kept her right hand over her heart as Hayward vaulted up the verandah's steps. Stepping before the microphone, he leaned in and said, "Please join our family in toasting the happy couple. If you look around, you'll see champagne being distributed among you."

Moments later, it seemed everyone held a glass in their hand. I saw John offer his arm to my grandmother, who walked up the stairs in front of Big John as the Foleys followed behind. Ten proud and smiling, we stood as a blended family, side by side on the verandah of the house in which I grew up. It came to me then that this was something the columned verandah had seen before. My parents' engagement had been announced in this same place, in the same way, under a similar, dark autumn sky.

I looked to where I'd last seen Little Tea. She stood beside her parents, waving at me, her glass in one hand raised in a gesture that shot straight through my heart and secured me to planet earth. Wilson Atkins wasn't in sight when Hayward skipped down the stairs toward her. He offered his hand, inviting her to follow him up the stairs. Somewhere in the foreground, the white light of a camera flashed, and my brother John admonished, "Hayward, you're missing it, get back up here with your family."

Laughing at Hayward's unpredictability, my mother put a stabilizing hand on John's arm. "That's so cute; he wants Little Tea up here with us. In a minute, I expect he'll call Rufus to share in this too. Dear thing can get so excited."

"Hayward grabs life's big moments with both hands. It's what makes him an artist," my father said. "Just a few more shots then let's get out there and dance." He waved his hand toward the stage, and the band fired up a rendition of Earth, Wind and Fire's "Celebrate."

Had I not been so caught in the thrall of my life's exuberant highlight, I would have paid more attention to the displeasure on John's turn of face. He shot a disapproving look at my grandmother, and the air bristled with telepathy, rife with a portent I might have paid attention to, were it any other time.

Heber Springs, Arkansas

My cell phone rang, but I didn't answer. Renny sighed and held out her hand to Ava. "All right give me a sip of that. If Tate Foley is going to motor up here any minute, I might as well." As though setting her sights on something else to be irritated over, she continued, "Celia, you know it's Tate calling you. Why won't you answer your phone?"

"I don't know that it's him," I pretended. "It could be anybody calling. Could be a wrong number, for all I know. Why ruin a perfectly fine day?"

"Especially since we know Tate's coming anyway," Ava stated, handing Renny her flask. Renny took a sip, and I saw her eyes water. "What's in this?" she winced.

"Wild Turkey. I siphoned it from the bottle Mark brought over the other night."

Renny leaned back on the striped towel she'd spread on the dock and adjusted her hat to shade her face. "Celia, we don't have to stay here if you don't want to. We can pack up and go any time, but I do think it'd just be prolonging the inevitable. Sooner or later, you're going to have to face Tate alone."

"Why do you say that?" I asked.

"Yeah, Renny. Celia doesn't have to do anything she doesn't want to. They were perfectly fine the other night when they saw each other. Why push it any further?"

"Because they're not healed, Ava, that's why. They can't dodge and weave forever. Celia and Tate need closure. Especially now. It's what you and I were talking about yesterday, remember? You were the one who said Celia needs it. By the way, you and Stan need closure too. Y'all need to settle what's between you one way or another. I hate to say it, but neither

213

of y'all is taking care of business. Ava, you let life happen to you, and Celia, you just conveniently run away."

"Wait a minute," I said, my dander rising. I couldn't admit it, but my feelings were hurt, which, of course, made my dander bigger. "Y'all were discussing *me*? Why?"

Renny looked taken aback. She shot Ava a complicit look that told me she wanted support in her reaction, and I saw the exact second Ava looked at her and gave it. And here I'd been years thinking of myself as the friend in the middle, the one who kept them from doing to each other what they were doing to me now. And it's worth observing how one infraction sets off the memory of another, until you're standing beneath an avalanche of wounds cascading from the past. I was just beginning a mental list of everyone who'd betrayed me when Tate Foley came roaring up to the dock, all blond haired and smiling in a borrowed boat. One look at him, and I knew his was the worst betrayal of all.

Renny leaped up and tugged her shorts over her bathing suit. She shielded her eyes from the unclouded sun. "Celia, I know you're mad, but we're going to have to park this for now. We weren't talking behind your back. We care about you."

"Okay, fine," I said, aware of a shift, and just like that, I felt my two friends rally around me. If body language means anything, then Renny and Ava created a force field from the simple act of stepping close. Ava placed her arm around my waist as though to claim me, every inch of her frame suggesting "if you want to get to Celia, you have to go through me." Renny stepped to the edge of the dock, and just as I thought this scene would go down one way, it went down another. When the roar of the engine grew louder as it approached the pier, Uncle Hank chose that moment to carry sandwiches to the dock in a white Coleman cooler. "Wait, Hank." Aunt Jean scuttled behind him. She let out a cheery, "You forgot the paper plates."

There's nothing more interminable than an event interrupted, when you know something's well on its way to happening, but fate presses pause because something else gets in its way. And the anxiety I put myself through in the name of common courtesy, when others are in the groove of their own agenda, oblivious to what's really in play. Maybe it was a good thing Renny's sanguine aunt and uncle weren't aware of the loaded dynamic into which they'd come carrying a cooler. As for me, I was resigned with a sense of fatalism, thinking this may be an interruption, but it's coming whether I'm ready or not.

"Tate, you're just in time for lunch," Aunt Jean sang, reaching into the cooler. "Isn't this wonderful? Look, Hank, we're having an unplanned picnic, isn't it a blessing to be with the young folks out on our dock? Just goes to show you never know what a day will bring. Now who wants something to drink? Tate, can I get you a co-cola? Renny, honey, go on hand Tate a co-cola."

"Here you go, Tate," Renny said, reaching her hand portside. Tate had angled the boat in and was tying it to a heavy post in an adroit cleat hitch, as the boat lurched on the rocking water. "Thank you," he said, popping the top, looking from Renny to Aunt Jean.

"Well, come on out, Tate," Aunt Jean encouraged. "We have chicken salad sandwiches, pickles, and chips. Here, sweetie," she said, motioning to me, "go on scoot over, let Tate sit down."

I moved over to Renny's towel. Once beside her, she intentionally elbowed me in the side. Wide-eyed, I turned to face her in an unarticulated, brows-raised question. Renny's mouth turned into a half-smirk as she nodded toward Ava, whose eyes I met just as she snuck a nip from her flask. Ava looked at us and stuck out her tongue. I lowered my head and started laughing. Two seconds later and the three of us were in it now.

"Girls, what's so funny?" Aunt Jean asked with enthusiasm.

"Probably nothing anyone will understand, Mrs. McCann," Tate said. "These three speak their own language. Always have." He took the sandwich Aunt Jean gave him and set about the business of unfurling its waxed paper, removing the pickle decorating its top and placing it inside.

Uncle Hank lowered himself to the beaten wood planks with an audible huff and helped himself to the cooler. "How long y'all girls known each other?" he asked.

"Too long," Ava said.

"Yes, it's been nothing short of awful," Renny chimed. "Ava, give me one of those before they're all gone."

"I'm tired of both of them, weary to the bone, in fact," I said, dodging the sandwich Ava lobbed at Renny.

"Jean, they're just funning us," Uncle Hank said. "Celia here hasn't been home in a while, so that's not true. She's been out in California for—how long has it been?"

Feeling the heat rise, I was in peril of being drawn into the flame of the last place I wanted this conversation to go. "Long time," I said, my voice low.

"Well honey, why so long? How'd you end up out there?" Aunt Jean asked.

I didn't have to look around to feel Renny, Ava, and Tate staring at me. It was as though the sky held its breath, waiting for my reply.

"Shoot, Aunt Jean," Renny said. "Celia isn't a small-town girl. Her life was always going to be bigger. I knew when she switched from UT to UCLA she'd never come back."

Ava scrunched her nose, the way she did whenever she was thinking deeply. She knew as well as anybody this wasn't the whole story. "Well, maybe Celia got a little push out of the nest." Her comment was so weighted with innuendo that Tate and I and Renny pretended to be fascinated by our sandwiches. Renny segued into a long, meaningless inquisition concerning how her Aunt Jean had made the chicken salad until my eyes glazed over. She used a tone dripping with such false interest that I thought I'd add my two cents by asking about the brand of mayonnaise. This led to more mind-numbing detail from Aunt Jean, including the price and market of where she'd procured the mayonnaise. And all the while, Renny and I shot each other looks that carried their own dialogue. I think we'd still be sitting there trying to ward off the inevitable had Tate not put a stop to it all.

"Well then," Tate said, standing. "Celia, you game to take a little spin round the lake?"

I rose slowly with all eyes on me and feigned a might-as-well indifference. "Sure," I said, and smiling at Renny's aunt, I added, "Thank you so much. This has been a wonderful picnic."

When I got in the boat, I was thinking my problem is that I go through the motions of what I think I should be doing, instead of following the inner guidelines of how I really feel. I wondered if I was normal, but then I thought of Ava's succinct assessment that normalcy is a myth. I wondered, as I clutched the bottom of the backseat of the careening Sea Ray 240 Sundeck, what my mother would do if she were in my place. If she were me, I decided, she wouldn't have gotten in the boat in the first place. But I knew the world had changed since my mother was alive. It had evolved into a lack of guidelines that tell women what to do. I thought we are now a species so genderless and unencumbered with definition that we are rudderless in a sea of equality. And yet I was aware that my mother still whispered in a Southern accent from the otherworld about pride and comportment and etiquette. Oh, the convenience of all this, were it applicable in this politically correct world, which shies from gender-specific identity. But there was hope for me here in this boat with Tate Foley—he was born in the South and had been raised in its ways. And then there was the matter of our history, which by anybody's standards packed a score to be settled. All these years later in the thick heat of a Southern summer and beneath an endless sky over a rippling lake, I watched the sinuous back of Tate Foley outlined beneath a Heber Springs Marina T-shirt, his thick hair buffeted from the wind by a navy cap worn backward. Oddly, it suddenly hit me that I didn't care about Tate as I once did. For years, I'd been holding on to what I thought I should think, given our story. It startled me to realize that, although I hadn't forgotten the story, by some miraculous feat, I'd managed to move on.

On the boulder-shored, evergreen-rimmed lake, Tate cut the boat's motor, and we swayed and drifted on concentric rivulets of frothy-white water every time a boat roared past, its occupants waving a hand in camaraderie as though saluting card-carrying members of the same aquatic club. Sound amplified sharply over the windswept water. Over blaring speakers, country music faded in and out at breakneck speed, then silence stretched unending, save for the rhythmic ripples slapping the boat's sides.

Tate swiveled in the captain's seat to face me. "I hope you don't think I'm cornering you, and I bet you feel ambushed. If you do, I'm sorry. Ava told you I was trying to reach you, right? I'm sure she did. I did try to call you a few times." He paused long enough for me to say something, but when I didn't, he continued with, "You're leaving tomorrow, I know, and it's important that—"

"The day after tomorrow, actually. We're leaving first thing in the morning to go back to Olive Branch. I fly out of Memphis the next morning."

"Are y'all doing anything tonight? I'd like to bring my wife around. We—um—we didn't want to just show up, so I thought I'd ask. It would—it would mean so much to both of us."

So this was it, then. Not what I'd anticipated at all. I couldn't have been more surprised. I'd scripted this meeting between us as one extended, healing, confessional monologue by Tate that I thought he owed me. I'd forgotten that after time and tide have their say, people don't change after all. Because they *don't* change, not really. Short of an act of spontaneous enlightenment, or after, perhaps, years of soul-searching, the cold, bare facts are that people are fundamentally incapable of being anyone or anything other than who they are.

Suddenly a vision of the night of our engagement descended. I felt the white heat of anger flare and almost screamed at Tate. Looking at him from behind my Wayfarers, I was glad he couldn't see the narrowed glare of my eyes. Behind them, I could say anything and be believed, if only I could keep my voice steady.

I happened to know Tate Foley had the facts of what was between us. There was no need for me to mention the evening we became engaged at the harvest party or anything else that became of that night. It had taken me years to quit blaming Tate for messing up my life, but I still gave him credit for trying. Resiliency, the ability to pick oneself up and reinvent oneself, the creative construction of Plan B, these are the things that define a life, and looking at Tate now, sitting there in the captain's chair in utter cluelessness, made me think I'd ended up much better off without him. I lowered my sunglasses, swept the hair from my face, and said, "Yes, by all means, bring your wife tonight. I'll run it by Renny and Ava, but I'm sure it'll be fine."

Como, Mississippi
Sometime in the 1980s

In the October air of the harvest party, Hayward led Little Tea through the whorl of dancers, dodging and weaving through the shifting dynamic, his arm firmly around her waist until they carved out a niche beside Tate and me. We'd followed the directive of my mother by positioning ourselves as the newly engaged couple on the center of the dance floor. I don't believe I've ever been so happy, nor anywhere near it since … Tate dancing in rhythm with the band, his blue oxford cloth shirt rolled off his wrists; Hayward and Little Tea dancing beside us; Ava, Mark, and Renny joining in. It seemed a five-person circle eddied in pageantry, closing intimate ranks around Tate and me.

"Tick-tock-the-game-is-locked," Ava called in my ear, and I laughed so hard, my head tossed back. It was then I saw the feral eyes of Wilson Atkins. I'd lost track of him in the crowd earlier but spotted him now, standing beside John, whose eyes cut through the dancing maze with a scrutiny so focused on Hayward, I could feel its serrated edge. From the look of things, the two were in serious conversation. Wilson's arms were crossed on his solar plexus, his eyes sharp on Little Tea as John gestured with more animation than I'd seen from him in ages.

Sensing movement on the verandah, I turned and saw my grandmother stepping her gingerly way down the steps then cutting a deliberate path to where the two stood. And then they were three, glaring at Hayward and Little Tea. With the lift of her gold-bangled wrist, my grandmother reached up and tapped Wilson Atkins on his shoulder. When he leaned down, I saw her shout something in his ear with seeming urgency. Straightening, Wilson marched forward, a man with a mission, and soon he was beside Little Tea. I couldn't hear much above the pulsing music but saw Little Tea balk plain as day. Whatever it was Wilson said hadn't gone well. Little Tea stepped back, her hand on her hip, and shouted something at Wilson then clasped her hand with Hayward's, and the two scurried away.

Renny put her hand on my arm and pulled me off the dance floor, leading me behind a six-foot speaker to the right of the stage. "I knew it," she said as we watched Hayward and Little Tea sidestepping around those in their way. "There's trouble brewing. Wait for it. This isn't over yet."

Ava came to my other side. "Look over there, Celia. Look at John. Someone needs to slap that smile off his face. If they don't, your grandmother's going to kiss it."

"What just happened?" Tate joined us. "Who was that guy?"

"I don't know. Someone Little Tea knows, that's all. I only met him once, a few years ago."

"Well, what the hell? Is he drunk? I couldn't hear it all, but I thought I heard him say the words *white boy*. Something like that."

Mark caught the last of Tate's words as he rounded the speaker. "You thought you heard that guy say *white boy*? He probably did. Don't have to be a psychic to get the gist of that one. Black people've got their side too."

"Side to what?" I said, irritated now.

"For heaven's sake, Celia," Tate reprimanded. "Little Tea was making a spectacle of herself. You know it, and I know it. You don't get out there and dance like that in public. She shouldn't have to be told."

"Why are you putting this on Little Tea?" Ava said, her voice sailing in rapid defense. "I swear, Tate, you're such a misogynist, and if you go into the black-white thing, I'll also call you a racist. This isn't the 1950s. It's the 1980s."

"Yeah, Ava? This is also Mississippi," Tate snapped. "I wouldn't want that to be my brother out there dancing like that in front of God and everyone."

Renny intercepted in a neutral voice. "Small town, small minds," she said. "Tate's got a point. Our kind doesn't mix this way, Celia, and you're bound to know it."

Miraculously, perspective descended to sway my better judgment, which isn't always the case, and rather than becoming further involved in the exchange, I pulled back and said levelly, "This is also the night of our engagement, Tate. We should drop this for now."

Were it not for Tate thinking it unusual to see Rufus making a beeline from the side yard straight back toward the pond, he wouldn't have said anything to me, and I wouldn't have asked him to follow. But my suspicions were raised, what with trouble brewing moments before and Hayward and Little Tea disappearing. My heart electrified my blood, pushing me with urgency to chase after Rufus in the dark without a flashlight.

"Wait, Celia. We're not going back there," Tate said, trying to catch up to me. "It's too dark. We don't know what scent that dog picked up. Could be anything."

"He's following Hayward." I didn't break stride. "You don't understand the way they are with each other. I'm going after him."

"So we'll go back there and call him, but I'm not following that dog into the woods."

"Fine, suit yourself," I said. "My guess is we won't have to go any farther than Little Tea's house. If I'm wrong, we'll take it from there."

Tate put his hand on my wrist, trying to stop me. "You're going to walk back there in those little shoes? God knows what's in that grass."

"My heels are low, and I know where I'm going. Come on, we're wasting time."

Beneath the half-moon, shadows wavered at hip level as we trudged through rye grass and broom sedge now harsh and brittle. When I found the trampled, narrow deer trail at the left, the pond's surface loomed black and vacuous, like a cutout hole to the center of the earth. I couldn't see clearly on the other side, but knew we were halfway to Little Tea's house when I saw the charred remnants of the shed strewn beneath an oak, an arrangement nobody had gotten around to clearing. As we marched forward, the trio of plastic gourds Thelonious mounted on a spike for the nesting purple martins towered high and stately, and I sensed we were nearing the far end of the water's edge. Just a few more minutes through this sightless trepidation, and there'd be safe haven on the Winfreys' front porch.

Scanning the distance in front of me, I looked for the glow of a house light, yet there was none to be found up ahead. But I could hear something marring the silence, it sounded like the beat of a drum, though it lacked all semblance of attenuation; a dead, stark slamming with an insistent rhythm, like something desperately trying to free itself. Reaching the Winfreys' porch, I realized my ears had deceived me—Rufus hurled himself against the Winfreys' front door.

I vaulted up the plank stairs and put my hand on his collar, yanking the squirming, powerful dog out of the way. I banged my open palm on the wooden door then tried its metal handle. Expecting nothing and receiving more than I anticipated, the door swung wide in an instant, and there, shaking in the living room's dim back light, stood a dazed Little Tea holding a blood-splattered knife.

Shock doesn't reach the senses visually, but from an audible, roaring cacophonous din that covers earth and air in shrieking timbre. In that moment, all my senses shut down, save for the deafening, amplified sound in my hypersensitive ears. Universal and primal, it was the wail of terror so overwhelming, it hit me physically, its ringing typhoon powers knocking the breath from my lungs. Then everything slowed to a standstill, as though time itself were arrested; there was too much of its harrowing impact in too little a window to let in another second.

I shut down. Became immobilized. Then creeping, as though coming out of a dream, my senses registered one piece of information after another as in the manner of the dawning of light. It was a preparatory crawl until I was strong enough to register the whole of it, coming to me in revelatory increments that seemed to have little to do with each other. A record clicked in a lock-groove from a turntable somewhere in the living room. Over and over, it spiraled in a perpetual vortex. It was Sisyphus with phonics, insanity without end. The half-moon eked through the drawn ivory draperies, illuminating the west end of the room in quivering silver that billowed from the wind kicking through the front door. Over Little Tea's shoulder, I saw upheaval in the way of overturned furniture, glass on the wooden floor, the base of a table on its side.

Rufus was inside now, circling and whimpering, and I sensed rather than saw something horrifically out of place, something strewn and shadowed and sprawled on the floor. At first, I didn't register that it was Hayward, that the blood in front of his inert body belonged to him even as I saw it pool from his body. With my acutely attuned ears, I heard it seeping into the grain of the floor as though being suctioned, washing and darkening, a black, spreading stain. Hayward's legs were akimbo. He lay on his side, top arm over his ribcage, the other stretched from his right shoulder with his palm half open, as though reaching for one last grip of the earth.

"Wilson," Little Tea said, in a catatonic trance by the door.

"Tell me which way," Tate screamed. "Call the police, Celia! Run get your dad!"

Presence of mind. I still marvel that Tate had it because neither Little Tea nor I could move. Until I did, and when I did, my movements were frantic, too rigid and constricted for my mind to catch up as I lunged to Hayward, hearing something clatter to the floor behind me, yet discounting it as I hovered over my brother, my fingers on his outstretched wrist, then both hands to his lifeless throat. Swiveling, I met Little Tea's hollow eyes before I saw the nine-inch, stiletto knife had fallen to the floor by her feet.

"Little Tea, *damn it*, which way did he go?" Tate put both hands on her shoulders to shake her into presence. She pointed to the woods and he flew off the porch.

High-pitched and wailing, Little Tea's voice trembled in a shuddering keen. "It happened too quickly for me to do anything, Celia. One second they were scrambling, the next..."

"He's dead, Little Tea," I shrieked. "What are you doing with that knife?"

"Celia, it's not mine! You need to go get your daddy! *Now.* Go on, get everyone! I'll make the call!"

My body was on automatic pilot as though propelled by muscle memory. I couldn't feel anything beyond my strained heart until blood was let from my ankles as I crashed through scabrous grass, in flight without fight, out-of-body propulsion, arcing round the back left of the house and bursting through the kitchen door.

"Elvita, get Dad," I shouted. "Y'all's house! Hayward's been stabbed!"

I hadn't noticed Thelonious in the room. I jolted when he flared, "*Thelonia*," and bolted out the kitchen door. On heightened alert, I followed Elvita's hurried steps through the foyer and out to the front yard in search of my father.

Tragedy never cooperates; it's neither sympathetic nor convenient. It seemed all forces worked against me when Elvita found Big John before either of us could locate my father. It was mayhem within the half hour, an explosion of sirens and dogs and lights and a rain that kicked up over the scattering party in the black October wind.

People are rudderless in the midst of confusion. Some try to take the lead; others duck and cover. The grounds were teeming with the chaos of people uncertain of whether to leave or get further involved.

Big John called the shots, mobilizing scores of men at the party who had known Hayward from birth and were quick to respond with retaliatory action. Once word had gotten out that Wilson Atkins was on the loose, they buttoned their coats and swarmed into the damp woods behind a battery of policemen. Big John's leadership emasculated my father. I heard my grandmother's hissing voice pronounce my father utterly useless. "Go stand over there with your wife and children," she directed. "Stay out of the way; let those who know what to do take charge."

It was Wilson's knife Little Tea let fall to the floor. She told me later it was reflex that made her grab it, and she was certain Wilson hadn't intended to use it. But Hayward had pushed Wilson then socked him in the jaw and a tussle had broken out of swinging attack and defend until the territorial war over Little Tea escalated into a fight for life.

Jealousy. Seeming crimes against nature hidden behind the air-tight closed minds of a cultural status quo. There were decades upon decades of hatred built upon dominance, racial mistrust, misinformation, and a lemming mentality that had caused this male-challenged, testosterone-fueled fatality, and I knew it. I sat on the Winfreys' porch at three in the morning beside Little Tea, too shaken to speak, but knowing the thing to do was be with my best friend no matter her involvement. We sat side by side for two shell-shocked hours while my grandparents and John went back to our house, and my mother and father followed the ambulance with Hayward's body. I thought Rufus sniffing around would break my heart until I realized I no longer had one to break. And Tate had all but abandoned me. He'd said nothing to me; he'd fallen in step with his blank-faced parents, leaving in a formation that told me a line had been drawn.

It was the Reverend Crosthwaite who walked me home through the field. He'd come out of the Winfreys' front door, held out his arm, and said, "Miss Celia, I best see you to home." It was the long, silent dirge in the dark that made it all suddenly real, my mind thrashing between the knowledge that Hayward wouldn't be in his room once I got to the house and the devastation of knowing why. The reverend's massive, man-of-God presence guarded me in the brittle grass world of which I no longer cared to belong. Blended into my despair were notes of shame, for crime always necessitates blame. I knew the ways of the region too well. I knew this would morph into something more than Hayward's death after the shock wore off and people settled into the account. It would come down to judgment on the wagging tongues of the community telling the story of a biracial relationship, how no good ever comes of it, in a case-in-point that would stain my family forever.

When I got to the front door, John stood on the verandah, his face distraught and his eyes on me as though waiting for me to say something, while my grandparents' voices drifted from the living room. One look at

John's face, and I saw the color red. I didn't care if it was displaced anger. In a flash, John's prompting in the night's grisly event roared over me as the incendiary catalyst it had been. I stomped past him and into the foyer without saying a word.

"None of us will ever be able to put this behind us. Hayward, the only one of us that shined," my grandmother said later, her tone heavy with despair. "I'll tell you what else is gone; did you happen to notice how that Foley family skedaddled out of here? They'll be distancing themselves, you mark my words. I know their kind. Never mind that it's murder, people will be talking about why. That family won't come near us. They won't allow themselves to be guilty by association."

"Cecelia, you always think the worst of human nature," Big John said. "They've announced their engagement. Why don't you give the boy a chance to come around?"

"I'll give him two weeks, but I want you to wait for it. He'll come around, all right, and when he does, it'll be to take back that ring."

I couldn't listen to another word. I couldn't think about Tate in the face of all this. I walked up to my room, closed the door, and got in bed, but no sleep came that morning. In the aimless, bottomless hours of early dawn, I waited for the sounds of my parents' return, knowing not one of us could console the other, and it remained so for days, while we drifted in the comfortless house, terrorized and shell shocked from loss.

★ ★ ★

Six days after Hayward's death, the Foleys came as a family to Hayward's burial in Memphis' Elmwood Cemetery. They even came to our house in Central Gardens afterward, yet they were stiff as boards and judicious in speech beyond acceptable formality. They may have donned tragic faces, but there were no supportive gestures beyond the obligatory, "Please let us know what we can do."

At the time, I was wretched and numb, too outside of myself to judge anything as it should be, much less for what was. That Tate hadn't called me once or come by in that first week was something I attributed to my family remaining in Como, until two days before Hayward's funeral. Once in Memphis, it seemed my family maintained an open-door policy. It was a constant flow of visitors bringing casseroles, flower shops delivering endless floral creations, and a telephone that never stopped ringing. If the reasoning behind the onslaught of activity was to keep my family distracted, it worked. Had Renny not pointed out Tate's arctic disassociation as we stood in the foyer after Hayward's funeral, it may not have entered my mind.

"Celia, what in the world is this?" Renny asked. "Tate won't even look you in the eye. Has he bothered to call you? And he won't give me the time of day either. He's bound to know I'm watching him."

"Renny, everybody's afraid of you," Ava said. "But yeah, Celia, *has* Tate called you?"

"No, he hasn't," I said, crossing my arms against the truth of it. "I haven't heard from him since ... He's probably too freaked out to know what to say." I looked at my two friends and felt the gray cloud of doubt rising off them, and for a reason perplexing to me now, I continued to justify Tate's behavior. "Tate saw it all at the same time I did. He's probably still getting over the shock." I looked at Ava, hoping she'd back me. "It was Tate who took care of business. He had to tell Little Tea and me what to do. You know how it is when something happens, and you process it later? Everything has been nonstop since that night. He's probably just giving me space."

Renny wasn't having it. "Space? Celia, you're excusing him. You need his support. He should be here beside you. He's over there in his black suit looking like he's not a part of this, when it's your family he's marrying into. He knows better than this."

Ava added, "Celia, I hear you, but the thing is he's had enough time to regroup. You need to go talk to him. See if you can get to him when he's not standing there by his mother."

"His father's worse," Renny said. "Look at them both standing guard around their boy. Let me go into the living room and get him. Celia, you stay right here."

While Renny talked to Tate, Ava and I stood by the front door, acting as though we weren't watching. I saw Tate turn his head my way, then say something to his father as everything in Renny's body language planted itself firmly. Presently, Renny put her hand on Tate's arm, leading him toward me. When they arrived at my side, Renny turned Ava around, and they both disappeared.

There was no mistaking the discomfort on Tate's face when he leaned in and brushed a dry kiss on my cheek. "I've been meaning to call," he said, letting his voice trail off in that way people do when they're hoping you'll interject. But I was mute, winded by the insincerity of his tone of voice. "I still can't believe it," he eventually said, after I'd said nothing. I looked at Tate but couldn't bring myself to comment. This was the boy who'd never gone a day without calling me, and here I stood now shattered on the remains of our broken pattern. When it was obvious that I wasn't going to say anything, Tate continued. "I haven't known what to do, Celia," he said, yet there was no indication of contrition. "My parents think it's best to let it all settle, you know. By the way," he said, straightening his posture. "I haven't seen Little Tea. Was she at the funeral?"

I shook my head, and the full, listless weight of my broken heart hit me. "She just couldn't. It would have been too much, and we all knew it."

"Do you know where she is?" Tate asked me.

"She's with her parents in Como. Even my parents said it's best this way. They all talked about it, I mean, about Little Tea coming. It was Big John who had the final say."

Tate nodded. I had the feeling he wasn't emotionally invested one way or another. He was merely interested in the logistics from a spectator's point of view. "Yeah, well, if it hadn't been for her," his words sailed and dangled, as though I'd intuit his accusatory point. His voice was flat, atonal, matter-of-fact in a way so insulting that my burning eyes seared his cowardly face.

"Tate, don't even—"

"Celia, I'll tell you what," he cut me off. "Why don't we talk about this next week? My parents are getting ready to leave now, and tomorrow I'm going dove hunting. I missed the season opening because of the party and … all this. I just decided to go on and go. Let me call you when I get back."

My grandmother had been right. What's more, she'd been right to the exact day. When Tate returned to Memphis after a week of dove hunting in Mississippi, he appeared at my door without warning. In my surprise, I did as I was taught to do; I offered him a drink and showed him into the living room.

Without the decency of preamble, he sat across from me as though in a formal meeting. "We can't have this between us," he began. "It's no way to start a life together. That everything fell apart the night of our engagement put it all into focus for me. Our families are just too different, Celia. I know this now. Hell, I think I knew it the second you introduced me to Little Tea; I just didn't want to admit it." I stared at him unblinking, while he continued with his prepared speech. "We have different values, different ideas about how things should work, and there's no pretending otherwise." He took a gulp of tea, suddenly in a hurry. He set the glass on a side table and stood, his words now running together. "Let me just say that in looking at your family, I'm not surprised Hayward came to the end he did."

Over the roar of rushing blood to my head, I stood at my full measure. I slid off the ring and met his cowardly eyes. And in that moment, I couldn't decide which was better: hand back the ring or slap his awful face.

★ ★ ★

There's only one way to summarize where events went after Hayward's death; my family fast-tracked into freefall and landed with a crash. Four months later my father died of a heart attack, an empty bottle of Scotch overturned on his desk. But the truth of it is that it was grief that killed my father, plain and simple. After Hayward's funeral, he went into a tailspin and quit trying to live. He quit his job, started drinking, and never stopped. Nothing nor anyone had influence over him—not John, not his parents, nor my mother's worried brow. Rufus seemed to be the only sentient being to reach him. He took that dog into his den and shut out the whole world. Worst of all, he couldn't bring himself to meet my eyes, but, truth be told, I understood his avoidance. Hayward and I had been so tied at the hip, whenever he looked at me, all he saw was loss.

The same congregation who sat in grief at Hayward's funeral came to my father's Memphis service. The only difference between the two was that, this time, nobody seemed surprised.

My mother soldiered on as she always did, as though the clouds would break any minute. But the golden light in her eyes was muted, and the very spark of her was gone. Little Tea's family packed up and moved from Como, leaving my mother to run the farm. She hired migrant workers because none of the locals wanted much to do with my family, being, as it were, that we were now tainted by tragedy. People are wary of tragedy and skittish about murder; the further one keeps, the less chance rubbing off.

★ ★ ★

"Celia," my mother whispered, leaning her head into my room. It was early evening, three months after my father's burial, and the two of us were alone in our Memphis house.

"Come on in," I said from my reclined position on the bed.

Lowering herself to the chaise lounge to the bed's left, she slipped off her heels and crossed her legs. "This came today," she said, handing me a light-blue envelope. "Looks like it's from Little Tea."

I sat up on the bed, crisscrossed my legs, and looked at her offering. The envelope's postmark was stamped Boston, but with no return address. Inside, a handwritten note read: *I'm so sorry to hear about J. T., Celia. May God bless your family. I send you my love.*

I hadn't heard anything from Little Tea since it had been decided her family wouldn't attend Hayward's funeral. In what seemed overnight, the Winfreys had vacated their cottage, as though they'd never even lived there.

I passed the note to my mother and waited while she read its brief lines.

"Well, that was sweet," she said with consolation, returning the note. I slid it back in its envelope, thinking pointing out the obvious would sound insensitive and self-oriented, but I said it anyway.

"On top of everything else, I lost my best friend."

My mother came over and sat on the edge of my bed. "Maybe not forever, honey, but I think things are as they should be for now. It's understandable why she'd want to keep her distance. Let some time pass. I can only imagine how guilty she feels, even though it may only be guilt by association. None of it was her fault, but I doubt she sees it that way." She studied her wedding rings for a moment, then added, "You and Little Tea can never go back to the way it was before; surely you know that. But what I know and you haven't learned yet is some things you think will last forever have a way of turning around." She placed her comforting hand in mine. "I do think this is Little Tea's call, Celia. I think you should give her the time she needs, even if it takes years. Do try to be patient with her."

"But I'm completely lost now. I have only you and Renny and Ava. I feel like the rug has been pulled out from under my life."

"Celia, there are solutions, and we have to find our way through this, which is what I want to talk to you about. And since you didn't mention John, I want to begin with him."

"Mom ... I haven't seen John since Dad's funeral, and that suits me fine. I know he's happy as a clam with his friends and job in Memphis, and that's more than what I want to know. Whatever you're going to say about John, just save it. I can't talk about him right now."

"Now hear me out," she entreated, but then I erupted, as years of baggage came tumbling out.

"I'm not going to excuse him anymore, Mom. I've done that forever, and I've been bitten every time. John's the most duplicitous human being on the planet, but you refuse to see it."

"He's your brother, honey—"

"Where is it written that just because someone's your sibling you have to get along? I've given him pass after pass on every condescending, snide remark he's ever made, and it only encourages him to keep on being nasty. Even Hayward had his number; that's what you didn't know."

"Hayward was always nice to John," she said.

"Nice? It was more like he suffered him. Once, when John was pretending to be nice, Hayward took me aside and said not to trust him, that it was all a facade. You and I both know Hayward saw everything clearly."

"But it's just the two of you now, sweetie. This is what I wanted to say."

"Why?" I asked, déjà vu descending. "I know you, Mom. What is it?"

"Why are you so suspicious? Do you not trust me now?"

"It's not like that," I said, exhausted. "I only know you cushion your blows."

"This isn't a blow. I'm considering something, that's all."

"Considering what?"

"Making a change. First, I need to tell you that Big John is going to let go of the farm."

"He can't do that," I exclaimed.

"Yes, he can, honey. It's his. He has title. Your father would have inherited it, but now, of course, that won't happen. And it was Hayward he had his sights set on for the future." Softening her voice, she added, "You know how he's always felt about John. I don't know why, but Big John has never been nice to him."

"With good reason," I snapped. I couldn't hold back. I was raw, overwrought, and suddenly lacked the filter I'd always used when it came to my gentle mother. "Big John has never liked John because he doesn't understand why he won't admit he's gay," I blurted. "You know that, right?

I'm not saying that's right, just that Big John isn't the kind of man to take it lightly. The one thing he's *not* is open-minded. In my mind, not admitting the truth makes John a liar. Big John probably sees it this way too. People like John are dangerous. He's dangerous because he's at war with himself. And I feel like he's been taking it out on me since I was born. Hayward felt the same way."

"Celia, now I'm going to be firm with you," my mother said, her jaw tightening. "Not only is John your brother, he's also my son. I won't have you talking this way because I think you may be getting ready to say something you'll regret later."

I said it anyway. "Mom, can't you see that were it not for John stirring Wilson Atkins up, Hayward might still be with us?" I watched my mother's face fall the second the words left my mouth. We were both depleted with the subject of Wilson Atkins, who'd finally been caught after three weeks of running, and who now awaited trial in a Mississippi state jail. I knew this, but I lacked the grace to stop there. "John was envious of Hayward, and he's always been prejudiced. He won't admit the real story about himself to anyone, so he judges everyone else. All I know is his venom's all over the place. Because he can't channel his discontent appropriately, it comes out sideways and damaging. I'll never understand his angry, twisted mind."

Tears flooded from my mother's eyes as though the wall resisting them suddenly crumbled. I'd never seen her so deflated, and the look in her green eyes was sheer despondence. Though I saw her cry over both Hayward and my father, this wounded collapse was the very definition of defeat, and I was sickened that it was my sharp jab that caused it. I'd never been so sorry about anything, nor instantly ashamed. In the most shameful moment I've ever had in my life, my mother stood, then left my room without saying a word.

When the door closed, the maligned, shattered pieces of my life were so scattered, I didn't know which jagged piece belonged to which shattered story. I crawled under the bedcovers, lost in despair over the first fight I'd ever had with the woman who'd given me life and then graced every second of it after until I realized the only way to end it was to rise and go find her. I thought she'd be in her bedroom, that she'd done as I'd done and taken to bed, but my mother was never one to reduce herself to such histrionics. Instead I found her in the kitchen, pouring boiled water into a china teapot, and when I looked at the counter, I saw she'd arranged Walker's Shortbread beside a pair of cups and saucers on a handled, wood tray. It was just like my mother to overlook my affront and tend to me, and it made the depth of my shame inarticulate. Because I couldn't find the right words to apologize, I followed her lead.

"Mom?" I began.

"Yes, honey."

"You started to say something about making a change. I didn't let you finish."

She set the tray on the kitchen table, sat down, and began to pour. "I'm not saying my mind is made up," she said, "but I wanted to talk to you about Scotland. I don't see that there's anything more for either of us here. Too much has happened. It's seriously more than I can bear."

"I feel the same way," I said. "I can't even think about returning to Knoxville. My deferring a semester at UT is a joke. I don't know what it is I think will change next semester. And even if I did return to school, Tate would be there. It's like there's nowhere to run."

"Well, this is it, isn't it?" she said. "Neither of us has much of a chance around here. It's all too painful. John seems to be doing fine, but I've been doing a lot of thinking about you and me. We really could move to Scotland. It's a viable option. We're citizens. We have cousins in Argyllshire. And Celia, you have a life ahead of you. You have a choice."

And I did, my mother was right, but my first reaction was to pause. At twenty-one and at the end of where I thought my life was going, I felt too disillusioned, too worn and jaded to stay tethered to my mother's apron strings. Now that Hayward, Tate, and Little Tea were gone, I had to get used to living in an anchorless world. I'd been so accustomed to viewing my identity in relation to someone else, I didn't know how to be self-sufficient. I was at a crossroads. I'd packed a lifetime of loss and betrayal into too short of a time, and knew, if I was to really start over, I better get it right. Turning my prospects over, I said the words that laid the parameters for the rest of my life.

"Let me think about this," I said. "The only thing I've got to build upon now is my education. I'm not saying no to Scotland. I know it would be perfect for you, and I could certainly visit, but …"

"But?"

"As far as the immediate future goes," I said, drawing in a breath and the scent of the tea neither of us had touched, "I've been thinking about transferring to another college." I tasted the tea and set the cup on its saucer. "I've been thinking—I've been thinking of moving to California and attending UCLA." I looked at her squarely and waited.

Heber Springs, Arkansas

Renny and Ava waited at the end of the dock when I got out of Tate's boat, leaving him to tie it. "What?" Ava demanded, as I started walking. "How'd it go? Tell us. What'd Tate say?" She twittered and bounced beside me, animated by the need to hear all.

"Shhh," Renny whispered, "Ava, lower your voice. Tate can hear you. He's going to return the keys to Uncle Hank. Can't you wait until he's gone? Here, Celia." Renny handed me the flask.

"Y'all are killing me," I said, laughing. "Alcohol cures everything, right? Y'all are priceless."

"You need a cure? I knew it," Ava said. "We should have gotten in the boat with you, but Renny wouldn't let me say it."

"It wasn't that big of a deal," I said.

"Not that big of a deal? You haven't talked to him alone since your mother's funeral, and that was only for a minute, ten years ago. Do you mean to tell me y'all were out there for an hour, and you didn't even clear the air?"

"I got the impression there will be no clearing the air with Tate. Ever. Still waters don't always run deep. Sometimes they're still because they're depthless."

Renny laughed loudly. "Touché, Celia. Come on, y'all, follow me." She led the way to the main walkway then turned onto a neighbor's covered dock. "These people live up north, they're never here. Celia, you told Tate goodbye already, right?"

"For now," I answered.

"Meaning what?" Renny said.

"He wants to come over tonight."

Ava and Renny met eyes, then Ava dropped down at the dock's edge, sinking her manicured feet in the water. "Typical. The timing couldn't be worse," Ava said.

"Now what?" I looked at Renny.

"Stan called while you were out. He's coming."

"Oh, this is perfect." I sat beside Ava.

Renny sat on Ava's other side. "I know. When it rains, it pours."

"Ava, you told me you had this all settled. What changed?" I asked.

"Hand me the flask," Ava said. She took a swig, passed it to Renny, and answered, "Well, for one thing, my daughter's life. For another, Mark's pressuring me."

I saw Renny roll her eyes. "Celia, don't even say it. I already told her she set herself up. Anyway, Stan's probably halfway here by now."

"So what's this mean? Ava, are you leaving with Stan when he gets here?"

"I have to," Ava said.

"She has to," Renny confirmed.

"What about Mark? What are you going to do with him, just press pause?"

"He understands," Ava said. "I called him and told him what was going on." She paused for a few beats. "It gets more complicated. Part of the reason Stan's coming to get me is Jessica dropped out of school. She's coming home. What am I supposed to do when my daughter needs me?"

"What's the other part of why Stan's coming?" I wanted to know.

"Stan's pissed off," Renny said. "He was worried for a while there, but now he's just mad."

"Ava," I said, "I'm not trying to tell you what to do, but I think you should get a plan. This is only an interruption of something that needs to be figured out."

"This is exactly what I said," Renny added. "The irony is both Ava and Jessica need to go home to their mother."

"The need for refuge," I said. "I get it."

"It's not as though I have the luxury of doing what I want to now. I have to take care of business," Ava said.

Renny leaned forward and winked at me. "God bless her, she's growing up."

Aunt Jean's voice called from beyond. "Renny, honey, can you come in here a minute?" Renny stood. "Y'all, I'll be right back, stay here. Keep that flask down low; they can see us from the house."

Ava watched Renny walk away. "She's making fun of me, and I don't deserve it. I know she thinks I'm screwed up, but how can she possibly understand?"

"But Renny's not judging you, Ava, keep that in mind. It's just her straight-shooting manner. We've known her long enough and well enough to know she's after our best interests, always."

"I know, but I still can't figure out whether I'm supposed to accept my plight, be grateful for what I have, or reach toward something more," Ava said. "I mean, doesn't there come a time when we simply outgrow something?"

"Yes," I said. "I think there can be."

"I know we've talked about this, Celia, but it's more for me than searching for happiness. It's bigger than that. I just don't want to stay in a rut because there are no other options. Am I making any sense? I mean, this is my life. When there seems to be no other options, what's wrong with creating an option for yourself? I know y'all have been trying to support me, and I appreciate it. You know that, right? I hope you know."

"I know." I trailed my feet in the water for a minute, thinking about Ava's words. "Thanks for saying so. I marvel at your ability to be so candid and forthright with your emotions. I've always found that so difficult. I admire this about you, seriously. I always have."

"Why be afraid of emotions? I've always been hell-bent on telling it as it is, so I don't have a heart attack and just keel over and die one day out of nowhere."

Ava's dramatic description struck me as funny, and when I started laughing, Ava joined in, sending us, once again, into uproarious circles. Ava flopped on her back and said, "Listen, Celia. I want to say this before Renny gets back and before Stan arrives because I might not see you in person for a while, since you live so far away." She turned her head sideways and focused on me. "I'm not trying to bring up any bad memories, but it took a lot for you to come down here. I don't know how to thank you. I feel bad about this, though. I don't think I've resolved anything by being here. And now Tate has a reason to come over, and I bet he's bringing his wife, which will be weird at the very least. All this effort you've made, and I've only put you in a weird position."

"You're right about that one," I said. "Tate will be bringing his wife."

"Did he tell you he was?"

"Yes. And when he did, I went out of my way not to react. The guy's so self-involved, the last thing I was going to do was get him talking about his life. All I wanted to do was portray my lack of interest. I'll just smile and say, 'Nice to meet you' then get on with my life."

"But that's all you're going to tell me? Can't you, just once, tell me how you feel about this?"

"You mean about Tate? I realized when we were out on the water that I no longer care."

"That's not what I mean. I mean about all of it."

"How I feel about all of it?" I had to check myself here. I was getting ready to do what I typically do, which is shut down, deflect, skirt the question, employ sarcasm—any defensive move that would get me out of the conversation. But Ava, who wore her heart on her sleeve always, didn't deserve it. I felt my breath dare to deepen, steadying, centering, expanding. I decided to rise to the occasion.

"I don't even know where to start." I paused for what seemed an eternity, looking for the first thread. "Have you ever felt powerless? I have. You really can be devastated in life, you know. As in permanently. As in nowhere to go from here. And it's not as though devastation happens once, and then it's all behind you. Repercussions are always endless. You just have to live with them. People talk about acceptance, as though anybody has a choice. We don't. Trust me on this: accept it or not, devastation doesn't evolve into something gentler. It only becomes a state of affairs. Everything becomes all about how you navigate from there. I'm telling you, Ava, I've been at the point where nothing surprises me. I'm not saying that lightly. Tate, his marriage, none of this fazes me the way it might somebody else."

"But that's not true, Celia. Anyone would be devastated over everything that's happened to you."

"Probably. The thing is, I don't take it personally. I'm just living in the paradigm. This might be the difference between me and somebody else."

"I'm not following you. What do you mean?"

"Okay, I'll put it this way. You've been talking all weekend about how to choose wisely from life's possibilities, and I understand what you're aiming for, but I'm so aware of life's inherent limitations, you know, that part beyond us of which we have no control. There's a bigger picture going on, which is what I call the paradigm. There are no promises within it, only the dynamic of cause and effect, good and evil, and then, of course, you have to factor in the mystery of the unknowable. I can't even say I'm fatalistic. It's more like I'm resigned."

"Well I'm never getting over what happened to Hayward," Ava said. "And, quite frankly, I don't know how you survived."

"After Hayward died, everything ended. Everything afterward was just more of it. Tate, my father's death, it was like three strikes, you're out. By the time my grandparents died, then my mother, it was as though I was used to being creamed. It's not that I expected it, it's just that I took it in stride. The thing is, you have to decide how you're going to handle this stuff. I mean, are you going to walk around thinking life is a series of bad events, with fate conspiring against you, or are you going to work within the paradigm? You need to pick a fundamental premise and stick with it. I've decided that working with life's limitations is the way to go. This way, I won't become jaded." I looked out over the great expanse of the metal-gray water, where bordering shapes of trees and tall grass and boulders rippled in reflection from the partly cloudy sky. "I will say one thing, though—it took me years, Ava, to get the vacant look out of my eyes. Ever tried avoiding mirrors?" I looked directly at her. "I have."

"Can't say I can relate. You know how vain I am."

"Yeah, well, if I had your looks," I said with a grin, "I'd probably feel the same."

Ava sat up and rabbit-punched me on the shoulder. "You're getting ready to sidestep, Celia. I know you."

"Ow, cut it out," I said, my hand on my shoulder. "Anyway, you're right. You know me well. Since I'm being uncharacteristically candid, let me say the fact that you and Renny have remained beside me all along has been an ineffable gift."

"What's ineffable mean?"

"Can't put it into words. Larger than life. And stop intentionally interrupting me. I'm in a rare groove here."

Ava's entire body shook before her laughter rang out, and again, I was pulled under. "We're both hopeless. You know this, of course," she said.

"Of course, but it's either laugh or cry at this point."

"You're an optimist. You got that from your mother," Ava noted.

"Thank God," I said. "Much more of my father in me than my looks and who knows what would have become of me?"

Ava's eyes softened. "But you reinvented yourself in California, didn't you? That's exactly what you did, and it worked."

"I don't know if it was reinvention. I just kept moving forward. I was lucky to find David," I said, knowing I meant every word.

"Celia, David was the one who was lucky to find you and that's the truth. I bet you amaze him, the way you've survived everything. And I'm glad you have someone you love that you can talk to about everything."

I paused for a second, considering. "I don't know, Ava. David knows the CliffsNotes of my story, but not all the gritty minutia. I think I got more from my mother than optimism. All those years of living with my father as he was, and she never really shared her feelings. It wasn't part of her internal makeup. She was old school, like most in her generation. I absorbed much of her ways by simply watching her. You know how today many women treat their husband as though he were a father confessor under the guise of making him a best friend, or maybe in trying to be understood? I can't bring myself to go there with David. Something tells me it'd be a mistake."

Ava's eyes grew wide. "Do you mean you don't share everything with him? I couldn't do that. It seems dishonest."

"It's not dishonest in the least, Ava. I wouldn't even say it's a lie of omission. Why be unnecessarily confessional?"

"I don't know, just because. Stan knows everything about me, even the stuff he doesn't like. So much that I wear him out. I know he thinks I'm crazy, but he loves me anyway. I have to give him that. I wouldn't call Stan my best friend—he doesn't know me the way you and Renny do—but I do tell him almost everything. I only stop myself if it'll come back to haunt."

"Yeah, well, how well does anybody know anyone? This is my point. I think my mother's generation thought the real question was how well somebody *should* know someone. It was an entirely different question."

"What's the answer?"

"I don't think it matters, as long as we know ourselves. Anytime we look for outside verification, that's where the trouble begins."

Renny's voice called from the front of the dock. "All right, y'all, let's get a move on. My aunt and uncle are going somewhere. They need to lock up the house and don't want us sitting out here unsupervised."

"Like we're little kids?" Ava called back, as Renny walked toward us. "What's going to happen? Do they think we'll drown in the kiddie pool while nobody's watching?"

"Yes, Ava," Renny said, reaching us. "When you get buck nekked and jump in the lake, they don't want to take responsibility. Y'all pick up the towels. I've already said good-bye for all of us. Get your stuff together. Let's go."

★ ★ ★

As Renny parked the Escalade in front of her kitchen's stairs, Ava turned to look at me in the back seat. "What time is it?"

I looked at the display on my cell phone. "Almost four o'clock."

"Stan ought to be here in about an hour and a half. I better go in and pack." Ava got out of the car and started up the stairs. "Y'all keep it light and breezy when he gets here, okay? And whatever you do, don't mention Mark."

"I wouldn't dare," I said, following behind her.

Renny gathered the towels from the back of her car. She snapped the back shut and locked it by remote, the beep-beep ringing the humid air. "I won't say anything," she called to Ava, "but hurry up packing, so Celia and I don't have to entertain him. There's a lot he won't ask us with you standing there."

I stepped inside then took the towels from Renny and loaded them in the washing machine partitioned behind accordion doors in the kitchen. "I think I'll take a shower and get my stuff together as well," I said.

"What time is Tate coming?" Renny asked.

"I didn't ask," I said.

"You didn't ask?" The look on her face said my answer didn't compute. "Well, how'd y'all leave it?"

"I said I'd ask y'all if it's okay for him to come over. I said I'm sure it'd be fine. My guess is he'll show up whenever."

"Awfully casual, Celia. I don't know how you do it." Renny walked into the living room, and Ava stopped at the top of the stairs when Renny said, "All right, y'all hold on a minute. Let me just say it now because this looks like the end of our weekend." I walked up beside Renny and gave her my full attention. "I wouldn't have taken anything for seeing y'all. I hope you both had as good a time as I did. And Ava, it'll all work out. I know you have to tend to business, but once you get Jessica settled, I'll be here for you. If you want to come stay with me anytime, I'd love to have you. Whatever you need."

"The same goes for me, Ava," I said. "If you decide you'd like to come out to California, my door will be open."

"Thank y'all so much," Ava said, the color of her eyes shining behind tears. At this, Renny and I rushed upon her, fumbling awkwardly, reaching for a place to land a comforting hand. Ava covered her eyes with both hands. Her tears were torrential. "I don't know what I'd do without y'all," she sobbed. "I mean it. We may not have solved everything, but I feel so much better than I did. I swear, y'all, I'll pull myself together. I'm just going to take it one day at a time."

"That's my girl," I said.

"Now you're talking. Way to go, Ava," Renny encouraged. "Go on get yourself together." She looked at the kitchen clock. "I'm going to take a shower. Let's meet up here in an hour. I'll fix us a drink."

"I'll be needing that," Ava said, then floated downstairs.

★ ★ ★

The first thing I wondered when Stan Theil burst through the door was what was he thinking by growing that unsightly beard? It was grotesquely thick, burnt brown and wild, and covered the lower half of his face.

Renny and I were in the living room at the time. Ava had yet to appear.

Stan clattered onto the kitchen floor in untied lumberjack boots, his faded jeans and black T-shirt rumpled from his journey. "Where is she?" he asked, his darting eyes searching.

"Hey, Stan," I said.

"Celia," he said in a clip, as though the last time he'd seen me had been ten minutes ago.

"Long time," I said, hoping my tone registered its implication that he was being rude.

"Come on in and sit down," Renny said to Stan. "Can I get you a drink?"

"No time for that. Ava and I should hit the road," he fired.

"Not even for just a minute?" Renny asked. "What's the rush?"

"Jessica's coming home later tonight." He rested his hands on his hips. "Did Ava tell y'all she dropped out of school? Now I've got *two* wayward women on my hands."

At Stan's words, I thought maybe I'd been hasty in encouraging Ava to patch things up. If I were Ava, I decided, I'd be on the fence about Stan too. "Ava's downstairs," I said, scooting off the sofa. "I'll run down and get her."

I couldn't get to Ava's room fast enough. "Guess what? Stan's here."

"How's he seem?"

"Mad. You done did it this time."

After Ava quit laughing, she said," I tried to tell you. I'm damned if I do and damned if I don't."

"Definitely a double-edged sword," I said. "One day at a time, didn't you say?"

"I did say that, but I was talking about drinking. I'm going to keep drinking one day at a time," Ava said, and when I started laughing, she waved her hand with a, "Sh, he'll be able to hear us down here."

"No, he won't," I said. "And so what if he did? He wouldn't know what we're laughing about."

"I'm supposed to be contrite."

"Well are you?"

"No."

"Here, let me help you with all this," I said, picking up her canvas beach bag. "You practice looking depressed and despondent."

"How's this?" Ava put on her sunglasses, dropped the corners of her mouth, and thrust her bottom lip out.

"The sunglasses inside are a bit much," I said. "Hurry up. He's acting like there's a fire to put out. Y'all have to get going. Stan said y'all are in a rush."

"I don't care if the world's on fire. I'm having a drink before I get in the car and ride for five hours with Stan. I'm also going to fill up my flask—

no, wait, Celia," she said, now digging around in her purse. "You have to fill it up for me and slip it to me when his back is turned."

"What diversionary tactic are you planning to employ while I do this?" I asked. "And by the way, how do you plan on sneaking a drink from your flask while you're sitting beside him in the car?"

"I told you he never pays attention to me. He won't even notice."

"All right," I said with a shrug. "You know him better than I do. Go on, get drunk and stay that way, but let me reiterate my offer for you to come out to California. This is ridiculous. I mean, really, you have to drink to be around your husband? How long do you think you'll be able to get away with that? Sooner or later it'll hit a head."

Ava draped the strap of her duffel bag across her chest. A pained look darkened her face, and for a second, I thought she would cry. "I don't know, Celia. I thought I'd made strides by coming here to be with y'all, but now it seems I'm right back where I started. Only now Mark is in the picture ... but he seems too good to be true. I know none of us can regain our youth, but when I'm with Mark, it feels possible. Since I've seen him here, it feels like I've created an option."

"Ava, you don't have all the facts here. I know what you and Mark had years ago like I know what Tate and I had, but people change. Things evolve. There's no way y'all can go back to what was. You might be romanticizing Mark. It's probably nowhere near the reality. I think you've got a choice to make. You either come to grips with the idea that it's over with Stan or not. You can't explore a relationship with Mark on Stan's time. It'd be duplicitous. Unfair to both of them. You know this."

"Yes, I do." She took a deep breath then exhaled dramatically. "I think what I'll do is just go on home and figure it out from there. It's really all I can do at this point." Ava walked out of the door and started down the hallway.

"Hang on a second," I said, thinking I'd better say what needed to be said now or never. "Ava, I'm taking a risk here but have to say it. There's something else you can do." I held up the flask. "You can quit drinking, like for real. I think you should get serious about this. It's adding to your confusion. I want you to get clear." Ava stopped and looked at me, her bottom lip starting to quiver. "I hope I didn't upset you," I said. "I can honestly say there's no judgment here. I get it. But the alcohol is in the way. You have to put it down for good." I shoved the flask back into her purse. "I wouldn't say it if I didn't mean it," I said. "I think it's the real problem. Everything else is an offshoot."

"I hate it when you're right," Ava said, and with that, she reached out and hugged me. Stepping back, a wicked gleam appeared in her eyes, and I knew I was in for something. "I promise I'll quit as soon as I get home, but I'm getting drunk on the way there." She looked up at the rise of the stairs. "Walk on ahead of me," she said. "I need a shield."

One foot on the stairs and the voices reached me.

My blood pulsed in my ears as I climbed into the inevitable. Fate lies in wait with two choices, whether we like it or not: we either fall into step or fall out of line. Tate Foley was in the living room with his wife, and I knew it. Though a list of infractions should justify a vise grip, sometimes the facts just don't hurt as they should.

"Stan, I don't believe you've met my wife," Tate said as I reached the top of the stairs. The late afternoon sun warmed through the window. Light flashed heaven-sent from the lake and in the midst of its glow, Little Tea stood smiling. Her dark eyes met mine as she held out her arms waiting to catch me.

I ran through the years … through the cotton fields … through the woods and across the wide verandah. I ran through the whole of Como, Mississippi, knowing, as I did, I'd never reach her fast enough.

Topics for Book Clubs

1. Celia, Renny, and Ava have a friendship that spans decades. What is it that keeps their friendship thriving? Do you have similar ties with your childhood friends?

2. Ava's marriage hangs in the balance at the center of this story. Do you find Ava's reasoning understandable?

3. Can you discuss how it might be that Celia and Renny have different views of Ava's marital predicament? What is it about their personalities and life experiences that shape their opinions?

4. What do you think about the appearance of Ava's ex-boyfriend, Mark Clayton, in this story? Is Ava trying to avoid her marriage by revisiting her lost youth?

5. What are Celia's feelings for Tate Foley during this story? Does she experience resolution at the end?

6. Discuss Celia and Little Tea's relationship. What are their differences? What is their common ground?

7. Celia has left the South to start anew in California. Do you find this reasonable? Can anyone ever outrun their past?

8. Celia's backstory is set in the 1980's South. What were the racial attitudes in the 1980's? How have they changed, now?

9. Discuss the nuances of the relationship between Hayward and Little Tea. What draws them together? Why, do you suppose, they kept their relationship under wraps from Celia and others?

10. How do the members of Celia's family shape the dynamic to this story?

11. Were you surprised by the ending?

12. What do you consider the ending point?

CPSIA information can be obtained
at www.ICGtesting.com
Printed in the USA
LVHW090435010520
654827LV00002B/646

9 781645 262596